# Numbers Don't Lie

# Numbers Don't Lie

Jane Honeck

REVERSING FALLS
PRESS

ISBN: 978-0-9845020-2-8 (Paperback)
ISBN: 978-0-9845020-3-5 (eBook)

Reversing Falls Press, Robbinston, Maine

# PROLOGUE

## ELLEN

300

297

294

Another sleepless night. Ellen expects them. Feels satisfied when three whole hours pass without stirring. On other nights, she wakes up after twenty minutes and knows. It's going to be another one of those nights. Tonight, her mental screenplay of a son lost at sea, and parents capsized with grief will not make room for even those scant twenty minutes.

267

264

261

She studies the latest sleep expert's advice. "Start at 300 and count backward by 3. It's boring and will put you promptly to sleep." But what does he know of an accountant's brain, one intrigued by numbers, one seeking out patterns until her number-oriented self solves the puzzle, tires of the game, and the countdown runs tandem with her other swirling thoughts.

216

She sees it now. The pattern reveals itself.

213

210

Every thirty numbers, the last digit is zero. The sequence repeats, another thirty float by, and the riddle is solved. Her analytical brain recedes, and other commentaries grow louder until the numbers are just white noise droning in the back row. Her worries take center stage.

Her doctor says to write down her concerns, to clear her head before crawling into bed. Easy to say for someone whose wife takes care of his every need, cooks his food, washes his clothes, attends to his children. All after his secretary and nurse have tucked in his office for the night. She knows men like that, works with them, watches their egos espouse things they don't know, things wiser men would keep to themselves. She dreams about a life like that, one she could shut down when she closes her office door at night. But that's not her. She packs her briefcase with unsolved mysteries the day's numbers bring her way. She brings them home. Brings them to bed.

Do her clients realize what they reveal when they share their finances? Do they know how they bare their hearts and souls when they sit across the desk?

96

93

90


No pattern of numbers will shut off the rumbling cadence from the day's last call. Dr. Reynolds finally made an appointment to see her. She expected it and knew that someday she'd have to face his tragedy and grief. She dreaded it, and now it was here. In three hours, she'd feel what she only imagined. Tom and Lucy Reynolds' son was dead. Their lives changed forever.

30

27

24

Why couldn't she be the quintessential boring, number-crunching CPA treading traditional, well-worn paths instead of veering off and digging deep to solve her clients' problems? Why couldn't she hide her heart behind rock-hard facts and refuse to go where souls connect? They didn't teach this at school or test for it on the arduous CPA exam. But this is what makes her practice different, what brings in her unique and beloved clients. Other CPAs are only about the numbers and sleep well at night. She does not. And neither does her staff.

Tonight, she'd give it all up for a few hours of sleep.

9

6

3

# CHAPTER 1

# ELLEN

ELLEN HARTMANN'S SCIATICA PLUCKED AS SHE rolled over to glance at the intrusive red glow of the alarm clock. 5:27. Three minutes before the alarm. Again. Always three minutes. Whether 4:30, 7:30, or even the occasional 9:30, three minutes before, she'd be fully awake and ready to face the day. But today, she lingered. She pictured her three sons down the hall tucked in their snug beds, in their cozy bedrooms, in a warm home. Tom and Lucy Reynolds woke each morning with an unused bed, in an empty bedroom, in a house flooded with grief. Their only son was dead.

Ellen gave herself an extra five minutes to prepare mentally for the day before slipping out of bed, sliding into her walking jeans, and tiptoeing down the stairs. She opened the dog crate in the kitchen to release Random, the family's Wheaten terrier. The dog knew the routine and stretched before following her outdoors. They let sleeping boys lie for another hour. With leash snapped on, they bounded down the six concrete steps from the front porch of the four-columned brick house and walked to the center of the road. There was no traffic, and in the still-brightening dawn, it was best to avoid the cracked sidewalks.

Ellen crossed from South Portland into Cape Elizabeth. Her property value would have doubled if her house had been there instead of in South Portland. Cape was filled with doctors, lawyers, and CPAs like her, but it wasn't her style. She was a townie from a tiny village in Wisconsin, where girls like her were admired by the farm kids bussed in. Unlike her sister, who thought Ellen had married (and divorced) beneath herself, Ellen knew she was a tiny fish in an even tinier sea.

She moved through unlit neighborhoods and thought of her morning's dreaded meeting with Dr. Reynolds. The last time she saw him was during tax season, when clients, like old friends, came to see her. For sixty minutes, they'd share more life stories than tax information. She loved her profession, or at least how she practiced, because it was about people, not numbers. Connections, not calculations. Money brought out the best or worst in a person, and her job was to help clients through the twists and turns of their finances. She walked beside them in good times and bad. This morning would be one of the bad.

Three months ago, Tom bubbled with pride for his son's upcoming adventure. Ben, a twenty-one-year-old, top of his class, three-and-a-half-year college graduate, was embarking on a solo trip on the family sailboat, the *Ocean Potion*. Ben came up with its name by merging his father's medical profession with the family's passion for the sea when he was young and thought everything coming out of his mouth was golden. They all agreed, and the name came along whenever the family boat was upgraded.

Together, the entire family, Tom, his wife Lucy, daughter Sarah, and Ben, dreamed and designed the seventeen-hundred-fifty-mile voyage down the coast of Maine to the Bahamas, where Tom would meet him. Ellen tried to join in Tom's excitement that day, but her fear of the ocean made it tough. When Tom shared his worries about Ben's one night alone at sea while he sailed from Miami Beach to Eleuthera, her anxiety resurfaced. She kept it all to herself.

She climbed the six steps to her front door and paused. The same trepidation that rose on a wave of uneasiness that day throbbed in her gut now, and her cold, stiff fingers lingered on the latch as she relived that hushed premonition. She heard her three boys rustling (or wrestling) on the other side of the door, and she packed it away. She breathed deeply and opened the door.

# CHAPTER 2

---

# TOM

TOM REYNOLDS NEVER TOOK BEN'S VOYAGE lightly. Ben and his daughter Sarah got their adventurous spirit from their mother Lucy, and it took a while before Tom relaxed into their mutual excitement. In the weeks after Ben's graduation, the four gathered around nautical charts to strategically plan the route, choosing the safest harbors on shores that hugged the waters they had previously sailed. Every marina was picked for the ideal one-hundred-nautical miles-a-day distance from the last. Ben was sailing alone, and this was not a race. Safety was paramount, and if their choice for a safe harbor was between 80 miles or a long 120, they always chose 80.

Logistics were planned carefully, but they didn't worry excessively about provisions. Each night, Ben could easily restock if he chose to cook at all. Tom was more concerned with spotty, inconsistent communication because he still didn't trust cell phone reception. Knowing his own proclivity for worry, before giving his full permission, he insisted that Ben would make or receive a call from home each night at seven o'clock. Nothing more, nothing less.

Ben's first calls home were exciting even though they were filled with answers to the same questions. How were the winds? Did you make good time? Any problems at the marina? Tom relaxed as the days passed and Ben's responses reflected just another typical day. Their last call was February 16th, two days before Tom would meet Ben in Eleuthera. He justified the two-day gap in phone calls because Ben would be on his overnight sail, the first and only night he wouldn't be tying up at a dock.

Ben's excitement and sense of accomplishment were still evident during that last conversation, but he sounded exhausted. Tom chalked it up to the solitude of a month-long journey filled with challenging work. He teased that soon they'd be relaxing together on a sandy beach. With his own list of things to accomplish before three long flights with layovers, Tom said his goodbyes and handed the phone to Lucy to say hers.

# CHAPTER 3

# BEN

BEN MISSED HIS FAMILY'S NIGHTLY, SOMETIMES bothersome calls and wished that when they spoke the night before, he had set up a call with his mom and sister while his father was traveling to meet him. Just a two-minute conversation would have reminded him that he was not alone, not alone last night, and not alone now. As the sun lowered to the horizon, he gazed at the endless ocean and tried to convince himself. It was hopeless. He turned from the setting sun and distracted himself by doing a safety check before dusk shifted into night: ditch bag, life preserver, fire extinguisher, and emergency lights. All where they should be.

Miami Beach unsettled him. Other nights at other marinas were uneventful. Last night was not; the two men had caught him off guard. Twenty-four hours later, he was still shaken. Ben slowed his thinking, deepened his breathing, and tried to fill himself with a sense of well-being that would carry him beyond his mental rehash of the night before.

Slowly, the tension leeched out of his body, and his mind's whirling dervish stopped. Dusk's cooling breeze enveloped him, filling his anxious spaces with a semblance of peace. The thugs' menacing faces began to pale and fade from his memory.

The night's forecast called for clear skies and calm seas, and by all indications, he would have a flawless night at sea. It would be a perfect end to his once-in-a-lifetime journey.

# CHAPTER 4

# TOM

TOM AND BEN CHOSE THE SPARSELY INHABITED town of Grand Harbour on the island of Eleuthera for good reason. Father and son missed each other and their uninterrupted togetherness on wilderness camping trips. Before Ben was gone at college, whenever Tom was overwhelmed and thought his son was too, he'd suggest a break from life to spend a weekend in the woods. As a teenager, it was tough to convince Ben to leave his friends, but whenever he did, it was equally hard to get him to pack up and return home. Their lives and father-son bond always flourished after a weekend in nature. Eleuthera was the perfect place to resurrect this longstanding tradition.

Tom arrived in Eleuthera with his LL Bean backpack, a gift from Lucy, after she complained that Tom's original pack from college days was simply too dirty and overused for this special adventure. She helped him fill it, added crucial things he'd forgotten, like toothbrush and toothpaste, and removed a couple of heavy books with a reminder that he was traveling to connect with his son, not his books. Tom landed at Governor's Harbour International Airport and chuckled at how its *international* name mirrored that of the International Jetport back in Portland. He was happy that Miami's airport had been truly international, with a duty-free store to prove it. The bottle of Veuve Clicquot, Lucy's suggested champagne for a proper celebration, was stowed in his new backpack.

Tom entered Grand Harbour's only upscale waterfront resort, glad that he had splurged with three nights in a two-bedroom luxury villa. Tom needed one night to unwind from his long day of travel and the busy medical practice he had left at midnight the night before. He was ready to forget yesterday's complex surgery and happy to slam the door on the ever-present office politics. One evening, all to himself, and he'd be ready to give his full attention to his son. Ben could then savor two nights of sleep in a top-notch hotel with a real bed and his own bathroom, complete with a real shower and toilet. One night alone for Tom, two nights in luxury for Ben, and they'd be ready for four nights of tropical camping.

Tom checked in, and following Lucy's urging to get more exercise, he climbed the stairs to his fourth-floor oceanfront room. The suite's balcony gave him a wide view of the harbor, and he visualized his son sailing into view early the next morning. His body relaxed, and his mind emptied. This trip was an elixir for his soul, and the soothing sound of the waves was already restoring his tired body and spirit. The *Ocean Potion* was doing its magic again. He stretched out on the bed and closed his eyes for a restorative, twenty-minute nap before dinner.

# CHAPTER 5

---

# BEN

THERE WAS NO MOON. NOT EVEN A SLIVER OF LIGHT from a waxing crescent reflected off the rolling ocean. The new moon had disappeared at sunset, and in its void, a deep, all-encompassing blackness surrounded Ben. His stuffed-down anxiety from last night's events stirred in his gut.

One hundred miles from shore, a passing seagull called out. Ben looked up into the star-filled sky. His erupting panic stilled. He remembered his mother's lessons as a child. *When things look down, change your view.* It was just what he needed to keep from slipping too far and too deep into his head.

Thanks, Mom. I needed that. He breathed in the twinkling starlight and pictured his mom at his side. Every new moon, weather permitting, she'd spread blankets on the back lawn and call for Sarah and him to join her. If they were lucky, his dad might be home, and the four of them would hold hands and stargaze. "There's the Big Dipper! I found the

Little Dipper first! Look, it's the bear!" they'd call out. As they grew, their guesses also grew more accurate.

He wished they were here with him. His first solo night on the open sea was not what he expected. He thought that after almost thirty days following the Eastern seaboard down to Miami, he'd be ready to give up the safety of busy marinas filled with fellow sailors high from a spectacular day on the water. Or just plain high. Either way, Ben loved swapping stories, sharing a cold beer, or smoking some weed. Tonight, he wished for all three.

He looked up and bathed in the starlight and his mother's words. He stretched his neck from right to left and dropped his shoulders. *I can and will relax. We humans turn to the dark side too quickly. It's all about attitude.* He learned that from his mom and from studying Viktor Frankl in school. He dredged up the familiar quote. *The last freedom we have is to choose our own attitude.*

Tonight, he would be in charge. He would not let last night take over. Tonight, he would let go of the fear that trailed him all day. Tonight, was his to savor, to relish. Tonight, he would be in control of the story he'd tell for the rest of his life.

And damn it, he would be the one to author that story, not the thugs from Miami. He climbed below deck for some rest.

# CHAPTER 6

# TOM

TOM MISSED DINNER AND WOKE DISORIENTED AT 3 a.m. Something had brutally aroused him. His sweat-soaked body and hammering heart suggested a nightmare, but his mind was blank to what his body remembered. He left the tangled sheets, opened the sliding glass door to the balcony, and scanned the harbor. It was vacant and peaceful after a day of bustling tourists freeing themselves from their trapped, landed lives filled with too many responsibilities, too many commitments, too many choices, too much of everything. Like him, they also needed days to muffle noisy lives stuffed with manufactured, me-made problems.

He looked beyond the harbor to the ethereal, limitless sea. Somewhere out there, the *Ocean Potion* was carrying Ben from busy college days to a new life not yet crafted, one made clearer by salty smells, calling terns, and wafting waters. He pictured Ben waking for the final leg of his journey, rubbing his eyes the same way he did as a little boy when he woke with a combination of curiosity and reluctance. Curiosity for what the day would bring and reluctance to leave the warm cocoon of his bed. With only a few hours until Ben's arrival, Tom stripped off his travel clothes and crawled under the blankets. Sleep came quickly. Soon, his son would be with him.

# CHAPTER 7

# TOM

TOM STOOD ON THE BALCONY STUDYING THE deep turquoise currents floating through the harbor. He marveled at the varieties of blues created by these Caribbean seas. The hues shifted over coral reefs, schools of fish, and deep underwater pockets crafted by the daily movement of incoming and outgoing tides. He looked at his watch. It was noon. Ben's arrival was long overdue. The trip from Miami Beach was only ten to twelve hours at most; Ben should have been here by now or at least tried to call.

His heart began to race, and he sucked in a long, slow breath to calm himself. I will not go there. I won't let my fears take me on a senseless ride. Right here, right now, I am fine. Ben is fine; there is nothing more. With a slow exhale, Tom almost believed it, but his anxiety was a runaway camel, loping over dunes, kicking up dry grains of worry, until he was miles away from any oasis of peace. His breath quickened, then shallowed, and he found himself panting with panic.

He stopped his rising terror by forcing in a long, slow breath. His heart slowed. Ben is not that late yet. Don't get ahead of yourself, or your fear will turn to anger when he does arrive. Tom remembered how his own mother's worry turned into a burning rage, searing everything in its path and leaving charred relationships behind. He would not do that to his son; he could not.

Tom walked to the bathroom, bent over the marble sink, and splashed chilly water on his face. He stood up and saw his image in the mirror. The color had leached out of his face, and his eye bags and sags had deepened. Snap out of it, shake it off, don't be ridiculous. But nothing lifted the thick, grey cloak enveloping him. It was growing heavier as the hours piled up. He turned away from the mirror.

It was well past noon now, and as each minute notched by, he produced and directed movie after movie of every possible disaster. He needed to act, to do something, even if it was only to share the turmoil brewing inside of him with another human being. He left the suite and headed to the front desk for help. The young woman standing behind it looked at him quizzically, but Tom couldn't find the words to explain. He staggered through the open-air lobby, turned left, and followed her directions to the police station.

# CHAPTER 8

# TOM

TOM APPROACHED THE SCARRED WOODEN DESK in the Grand Harbour police station. A slow Caribbean smile spread across the police officer's no-worry face as he lifted his head from a two-day-old newspaper. Tom took that as his cue to speak. "My son was supposed to arrive this morning on his sailboat. It was only an overnight trip from Miami Beach; he should have arrived early this morning. I'm worried." Tom rubbed his brow and waited for the man's response.

"Ah, no worry. It's only noon. He'll be along," the officer drawled. "I've heard this story before, and it always turns out good. Let's wait a bit, shall we?" He smiled broadly.

"I'm worried that something isn't right, something is off. If we don't do something now, it'll get too late, and we'll have to wait another day." Tom tried to speak in the laidback, unhurried style of the island. He wanted them to think he had thought this through carefully and wasn't panicking. He failed miserably.

"It's too soon. We must wait. There is a protocol to follow. We must wait before I can call the Royal Bahamas Defense Force. There is nothing I can do today." The police officer lowered his head to his newspaper. Their meeting was over, and Tom had no choice but to leave the station. He couldn't fault the guy for refusing to jump into Tom's fear-ridden world. To an outsider, it was too early, but to a parent, it was already too late.

Tom followed the street to the harbor, and as he walked, he scrutinized every approaching boat, but after falling prey to hopeful delusions and being duped by a sailboat twice as long with twice the rigging, he knew his judgment couldn't be trusted. He continued to the dock toward a leathery-skinned man sitting on the pier basking in the salt air. The man, oblivious to him, looked like the stereotypical islander: dropped out and lost in a weed or alcoholic haze. Tom kept walking. As he passed, the guy squinted into the sun and asked, "What can I do to make your day better?"

Tom's words tumbled out. "Not much unless you can magically bring in my son's boat. He should've been here hours ago. I'm worried, but the police aren't, not until tomorrow they say. So, there's nothing you can do to make my day better. I just want to see my son's face."

Tom squinted back at the man, not from the sun but from the pain of his worry. "Sorry, that got away from me; I didn't mean to burden you." His hand rubbed the back of his neck, and Tom wished his OR nurse was there to wipe his brow.

The man stood up, and his eyes searched Tom's.

"I get it," he said. "A parent's worries shouldn't be taken

lightly. But I'm afraid the officer is correct. The Bahamian Government won't help, at least not for a couple of days. But BASRA won't wait. They'll help now." He offered his hand.

Tom grasped it. The guy wasn't as out of it as he looked.

"Wait. What? BASRA? I don't understand." The man grimaced, and Tom dropped his hand. His own fingers hurt from his over-squeezing.

"Bahamas Air Sea Rescue: BASRA. We do more than the official rescue any day of the week. Come on, I'll take you to my office." He lightly jumped off the dock and onto the bow of the midsize powerboat he was sitting close to. He signaled for Tom to follow.

They stood on the open deck of the boat while the man explained that BASRA was a nonprofit organization committed to helping distressed pilots and sailors in the Bahama Islands. They existed because of the lack of urgency from government agencies. They existed for family members like Tom, who couldn't wait another day. They existed because they knew that when it came to sea rescues, sooner was always better than later.

"I'll make some calls, and within an hour, we'll be operational, long before sunset, and in plenty of time to escort your son into the harbor." The man's confident, competent, and reassuring self materialized from his ragged shorts, dirty T-shirt, and the skunk-like aroma surrounding him. Tom's shoulders dropped as he considered turning things over to this burnt-out hippy. Remembering that his other choices were null and void and that first impressions could be deceiving, he accepted the stranger's help.

"Thanks," Tom blurted. "By the way, what's your name?"

"Marley. Marley Roberts. Yeah, my parents had a real sense of humor. Just call me Bob." He smirked, turned to his radio, and sent out the SOS to his fellow searchers.

# CHAPTER 9

## LUCY

LUCY HAD EXPECTED A CALL BY NOW, EXPECTED IT before dinner, and despite her growing concern, she waited. She told herself they were busy partying, that as soon as Tom and Ben were done patting themselves on the back, had finished draining too many beers, and the celebratory champagne, they'd contact home. She didn't blame them; she sometimes forgot to check in too. Tom, the worrier in the family, was not like her and rarely forgot, but she told herself this time was different. He was simply caught up in the moment and would call soon enough.

This afternoon, Lucy needed to fill her head with something else, anything. It was just Sarah and her for dinner, and although the refrigerator was filled, a trip to the grocery store was a good diversion. She could pivot and make her daughter's favorite meal. It wasn't often that it was just the two of them, and cooking something special would keep Lucy busy and give Sarah the extra attention she deserved. She should have thought of it sooner.

After a dinner of fresh scallops on a bed of baby spinach smothered in Lucy's famous alfredo sauce, Sarah hugged her mother and went to her room to study for tomorrow's history exam. Dinner gave Lucy a break from her nagging unease, but enjoying the rich meal was still difficult. If Sarah noticed the remnants on Lucy's plate from her minuscule portion, she said nothing. Neither had she asked about Ben. They both seemed not to want to talk about it.

It was now seven o'clock, and Lucy couldn't wait any longer. She picked up the phone and dialed the number for Tom's hotel, one of many numbers on his long list of things she might need while he was gone. The phone rang. No one answered. They were most likely at dinner.

Eight o'clock. The phone rang. No one answered. Surely, they would phone home soon. This was getting unfair.

8:30. The phone rang.

8:45. The phone rang.

9:00. The phone rang.

# CHAPTER 10

# TOM

10:15 P.M. TOM SNAKED HIS HAND DOWN THE WALL, fumbled for the light switch, and hurried to pick up the clanging phone in the cavernous hotel suite with the empty bedroom waiting for his son to luxuriate in its safety. He had spent the afternoon and night with Bob waiting for something, anything to explain Ben's vanishing. He couldn't bring himself to call Lucy until he knew something, anything. Lucy's frantic voice dissolved his last shred of hope. "Why haven't you called? I can't believe you put us through this. Sarah and I have been waiting for hours. Put Ben on the phone, I don't even want to talk with you. I'm so angry."

Tom's throat spasmed. He raked his trembling fingers through his salt-filled hair. He struggled for words. "I can't put Ben on the phone, not yet."

"Why? Is he still on the boat? Still buttoning it up? Shouldn't you have done that long before you started celebrating?" Lucy's accusatory tone buzzed in his brain as he slid open the balcony doors and scanned the empty harbor.

"No, Ben can't come to the phone. He isn't here. We don't know where he is. We're looking." Tom's words croaked from his tight, dry throat.

"What do you mean you're looking, looking where? I don't understand. He should have been there at least twelve hours ago. Where is he?" Lucy's voice rose in pitch and volume. "Tom, what are you saying?"

"Ben didn't arrive, I don't know what else to tell you. The police wouldn't do anything, but Bob, this guy I met, is on it. He and his friends are looking. It's the best we can do right now." He turned away from the unforgiving ocean and slammed the balcony door shut.

"What do you mean, a guy you just met and his friends are looking? That's the best you can do? Our son deserves better than that. You're better than that Tom. Call someone who can really help!" Tom flinched. Lucy was saying everything he felt. He slumped into the tropical-colored, over-cushioned chair in the corner of the suite's living room, wishing it were a hard, punishing bench. That was all he deserved.

"Bob is someone who can help, the only one right now. He's part of a volunteer rescue group that steps in when the authorities won't get involved. They've been hunting for Ben by air and by sea for hours. They'll start again in the morning. The Bahamian government won't even consider getting involved until tomorrow." He tried to keep his voice even-keeled and confident. Lucy didn't need to be exposed to the terror he was carrying.

Tom paced as the silence grew between them.

"I'm too angry, I can't talk anymore," Lucy's voice trembled. There was a single click, and she was gone.

It's what he would have done; it was the only thing to do. There was nothing either of them could say that would ease their pain. With dreams demolished, he too wanted to hang

up on this nightmare, to wake to a new day when a sparkling blue morning and a glorious sun would illuminate the white sails of the *Ocean Potion* as Ben sailed into the harbor.

# CHAPTER 11

# THE OCEAN POTION

SHE COUGHED AND SHUDDERED ONE LAST TIME and then went silent. The last of the fuel sucked from the emergency reserves through the pistons of the engine. Her propeller turned once more and stopped. The early morning dew had long since dried up, the noon sun beat down upon her deck, and the planks creaked and moaned as the wood dried. Like a yellow ducky bobbing in a toddler's bathtub, she waited to be corralled, taken in hand, set on her course once again. But nothing came. Nine o'clock, ten o'clock, eleven o'clock, twelve o'clock. And still, he didn't rise. She was alone. She felt it. Her magic was gone, and she bobbed with the rhythm of the sea.

# CHAPTER 12

## ELLEN

WORD PASSED QUICKLY THROUGH HARTMANN and Associates to steer clear of Ellen until after her morning meeting. Katie alerted them to what she was facing, and they all knew how tough this kind of meeting was on their founder. They knew because Ellen hired carefully and chose people based more on their emotional intelligence than on their accounting skills. Accounting could be taught, managing your own and others' emotions, not so much. Ellen started the firm fifteen years before as a solo practitioner, and it steadily grew and expanded under her guidance. Now, its ten accountants and two support staff all contributed to its high regard in the community.

Ellen waited for Katie to buzz that Dr. Reynolds had arrived. She started to hyperventilate as she struggled to keep her emotions in check. Was it even possible or desired? She wasn't sure. Her clients counted on her for open and honest interactions, even if it meant wading into uncomfortable waters, and her staff quickly discovered that she didn't know how to connect in any other way. She rested her head on her cold desk and tried to halt her endless and pointless meanderings by recalling her long history with Tom.

Ellen first met Tom twenty years ago. She was one of three women in the Portland office of an international accounting firm and was trying to fake a lack of intimidation as she forged her way through the masculine world of money. Dr. Reynolds was her first face-to-face client meeting. His striking blue eyes sparkled, a smile flooded his face, and he reached out his hand and said, "Hi, I'm Tom." Ellen sighed, remembering how this kind, quiet surgeon with solid values and unusual humility had innocently defused her fears. Could she do the same for him today?

Ellen had spent hours, days, and weeks imagining the despair that Tom and Lucy had faced over the past grueling months. How does a father, or even worse, a mother, cope with the death of a child, the child they nurtured and worried over? They would never again squeeze him tight, stroke his soft, silky hair, or kiss his sleepy head goodnight. It didn't matter if that child now had a deep voice and was taller than you; he would always be your baby. Her imagination ran wild through places she didn't want to visit, scenes too horrifying to picture, and possibilities too close to home.

Enough. She sat up, stiffened her back, and adjusted herself at her desk. She slid open the center drawer and pulled out the newspaper article resting there since she first read the shocking news. She was still annoyed by how she learned about Ben's death from the small article in the *Portland Press Herald.*

> After a seven-day extensive search, Benjamin Reynolds was found dead on his family's sailboat, the Ocean Potion, after he failed to arrive at Grand Harbour, Eleuthera, where his father was waiting to meet him. Death was caused by mechanical failure.

Why didn't anyone from Tom's office call to warn her? Or call Julie, her right-hand senior accountant? She understood accountants weren't usually on your first-to-call list, but their relationship with Tom's office was different. She had been part of his growing practice since its inception, and both she and Julie worked with the families of most of its physicians. Surely, one of them could've called. Ellen's chest tightened as anger muffled her sadness and grief. She turned to the window, and her mental grinding paused as she noticed the bright and cloudless morning. It annoyed her in its perfection. She returned to the story she had read between the lines that day, the one with Ben facing a slow, torturous death surrounded only by squawking seagulls. She closed her eyes. Not now.

Her eyes popped wide at the buzzing of the phone. She didn't pick it up. She knew what it meant. She sucked in a deep inhale, counted to five, and exhaled. Ready or not, Tom was here.

# CHAPTER 13

# ELLEN

ELLEN FACED TOM ACROSS HER CHERRY DESK. The huge executive desk felt like the conversation she was facing: a two-hundred-twenty-foot-deep abyss to be dropped into and trekked across before coming up the other side. She took a moment to gather herself and to give Tom time to settle into his chair and himself. Ellen tried to reflect comfort and understanding when she saw his eyes searching hers. She leaned in, rested her chin in her right hand, and cupped her cheek. "Oh Tom, it must have been awful. I never learned the details; do you want to talk about it?"

"I do. Thanks for asking." His eyes disengaged from Ellen, and he looked down at the abyss. He paused, then looked up. "It was awful. I'd be lying if I said it wasn't. The worst was being alone, waiting. Me in the Bahamas, Lucy here in Maine. After two days, we decided Lucy and Sarah should join me. We needed each other. No matter what happened, good or bad, being alone made the wait torturous. My luxury suite was swallowing me alive. It was never meant for one, and I got them on the most direct flight the next day." He looked up and wiped his watery eyes. Ellen missed their usual twinkling blue; today, they were red roadmaps of grief.

"I was so overwhelmed, so angry, almost irrational. I wasn't supposed to be waiting for my wife and daughter. I just wanted my son. I wanted four days around a raging campfire, trading foolish stories and slinging wisecracks across the flames. I wanted my new adult son at my side, dreaming about his future. I hated that empty bedroom." He slumped in his chair and closed his eyes. "Ben was supposed to be there, not Lucy and Sarah. It wasn't comforting to share my bed with my wife or have my daughter in the other room. I just wanted the nightmare to end and for Ben's journey to be the way we'd planned it."

Ellen absorbed the family's torment, and her maternal fear stirred. It was just the luck of the draw as to which family would face tragedy next. Her sons weren't risk-takers, but her motherly fear bubbled up whenever they crossed Ocean Street to go to school or pulled out of the driveway with their grandmother behind the wheel. Her minor parental heartbreak and worry hinted at the eternal ache that would be Tom and Lucy's uninvited companion forever.

Tom ran his fingers through his salt-and-pepper hair and shifted in his chair. "On the third day, shortly after Lucy and Sarah got there, the official government's rescue force got involved. I still can't believe that they rely on a volunteer organization to do their search and rescue." He leaned in and locked eyes with Ellen. "I insisted we call it search and rescue. I've listened to too many heartbreaking television news stories where frantic parents listen in agony as officials announce they have changed from search and rescue to search and recovery. I refused to admit that we might be going there."

Ellen nodded, but he had lowered his eyes again and didn't notice. She waited for him to continue. She wasn't going to interrupt or hurry him. She gave him all the time he needed.

He sat back and cleared his throat. "Lucy and I met with the Royal Bahamas Rescue Force to hear their plan, but they only gave us lip service. They were relying on BASRA and the volunteers to do the real work. Can you believe the government only sent two men? There were hundreds of volunteers out in boats and planes. It was obvious the government was only there to coordinate the effort." He paused, his eyes looked up to the right. "It was better than nothing. Bob couldn't do it all alone. He was overwhelmed with organizing his volunteers and answering my questions. And now he had to field those same questions from Lucy and Sarah. What would we have done without him?"

Ellen hesitated to interrupt the flow, but she was curious. "Who's Bob?"

"Marley Roberts, call me Bob." Tom laughed, and his eyes lit up. "That's how he introduces himself. He looks like the typical nonfunctioning island hippie lounging on the docks. Boy, was I wrong. He heads up BASRA, the volunteer force, and he stepped right in when the police said I had to wait. Believe me, he's a force to reckon with. The quintessential velvet glove, if you know what I mean."

Ellen did. She tried to be like that, not like the hippie, but the velvet glove. She worried at times that she came across as too strong and aggressive. "I know exactly what you mean.

What's the saying? Speak softly and carry a big stick? My kind of people."

Tom shook his head in agreement. He picked up his coffee cup and took a sip of his coffee. His nose wrinkled. It must be old and cold.

"Do you need a fresh cup? I can have Katie bring one?" Ellen reached for her phone.

"No, no thanks, it's fine." He set down his cup and pushed it away. "Where was I? That's right, the three of us prayed that Bob would find a miracle. All we could do was wait. It was excruciating. I latched onto Lucy for spiritual and emotional strength. She's the real power in our family, and she anchors me." He rubbed his chest slowly with his hand. "When we returned to the suite each night, Lucy, Sarah, and I would sit in purposeful silence. We waited for the grace of God to intervene." His hand rested on his heart.

Ellen held her breath, and an unexpected tear dropped into her lap. She worked to pull herself together and be strong for Tom. Maybe if she had a bit of their faith, life would be less painful.

"It took seven days to find the *Ocean Potion*. Seven full days. Bob said it was like looking for that one emerging hair on a bald head." Tom rubbed the thinning spot on the back of his head. On another day, in another meeting, Ellen would have teased him. "Every millimeter looks the same, every hair follicle just like the rest, and even when you think you've found something out of the ordinary, it might not be what you were looking for.

"They found the *Ocean Potion* two hundred miles off course, bobbing in a tight circle. Her rudder was pushed to the right, and in spite of that, the waves were pushing her farther and farther into the open sea. Her sails were down. Ben must've lowered them when he went to sleep. He always felt safe listening to the quiet hum of the motor and loved hearing it as a boy. The steady drone of the engine always sent him straight to dreamland." A sad smile skimmed across Tom's face. "I hope he was content knowing he'd see me in the morning. Who knows? I like to tell myself he was happy, that he died quickly and easily."

Tom was losing steam, and his voice was a creaky whisper. Ellen leaned in to hear better.

"They found him on deck with no signs of injury. He was lying there for the seven days we were searching. The sun and the wind do awful things. They told us not to view his body, that they could identify him from a picture."

"Oh Tom." Ellen reached across the desk to grab his hand. At the same time, he yanked a handkerchief out of his pocket and blew his nose. She pulled her hand back into her lap.

"I assured them I was a doctor. I could do it. In hindsight, I wish I'd taken their advice. I forgot that being a parent trumps the doctor in me. A parent should never have to see that. I could identify him, but my fear and anxiety turned into physical agony for my beautiful boy. It will never leave me. I know that." His eyes squeezed shut.

"How did he die?" Ellen asked gently. Tom looked up and straightened his back. His confident physician-self reappeared. He slid into medical lingo the same way Ellen used numbers and finance to rescue uncomfortable conversations.

"No blunt force trauma, no inherent signs of injury. We had to wait for toxicology reports for the official cause of death: carbon monoxide poisoning. They never said why. It appeared Ben was below in the cabin and made it up the ladder to fresh air, but it was too late. The carbon monoxide replaced the oxygen in his red blood cells. His brain, heart, and body were starved of oxygen, and he expired."

Ellen waited for more. Seconds felt like minutes felt like hours. "I'm so sorry." Whispering those three words felt incredibly inadequate, but she had to say something. Her heart spasmed like an overused muscle. "How's Lucy doing? And Sarah?"

"We don't talk about it much, but I suspect they feel the same. We're all doing the best we can." Tom stroked his forehead. "Some days are better than others. It's weird. On mornings before I'm fully awake, the day is new, and I dream of dancing waves under a blue cloudless sky. It's a perfect sailing day, and I smile. But then I wake up to my hellish life where oceans swallow your son, your life, your happiness. Reality sets in." He shook his head as if rattling loose the memory.

Then his face relaxed, and his shoulders dropped. "Thanks for listening, Ellen. I mean it. Most people can't go beyond saying I'm so sorry for your loss. No one wants to imagine, much less hear about a life lost before it barely got started. I get that. But it helps to talk about it. Somehow, it brings Ben closer even as it makes everything more real."

Tom closed his eyes, and they opened with a different kind of intensity. "There's something else I need your help with—the other reason I came in today. You know I took a few months away from the office to deal with things." Ellen nodded and relaxed against the back of her chair. "When I returned, they fired me."

"They what?" Ellen's body jack-knifed, and she slammed her hands on the desk. She picked up the phone and buzzed the front desk. "Katie, can you bring in two cups of fresh coffee?"

# CHAPTER 14

# JULIE

JULIE WAS BURIED IN FILES, AND HER HEAD WAS spinning from the new forensic case Ellen had delegated to her. Tracing errant numbers through a mishmash of bank and investment statements at too many institutions and searching for a *gotcha* was her passion and her forte. It was also her bane. After sleuthing for five hours, she'd disappeared down too many rabbit holes and turned up nothing. No smoking gun to prove their client's belief that her husband was hiding money. But just because Julie didn't find it the first time, didn't mean it wasn't there. She squeezed the back of her neck and pinched her eyes shut to relieve her tension and clear her mind.

The buzz of her phone interrupted her reverie. "Daniel from Portland Surgical on line two." Katie's voice was always professional.

"For me? He usually talks with Ellen. Oh yeah, she's in that meeting with Dr. Reynolds." Julie looked across the staff bullpen, through the glass sidelight in Ellen's door, and saw that Ellen was still meeting with Tom. Ellen's pained expression told her it was rough going.

"Can't he wait for her to finish? Can you take a message?" Julie asked.

"He asked for you. Never said anything about Ellen."

"Okay, give me a sec." She needed to clear her head from the puzzle in front of her before moving to a new one. Why was Daniel, the manager of Portland Surgical, Dr. Reynolds' practice, calling her? Yes, she was the staff accountant for this important client. And yes, she sometimes talked with him about complicated transactions when she prepared the company tax returns. But no, he never made unsolicited calls to her for anything; he always went through Ellen. She honestly thought he didn't like women, and most definitely not a second-in-command one. He still thought business was a man's world, and since that wasn't much of an option at Hartmann and Associates, he only talked with Ellen, the head honcho. Julie pushed the blinking button on her phone and cradled the receiver on her shoulder. She was curious. *Let's see why he called lowly me.*

"Hi Daniel, what a pleasant surprise. What can I do for you?" She spoke in her best professional voice but couldn't resist a jab. His full-term pregnant pause put her on notice.

"Julie, this is a difficult call for me to make, but it's important that I speak with your firm this morning." She met Daniel's pronouncement with silence. Ellen trained her well to mind the gap.

"I know we've worked with you guys for a long time. You've seen us through a lot of big decisions with new doctors, complicated mergers, and such. And we've always appreciated the business and tax advice you've given us over the years."

Aha, a shit sandwich! She smirked. First, a compliment, then bad news, followed by more praise. Julie waited.

"We've decided to go in a new direction, and we've found another accounting firm to take over our accounts, one with fresh eyes. They have our signed letter authorizing them to get access to whatever workpapers and files they'll need from you."

Jerk, now I know why he's talking to me instead of Ellen. What a coward. He's making me do his dirty work. She raised the third finger of her right hand and pointed it at the telephone receiver. Asshole. The shitshow continued.

"You're such a professional firm, one of the best around, and I know you'll cooperate to make this an easy transition. I have nothing but the highest regard for all that you've done. I mean that. Both you and Ellen."

Julie paused to collect herself and to let the bastard dangle. She never liked him since he had replaced Angela, Dr. Reynolds' office manager, the one who had been at Tom's side since the early days of his practice. Sure, Angela didn't have the college degree or credentials Daniel relied on to shore up his ego. But she had real-life experience. She had managed Dr. Reynolds' practice through years of challenges when the practice and medical industry changed from independent doctors to large group practices. Julie never understood why they got rid of Angela, and she always suspected that the younger doctors had pushed her out. And knowing Dr. Reynolds' avoidance of conflict, she knew Tom would've rubber-stamped the decision.

The pause gave her just enough time to hold back and stay professional. "Really? I'm surprised to hear that and dismayed that you didn't give us an opportunity to address any questions or concerns you were having. I'd be lying if I didn't say this seems to be coming out of left field." Julie heard him gulp in response to her thinly veiled zinger.

"It's been the topic of conversation for some time," he said, "but the partners didn't want to involve you until it was a done deal. It was tough for some of them, but ultimately, the majority rules, and I was drafted to call you." He minded the gap this time and waited for Julie to step across it.

"I guess there's nothing more to say. You obviously made up your minds before today and didn't find it necessary to extend the courtesy to let us respond to your concerns." Julie tried to be as civil as possible when *what the fuck* was what she'd prefer to say. She couldn't go that far but didn't see any point in making him comfortable. She let him squirm in the silence.

"Please give my regards to Ellen and thank her for a job well done. And thank you, Julie, for making the transition as smooth as possible."

Julie didn't say a word. She waited for the click of his phone before slamming the handset down. She stood up with her hands on her hips and shook her head. Unbelievable. What the hell?

# CHAPTER 15

# DANIEL

THERE. IT WAS OVER. DESPITE HIS REPUTATION as Practice Manager, firing someone, even an accounting firm, was not something he relished, but after letting Dr. Reynolds go, it was the easy part of this whole fiasco. Daniel wasn't sure it was the right decision, but Dr. Green wouldn't listen. He was almost irrational in pushing Tom out after the death of his son, and as the practice's Managing Physician, he somehow convinced the others to agree.

Daniel knocked on Dr. Green's office door and opened it. "It's over. I did it. Good idea to call when Tom was meeting with Ellen. We're lucky Tom asked his assistant to schedule it before he left yesterday. It was much easier to talk with Julie. She was angry, but Ellen would've asked me to 'be curious and consider another viewpoint before proceeding with caution.'" He used air quotes to show that he hated this annoying habit of hers as much as Dr. Green did.

Dr. Green pushed back from his desk and grinned. "Good job Daniel. Send an official email to the entire staff introducing the new accountants. Make up something about a conflict of interest now that Tom's gone and that it was Ellen's decision." He leaned back in his chair and put his feet on his desk.

"Really?" Daniel knew by the look on Dr. Green's face that he wasn't kidding.

"Some staff got a little too close with Julie and Ellen over the years. I hated that; no need for it. If they'd just been typical accountants interested in only the numbers, we might've been able to keep them. Too late; their loss. The new accountants you found are perfect. Just the facts. No time to fool around with emotions or relationships. Just what we want."

# CHAPTER 16

# ELLEN

ELLEN GRABBED A MUG OF STEAMING COFFEE from Katie and pushed the other over to Tom. Black for her, regular for Tom. Here in Maine, *regular* coffee meant cream and sugar. In Wisconsin, where Ellen grew up and learned to drink coffee, black was the regular choice. They both took long sips from their respective cups.

"Much better," Tom exhaled and set the mug down on Ellen's desk.

"I'm sorry, my emotions got away from me." She took another sip. "They really fired you? Unbelievable."

"No need to apologize. I've had a day to process this. Believe me, I blew off some steam with Lucy last night." He cradled the cup of hot coffee in his hands. "I was gone from the office for about three months. Two weeks in Eleuthera dealing with Ben's death, ten weeks after. I needed to bring Ben home and cope with his death. I thought the funeral and time off would give me closure. They didn't. I knew I had to go back eventually. Better sooner than later. Time doesn't heal all wounds, but I could tell more time off would just keep me from getting back to normal life."

His chest expanded as he filled it with a deep sigh. "Whatever that is.

"I could feel something was off as soon as I walked in. Everyone looked away as if I had the plague, and they'd head into exam rooms or down another hallway when they saw me coming. I know people are uneasy around tragedy and that three months is long in the life of an office. But this was different, something else. In hindsight, it was obvious that everybody knew. Everybody except me."

Ellen shook her head from side to side. The left corner of her mouth turned up in disgust. She said nothing.

"I hadn't even sorted through the pile of mail on my desk when Daniel showed up. He didn't knock or ask if I was busy. He just perched on the arm of the closest chair and said, 'We need to talk.' I was immediately on alert. Daniel never interacts with any of us, just with the Managing Physician, that thankless job I deep-sixed when they replaced Angela the year before." Tom picked up his coffee cup for another gulp. Ellen did the same.

"Daniel mumbled something like, 'This is tough for me, but the practice has decided to let you go.' And then, he spouted an obscure clause of our partnership agreement that allowed them to terminate a partner for not officially asking for a leave of absence."

"Wow. Talk about taking advantage of a tough situation. How low can they go?" Ellen was shocked that fellow human beings could be so cruel. She stared into her coffee cup as if it had the answer to why someone would do this to an already grieving family.

"I couldn't believe it, but at this stage of my upside-down life, I wasn't surprised. God had something else in mind for me, something that was going to shake me to my core. Ben's death was just the start of a journey I didn't want to be on, but one, nevertheless, I was." He glanced down into his empty cup, wishing it had tea leaves to read.

"I didn't bother to ask why or how many of the doctors I recruited were behind the decision. It was the same when they fired Angela and hired Daniel. My opinion didn't matter. Just like before, they all fell under the spell of Daniel's resumé, polished words, and inspirational plans for expansion. Back then, I said what I needed to and abstained from voting. I took the coward's way out to avoid any backlash, but they knew I was upset. Do you think they fired me for revenge?"

"Hard to know what motivates people. Believe me, I've tried, and I'm always surprised." Ellen leaned her right elbow on the arm of her chair and covered her lips with a loose fist. She was trying to absorb all he was saying.

"Anyway, Daniel stood up, signaling there was no need for further conversation. He told me my calendar was clear, no appointments or surgeries were scheduled, and to feel free to leave anytime. Then he handed me my final paycheck and said my share of the practice would be bought out per the latest signed partnership agreement. I was so angry that I refused the paycheck and his offered hand. He tossed the check on my desk."

Ellen's face flooded with fiery anger. How could they? She started tapping her pen on the desk. Tom's glance put an end to it.

"I was speechless and simply thanked him. I said I'd be gone by the end of the day. Before skulking out the door, he told me that if I had any questions, I should call him directly. The other doctors asked him to manage all the details and said I shouldn't bother them or the staff. And then he was gone. When he walked by my nurse's desk, he mumbled something like, 'It's done.' At least she hung her head in shame when she saw me watching."

Ellen was flabbergasted; there was no other word for it. "Unbelievable. Simply unbelievable. There is absolutely no place in my psyche that imagined this is what we'd be talking about today. I am simply dumbfounded. I had no clue. I don't even know what to say because if I said what I really want to, my image would suffer."

Tom's laugh stopped Ellen's rant, and they both took a deep breath.

"Now, what?" Ellen leaned back in her chair. "What are you going to do? How can we help?"

# CHAPTER 17

# LUCY

LUCY WAS LIVID. TOM REFUSED TO LET HER GO to the meeting with Ellen. She knew they had a special relationship, that Ellen and Tom knew more about his business and finances than Lucy ever would, but this was Lucy's life too. She should be allowed an opinion.

Tom hadn't wanted her there because he guessed Lucy would try to enlist Ellen as a co-conspirator to push him to fight his colleagues. Without Tom, the surgical practice wouldn't exist, there would be no young doctors vying for his position, and it certainly would not have the professional reputation it enjoyed in the medical community. Because of Tom, referrals flowed continually into the practice. Lucy knew Tom was not a fighter and that his fallback position was just that. Fall back. So, he was right; that's exactly what she would've done.

Her grief and rage coiled into a bundle of indignation. How could they so offhandedly do this to the man who created their medical empire? How could they do this on top of Ben's death? Where was their compassion? Watching her husband back away from their unconscionable act filled Lucy with sorrow-fed rage. This wasn't just unconscionable; it was evil, a battle between good and evil. She was not going to walk away.

Tom was a good man—that's why she fell in love with him—but his goodness sometimes covered up his inability to stand up for himself. He had no problem standing up for others. He gave others the benefit of the doubt to help them pave an easy way forward, but too often, it was at the expense of his own family. His soft, calm, logical voice would advise them that it was more important to be good than right. Most of the time, she agreed.

But not this time. What they did to Tom was not good or right. And if he couldn't stand up for himself, Lucy would. She would fight for Sarah's inheritance and for Ben's memory. Tom's career was their family's legacy, not just his. Watching him walk away from it was one loss too many.

She picked up the phone and waited for the connection. "Hi Katie, this is Lucy Reynolds. Is Ellen free?"

# CHAPTER 18

# ELLEN

ELLEN WAS LOST IN THOUGHT AS SHE WALKED back to her office after escorting Tom out. She ping-ponged from anguish to fury and vibrated with grief. She didn't notice Julie standing in the doorway until she bounced off her.

"Julie!" Ellen looked at her in dismay. "Sorry. What a meeting, my head is spinning. You're not going to believe what Tom Reynolds told me."

"I know." Julie flopped sideways into one of Ellen's client chairs and threw her legs over the arm. "Daniel called when you were behind closed doors. I think he planned it that way. Too much of a coward to tell you himself. What an asshole!"

"I know, can you believe it? How could they do such a thing?" Ellen joined Julie's bursts of rage. "My next call is to Daniel. Boy, I really want to let loose; tell him what I'm thinking. But they're still clients, and I have to be civil. I need to get to the bottom of this."

"What are you talking about?" Julie swung her legs down and sat upright in the chair. She leaned in, crossed her arms on the desk, and stared at Ellen. "Still clients? I don't understand. What did Tom say?"

Ellen slowed down to explain to Julie. "They kicked Tom out of the practice. Fired him. Can you believe it? How heartless can people be? Your son dies, so now's a good time to kick out your founding doctor? I just don't get it. I'll meet with Daniel to see what's really going on. There must be something they haven't told Tom." She picked up her empty coffee cup. She could use another, although her hands were already shaking.

"Well, you're going to have to find another way," Julie said. "Daniel fired us. No explanation. Said they're going in another direction and asked for us to help their new accountant make a smooth transition. Can you believe that bastard? Refuses to talk to lowly me for years but takes the asshole way out to give us the hatchet; he didn't even try to talk with you. I never liked the jerk. Not that I needed to. He has enough admiration for himself. But why wouldn't the other doctors stand up for Tom? Or, for that matter, us? I mean, we do their personal tax work too! What the hell?"

Ellen was blindsided by this news but let Julie complete her harangue. After ten years of working with her, she knew Julie needed to dump her frustrations before she could take in anything new. Eventually, Julie stopped. Ellen waited for what was coming next; she'd been here before.

"Wait, they fired Tom? Back up. Did I hear you right? They fired Tom! What the fuck!" Julie jumped out of her chair, spun around, then sat back down. Ellen laughed.

"Aah, you did hear me. They fired Tom for taking time off without prior notification. Yesterday, on the day he returned, the minute he returned. Told him to pack up and be gone by the end of the day." It was Ellen's turn to rant. "Can you believe it? I mean, what's going on over there? What triggered this crap? This is too odd, too off-kilter. What happened? Is this connected to Tom's dismissal, or did we do something wrong? Is there something I've forgotten, something troublesome?"

"Wait. Wait. Wait. Let me think." Julie's eyes closed for a short second. "There was that one thing about travel expenses. They spent a lot of money on international conferences last year. It caught my attention because it's been getting bigger every year, and last year, it almost doubled. You know how the IRS feels about international travel; they want detailed documentation, and I thought I had better have the answers. I asked Daniel. But he was annoyed, kept evading my questions, and said he'd have to check with Dr. Green. I never heard back and decided to drop it."

"I remember now; you were questioning those conferences. Travel costs had been escalating for years." Ellen rubbed the back of her neck while nodding.

"We did our due diligence and reported everything correctly for the tax return." Julie tossed her long, curly hair over her right shoulder. "I know we represent the client, not the IRS, but it always bothered me. I was going to look at it again this year. Now, I'll never know."

"That seems awfully minor to fire us about. But maybe you were getting close to something they didn't want to explain. It's going to be hard to let this go. But we'll have to;

we're not their accountants anymore. Just one more thing to keep me awake at night," Ellen laughed despite being tired after last night's sleepless night.

"You and your sleep. You need to be like me. I sleep like a log. Always have, always will. But you know what they say: no rest for the wicked. I guess we know who's the wicked one in this room!"

Julie's poke didn't lighten Ellen's mood for long. She was stuck in her head. She kneaded her right shoulder to relieve the chronic stress living there. She looked at the pink phone messages in her hand and noticed a call from Lucy. She showed it to Julie. "Maybe she'll shed some light."

# CHAPTER 19

# ELLEN

ELLEN SAT AT HER DESK AND SHUFFLED THROUGH her accumulated phone messages before going home. She was talked out and didn't want to return any of them. Most could wait until tomorrow. She looked again at the one she wished she could avoid and knew she'd sleep better if she got it over with. She punched the number into her phone.

"Lucy, it's Ellen Hartmann returning your call. How are you? Sorry, stupid question. How could you be anything but devastated."

Ellen's stomach muscles contracted, and she felt even more tense. "Tom told me everything. God, it must be awful. How are you holding up?"

Ellen had sent a card and flowers from the office and received a note of thanks from Lucy in return, but a written transaction and an actual conversation were two different things. Her abs pulled even tighter as she babbled. She wished she could stop both.

"It's rough. But it is what it is." Lucy sighed deep and long. "Damn. I hate it when people say that. But what else can I say? It's horrible. Every day is horrible."

"I'm sure it is. I don't know how any of you carry on. I wouldn't have the strength." Ellen was overwhelmed and exhausted, and mindless platitudes kept spouting from her mouth. There was only one thing to say that would stop it. "What can I do to help?" Maybe if she tossed the conversation back to Lucy, the grieving mother would say more about Ben or move on to the reason she had called her. Ellen dropped her head, and her overtight shoulders rebelled against the stretch.

"Tom didn't want me at your meeting this morning. He knows I'm still riled up. I had to call to give you my two cents' worth. I want him to do more than just walk away. I love Tom, you know that, but sometimes I wish he would fight for himself as much as he fights for others."

"I hear you. When Tom told me he wasn't going to fight, it seemed like he just couldn't find the energy." Ellen shifted in her chair. Too much sitting today. "I can't say I blame him. It must be painful having your entire life's work stripped away. Frankly, I'm surprised he wants to keep working at all. But then, we both know his practice is his life."

"For sure. He's not ready to quit surgery, and I can't imagine when he ever will be. He loves his patients, the new technology, and everything about it. It's how he tunes out the rest of the world. And with Ben gone, he needs it more than ever."

Ellen heard Lucy take a long sip of whatever she was drinking. Was it tea? Wine? Ellen wouldn't blame her if it were wine.

"He wants me to help him set up his new practice again," Lucy continued. "I'm not sure I have it in me."

"I get it," Ellen nodded. "I'm not sure I'd be up for it either if I was in your place. His surgical practice was as much your baby as his in the beginning. But it's your loss, too. You were there from day one, filling the roles of receptionist, nurse, office manager, everything. I still remember training you." She glanced at her sliding patio door and looked for her friendly seagull. He had flown the coop. She wanted to follow.

"How could I forget," Lucy laughed. "How will you be paying today? Then, keep my mouth shut. You said the next one to speak loses. You were so right. Most people won't answer *I'm not*. The silence made them reach for their wallets. Oh, how I wish we could go back to those days. You helped me with so much more than finances. You helped me maneuver through life with a doctor at my side."

"I know; it's not easy. It was the first thing I learned." Ellen chuckled. "I never forgot the joke my first boss told me when I started working with doctors. Something about a guy pushing to the front of the cafeteria line. The guy he cut off turns and asks the guy behind him, 'Who does he think he is—God?' The answer? 'No, a doctor!'"

"I remember. It was just what I needed to remind me that part of my job was to keep Tom humble." Lucy's laughter bubbled up again.

"It was supposed to remind me not to let doctor clients push me around. It worked, but I have to admit, sometimes when I nudge them to get off their high horse, I feel like their mother." Ellen appreciated that she could be honest with

Lucy. She always liked her and regretted that she hadn't had the chance to know her better.

"I know. It's exhausting reminding men to grow up and be real. But someone's got to do it, right?" Ellen heard the distinctive clink of a wineglass. She didn't judge Lucy; she was ready for one herself.

"Hence, I'm single," Ellen confessed. "Easier for me to dole out tough love across my desk than the dining room table. I think it's God's cruel joke that men and women try to live with each other. And besides, I have my three sons to shape into men for the next generation."

She immediately regretted bringing her sons into it, but Lucy's laughter didn't stop. They both needed a breather from Lucy's shock and sorrow, but now it was time to stop jabbering and get serious.

"Lucy, what are we going to do with this mess?"

# CHAPTER 20

# ELLEN

ELLEN SNAKED HER WAY THROUGH THE STAFF cubicles to Julie's office. As she moved through the desks, the newest staff accountant caught her eye. He blinked and straightened his spine. "Do you have a minute for a quick question?" His glistening forehead and halting speech hinted that asking wasn't easy for him. Ellen wondered what his mother was like.

"Of course I do. Can I stop on my way back to my office? I need to talk to Julie first. It shouldn't take too long. If I forget, just come to my office and remind me." Ellen knew that as leader of the firm, her first job was to be available to the staff. Without each one's two thousand eighty billable hours plus overtime each year, there would be no fancy waterfront office, no fringe benefits, no accounting firm at all. She may be the firm's owner, but without the staff, it was worthless.

Ellen stood at the half-open door watching Julie study a tax return. She traced numbers from one schedule to another and jotted down notes on a yellow, wide-ruled pad of paper. The deepened furrow between her brows said she needed a break. Long hours staring at tiny numbers weren't conducive to a smooth complexion devoid of wrinkles, and it didn't take long to learn that number crunching went beyond a tired mind, creaky back, and tunnel vision. Excessive worry lines were part of the profession.

Ellen tapped her mechanical pencil on the door frame. "Sorry for interrupting again. This Reynolds crap won't quit today. I just got off the phone with Lucy. She wants our help."

Julie peeled her gaze from the tax forms spread across her desk. She squeezed her eyes shut, then widened them. More crow's feet; in another ten years, she'll look like me.

"Lucy asked to come to the meeting this morning, but Tom wouldn't let her." Ellen sat down in one of Julie's client chairs. She slipped her shoes off and rubbed her feet on the carpet. "She called to give me her part of the story. She's livid that he doesn't want to fight. From the tone of her voice, she's got enough fight in her for both of them."

"Of course, Tom doesn't want to fight. He never does." Julie stretched her neck from side to side. "I saw that every time he caved on contract negotiations. A new candidate only had to hint at something, and Tom gave it to them. I always chalked it up to his need to be the nice guy, but I think it's more than that. He clearly hates conflict."

"In his defense, even if he persuaded them to change their minds in or out of court, it'd be tough to work in an environment where you're not wanted." Ellen's toe played with her empty shoe. "He thinks that as hard as it'll be to walk away, it's easier to just start over. He wants Lucy to set up a new office for him. She's not sure she has it in her to do it again."

"Oh sure. Easy for him to say, 'You do it Lucy; I'll just keep doing surgeries. You do the rest.' Doctors, even great guys like Tom, don't think about what happens behind the scenes." Julie was on an unforgiving rant. "They forget about scheduling appointments, booking ORs, hiring and training staff, filing and refiling insurance forms. They think everything exists because of their doctoring and forget that without everyone orchestrating their life, they'd be sitting with their thumb up their ass."

"Whoa, don't get carried away. You're a bit testy. Working on a tough client?"

"Hell yes. I'm just trying to gather data to stop a mutiny over at Hampton Industries. Management is pushing for a big wage increase. I'm on their side, but the owner won't budge. As much as I'd love to tell him he's wrong, I know that if I do, he'll dig in his heels even more. I'm pulling historical numbers to support management's position and show him what losing crucial staff will do to the bottom line. Losing money is the only way to get this guy to listen."

Ellen stared over Julie's head at the boats bobbing outside of her window. She nodded in agreement. "I hear you. If anyone can do it, you can. You know how to use numbers to get their attention." She slipped her right foot into her shoe. "Anyway, I've scheduled a meeting for the three of us. You, me, and Lucy. Tomorrow morning at 10. She told Tom she needed to talk to us before she'd commit to setting up his office, but that's only an excuse. You won't believe why she really wants our help." Her left foot found her other shoe.

"Oh yeah? What's that?" Julie had drifted back to the problem spread across her desk and looked up again at Ellen.

"Lucy thinks Ben's death wasn't an accident." Ellen had Julie's full attention again. "She thinks Tom's firing is somehow connected. We didn't get into details on the phone because, frankly, it felt like a stretch, and I wasn't about to argue with a grieving mother. The least we can do is hear her out." Ellen stood up. It was time to finish and go home.

The creases at the corner of Julie's eyes deepened, and a slow smile spread across her face. Julie's inner Watson was resurrecting. "That's one helluva thing to drop on your friendly accountant. Whoever said accounting was boring? Every time I get a break and settle into mundane tax returns, you spring something new on me. This time you really outdid yourself!"

"Slow down, let's hear her out first. I'm not about to waste our time and their money chasing something that has no basis. We'll see what she tells us tomorrow. It needs to be more than just assumptions. Remember what assume stands for?"

Julie rolled her eyes. "Yeah, yeah, you remind me all the time. It makes an ass out of you and me. I get it. I'll try not to get ahead of myself this time. Ten o'clock it is. I'll be ready."

"You always are!" Ellen returned Julie's door to its half-closed position and laughed. She meandered back through the cubicles to her office and failed to notice the hopeful young accountant trying to catch her attention.

# CHAPTER 21

# LUCY

THERE, IT'S DONE. SHE SAID IT ALOUD. NOT TO Tom, lost in his bubble of misery. Not to herself. She'd already heard it too many times. But to Ellen, someone she knew would listen and not think she was out to lunch. Lucy had given in to her inner voice, begging her to do something. Anything. She had to try.

She sat at the kitchen island and rested her head on her folded arms. They absorbed the iciness of the unforgiving quartz countertop, which could instantly shatter any fumbled glass or plate. It was like the permanent chill that had invaded her since Ben's death. It, too, could shatter her into a million little pieces. Today's phone call had cracked open Pandora's box, and tomorrow, she and Ellen would lift the lid to peer into its depths.

Lucy had one day to gather her rootless thoughts into a coherent argument that would convince Ellen to help her. She didn't know who else to turn to. Last week, when she hinted about her suspicions to Tom, his solution was to take her in his arms and tell her it would be fine. He didn't notice her body recoil from his deflection as she remembered her father's pats on the head and his implied and too often spoken words, "There there, Lucy, don't be foolish." She didn't want to interpolate too much into Tom's embrace, but she didn't want or need to be placated or silenced. His gesture reflected what he needed at the moment. The hug was for him, not her. He just didn't realize it. She let her anger go, hugged him tightly, and decided to turn to Ellen.

Lucy thought back to the events she brushed off as unimportant. Her uneasy hindsight was unforgiving in its quest for answers. Why did Ben change his Rocky Mountain skiing adventure into a solo Caribbean cruise so quickly? There was no hint that Ben was even considering it until he announced it Christmas morning. In the moment, she chalked it up to his desire for winter warmth and the unpredictability of youth. But was it?

She recalled the Christmas Eve party at Dr. Green's house. Gary Green, Ben's godfather, was Tom's first partner and a close friend of the family. Lucy was close to his first wife Patty. Three years later, Lucy still bristled around his second wife, Gary's former assistant. Rumors of clandestine couplings in supply closets had sounded more like *Grey's Anatomy* than real life. Then Patty found them in the act when she surprised her husband with his favorite lunch. The scene was over-the-top real, and his public humiliation made their divorce quick but not easy. Lucy was still angry when she remembered. Because of office politics, they always accepted the Christmas Eve party invitation even after Patty was replaced. Lucy went to the party with Tom but didn't even try to compete for a role in Dr. Green's pretend world. He deserved an Oscar for acting like nothing had changed.

This past Christmas Eve, he spent a lot of time talking with Ben. Lucy watched from across the room and noticed the intensity of their conversation when Dr. Green laid his hand on Ben's shoulder. Lucy sensed its persuasive weight when Ben looked up and slowly nodded. Later that night, she asked Ben about the conversation with his godfather. He brushed it aside, "I don't remember. I talked to so many people tonight. Must not have been anything important."

The Christmas Eve scene popped into her mind when Dr. Green and his blonde bimbo showed up at the pier to send Ben on his way. Lucy was annoyed when Gary shouted to the entire marina, "You don't think your godfather would send you off on this adventure without a few words of wisdom and a care package, do you?" He handed Ben a smallish box labeled with a thick red Sharpie: *OPEN AT YOUR FIRST PORT.* He squeezed Ben's left shoulder with that same heavy hand and held out his right for a final shake. Lucy saw Ben's head notch down before he ratcheted up, smiled, and stammered a quick thanks.

*Just something to enjoy at your first stop* were Dr. Green's inappropriately loud final words. Then he grabbed his wife's well-manicured hand and dragged her up the low tide gangplank, its steep and unmanageable angle a challenge for the stilettos climbing at his side.

At the time, Lucy tried to appreciate Dr. Green's gesture. Today, she wondered why. Where did this thoughtfulness come from? His ex-wife Patty was the one who kept relationships alive with considerate gifts and cards. Even though Patty was relegated to the fringes of Lucy's family life, Patty sent Ben a bracelet to wear on his voyage. It was handcrafted from a Maine lobster gauge and engraved with the coordinates for home. Patty was the one, not her ex, who thought of farewell gifts. Lucy distrusted his visit that day and everything about him since he went into that closet.

She lifted her head from the icy island and cradled her tear-moistened cheeks in her hands. How does one move from a mother's intuition to concrete facts? How could she enlist Ellen's logical mind and staff resources? She knew Julie was quick to act, and just a hint of Lucy's misgivings would be enough for Julie to begin the attack. But without Ellen fully on board, Julie wouldn't be available.

Meeting Ellen's logical side on an even playing field was the answer. Facts that didn't line up or showed only what, not how or why, wouldn't impress Ellen. Facts had to be concrete and multi-dimensional. She knew Ellen's modus operandi from other times when she helped analyze CVs for new doctors to hire for Tom's growing practice. If the facts in the candidate's professional resumé left gaps too quickly filled with speculation, Ellen went beyond them. She followed her logic-based insight to uncover the hidden side of the candidate. The practice owed Ellen big time for all the times her tenacious digging of how and why had saved them from inviting the wrong person to join. Lucy needed to jumpstart Ellen's usual routine; she needed to emulate Ellen.

She walked across the room to her favorite easy chair. She sat down and ripped out a college-lined sheet from Ben's half-filled school notebook, which was resting on the small table next to her. She used the notebook for her morning journal and was comforted to know Ben once carried it to classes. She used it now to fill the page, trying to transform her mother's intuition into specifics. First, facts. Then, questions—questions that Ellen couldn't resist finding answers to. She ripped out another page and kept writing.

# CHAPTER 22

## ELLEN

"TOUGH DAY, HUH." KATIE INTERRUPTED ELLEN as she walked past the front desk to grab her coat from the closet.

"Amen to that. I knew it would be rough, but I had no idea. I'm exhausted. I'm going to head home a little early."

"Right. Five minutes before the rest of us. Your idea of early." Katie turned back to her desk.

"Believe me, if I could have gotten out of here an hour ago, I would've. Thanks to you, the calls just kept coming, and coming, and coming." Ellen grabbed her brown raincoat and an unclaimed umbrella left behind by a client. It was another rainy day in Maine's spring season, not really a season, but a long, endless transition from a never-ending winter into the brief, speeding days of summer. On days like this, she wondered what she was doing in Maine.

"I think your clients decided to make this national Call Ellen Day." Katie laughed and then scolded. "You do know, just say the word, and I'll cover for you. I can tell clients you're in a meeting or out of the office. You are entitled to a break and a little alone time." She switched off her computer monitor.

"Now you tell me. Next time, remind me. There'll be no alone time or peace and quiet when I get home. Not that I'm complaining." Ellen's mood lifted as she thought of her three sons.

"What's up with the boys tonight? Anything exciting?"

"Not much. Between seasons, the lull before the storm. This year, they're on three different baseball teams. That'll keep life interesting!" Ellen stepped into the elevator and blocked the sensor so the door wouldn't close. "See you tomorrow, Katie. Enjoy your evening."

She leaned against the back wall and enjoyed ten seconds of rest as the elevator slid to the first floor. She stepped out and opened the door to the cramped first-floor parking garage. Parking was a premium on the waterfront, and the spaces were narrow. Only Houdini could maneuver a car between the huge concrete columns supporting the four upper floors. Her car wasn't the only one bearing evidence of backing out with an unfocused mind. Tonight, she knew she was preoccupied and exhausted, and sat for a minute before starting the car. She backed out carefully and decided to take the long way home. She needed time to transition from boss to mother.

Five minutes early meant she'd be ahead of the stream of cars crossing the drawbridge from Portland to South Portland. It was the same reason she arrived shortly after 8 a.m. most mornings. Her eight-minute commute could turn into twenty minutes if she didn't time it right. Twelve minutes was too much to waste in traffic. Of course, if those same twelve minutes stretched to twenty or more because the bridge was raised for an oncoming ship, she was an expert at relaxing and waiting. Traffic was one thing, a drawbridge another. She could only control so much.

Instead of a straight shot home tonight, she meandered the back roads through Cape Elizabeth. She never tired of the centuries-old massive brick and stone homes on the waterfront side of Shore Road. When she first moved here from Wisconsin, she couldn't imagine who had enough money to own and maintain those properties. She never dreamed that someday those owners or those living in McMansions filling the once lush farmland would be her clients. Tonight's longer route circled through affluent neighborhoods, a few modest left-behind middle-America homes, and then around the one remaining farm field divided by the road she and Random occasionally walked.

Thirty minutes later, she pulled into the driveway, marginally refreshed from dropping her work worries along the roadside. Jack and Kevin, her first and second sons, were on the front lawn. Jack was pitching to Kevin, squatting in the catcher's crouch his father had taught him. They both dreamed of following his failed footsteps into a professional baseball career. Ethan, her youngest, bored with the whole thing, ran to meet her.

"What's for dinner? I'm starving!"

The other two threw down their well-oiled gloves and joined in the whining. "Are you too tired to cook? Can we go out?"

She knew they took advantage of her propensity not to cook. They didn't understand her lagging spirit at the end of the day, but they knew she'd give in if they begged a little. "Not tonight, guys; I don't have it in me to go out again. How about we just make our family's special recipe? You know, the one from Ethan's First Grade Family Recipe Book?"

"I'll make the phone call," Jack volunteered.

"I'll set the table," Ethan added.

"And I'll go with you to pick it up." Kevin sealed the deal. The only thing better would be if she could toss the car key to one of them. That time will come; no point rushing it.

"Sounds like a plan. Pizza it is." She threw her raincoat on the back of the kitchen chair and opened the fridge for a club soda. She placed a slice of precut lime in it and climbed the stairs to her bedroom to complete the switch from Certified Public Accountant to just another tired mother.

# CHAPTER 23

## JULIE

JULIE WAS OVERFLOWING WITH QUESTIONS FOR tomorrow's meeting with Lucy. What did Lucy know that she hadn't shared with Ellen yet? What was stirring her suspicions? Julie's mind ran wild with the rumors and innuendos she had picked up but ignored when she worked at Tom's office. With Lucy's nudge, all the small inconsistencies became dying dandelion seeds waiting to be blown apart. Julie needed to get them down on paper before a gust of wind scattered memories she didn't want to lose.

She left the Hampton Industry project open on her desk along with tax returns and workpapers spread around the floor in a pattern only she could read. She knew Bobby, their office cleaner, would leave them as is. Cleaning their offices and other professional offices was a different kind of cleaning. No errant paper, whether balled up or flat, could be tossed. Only those firmly residing inside the waste basket made it into Bobby's trash bin. She mentally added *dust desk* to her list of things to do when, and if, it was ever clear. By the looks of it, it hadn't been clear for a while. Bobby knew to never, ever touch the desktop, no matter how dusty.

With nothing calling her home, she decided to head to her favorite bar. Julie gently backed out of the garage and moved her car to the empty parking spots on the pier outside of their office building. "I don't trust myself after a few beers. I'll make it easy on me and my car." She hoped no one overheard her mother's habit of talking aloud to herself.

She breathed in the salty air, stinking from the ebbing tide that exposed lobster bands, decaying ropes, and other junk from the now-illegal practice of pushing the city's snowstorms off the deep end of the pier. How did no one have the foresight to question the damage being done? She remembered the article she read about the still expanding islands of plastic in the Pacific. "They just don't get it. Damn humans!"

She pushed the tarnished brass hand plate on the glass door to J's Oyster Bar and carefully stepped onto the just-a-bit-too-high threshold. She looked left towards her favorite spot at the curved end of the large, u-shaped bar. It was still available. From that vantage point, she could watch new arrivals as well as the dexterity of tonight's shucker. It didn't matter how often she watched; she relaxed, almost meditated, to the repetitive motion that released the bivalves from their sharp, rugged shells. Watching was one thing; eating them was another. Having grown up in Aroostook County's potato fields far away from Maine's salty coast, she found the slimy crustaceans disgusting. She never indulged.

"Hey J." She called to the tall, fifty-something owner wearing a revealing red tank top and overly tight jeans. 'Give me the usual. How's it going?" Julie removed her coat in the warm, soon-to-be-packed bar. She tossed it on the top shelf of the hangerless coat rack.

"Another day, not enough dollars." J drew a Shipyard draft from the row of attention-getting taps trying to capture new fans. The gold, oar-shaped tap filled the frosty mug with brown ale.

"There you go, I'll open a tab."

"You know me too well." Julie wrapped both hands around the icy glass. She knew the smooth, dark beer would refresh both her mind and body. "I've got some thinking to do."

"I knew the minute you walked in. You're stuck in your accountant's head, and it's not even tax season! What's got you discombobulated tonight? Do you need a stack of napkins?" J asked.

"Sure do. You have no idea how your napkins help me, my clients, and, not to be egotistical, the world. Who knows where the universe would be without J's Oyster Bar and its napkins!" Julie downed another slug of beer.

"Here, have at it. Do your magic. I'll leave you alone." J slid Julie a pile of white cocktail napkins and a second beer. She moved across the bar to serve the latest group of work-weary fishermen.

Julie removed the banana clip that, by day, held her long, unruly, dark curls into a quasi-professional updo. Combing the tangled ringlets with her fingers, she let the thick curtain of hair cascade around her shoulders. She looked across the bar. The gawking fishermen nudged each other as her lifted arms revealed her remarkable cleavage. Her Mona Lisa smile didn't encourage or discourage their appreciation.

After draining the second Shipyard Blue Fin Stout, she pushed the empty glass to the rail and picked up a napkin.

*International Conferences*. Julie underlined the topic.

*When did they start?*

*Where?*

*Always the same place?*

*Who went? All the doctors, a few, the same each year?*

She grabbed another napkin from the pile.

*What kind of conference? New medical techniques? If so, what?*

*Management techniques? If so, why in a foreign country?*

*Who is the sponsor?*

The answers would give Ellen information to back up the numbers in the historical financial analysis Julie intended to do before tomorrow's meeting with Lucy. Why did these expenses always seem questionable? Why did her memory refuse to drop them when so many other transactions for this client and others were lost in the catacombs of her brain?

New napkin.

*Ben's death*. Julie traced the letters over and over until they were black and bold.

What questions or answers were too boilerplate, too off the cuff, too easily brushed off? She poked into the corners of her mind. Not being privy to the entire story that unraveled during Ellen's meeting with Tom kept her unhindered by others' assumptions about what happened. She took advantage of her limited knowledge to fill the blank slate of the logoless five-inch square.

*Mechanical failure? What, how, why?*

*Ben's body? Where? How long? Any unusual marks?*

*Medical examination? Where, who? Confirmed by another?*

*Why does Lucy think they're related?*

Julie didn't limit fact-searching to balance sheets, income statements, or tax returns. Numbers were just a piece in a much bigger jigsaw puzzle. There was a place for everything. And until everything was in its place, the puzzle wasn't complete. Pieces forced into the wrong places would pop out until the puzzle was rearranged and everything fit effortlessly.

She began to fill the fourth napkin.

*Tom's Firing*

*Who decided? All the doctors or just some?*

*Why now?*

*Was there any hint in the past that they wanted him gone?*

*Who benefits?*

Julie grabbed another napkin for the final, most important questions.

*How do I get the records? We're fired!!!!*

*Who has inside information?*

*How do I get it?*

She placed the unused napkins back on the pile, waiting for other drinkers. She arched her back to relieve her shoulders, which were tight from hunching over her desk and the bar. She met the man giggles and elaborate elbowing across the bar with a raised middle finger and infectious smile. The guys were embarrassed and confused by her two-sided reaction and pretended they didn't see.

"One more for the road." She grabbed the dark ale that J slid down the bar to her. "No more work, just pleasure." Julie grinned across the bar at the deeply tanned, weatherworn faces made ruddier by her inviting smile.

She called across the bar, "How you guys doing tonight?"

# CHAPTER 24

# TOM

LUCY CUDDLED INTO HIS ARMPIT. THIS WAS Tom's favorite time of day. She was all his. In bed without distractions, his mind was open and expectant, ready to hear about her day, ready to share his.

Tom snugged Lucy closer. The lavender scent of her evening bath relaxed him. "It's so strange not to go into the office; I was always so excited about an upcoming surgery. And even these past three months, when I was gone, thinking about the office distracted me. Now, there's nothing. Nothing but a deep crater left by the bomb Daniel dropped on me. I still can't believe it."

Tom kissed Lucy's head and waited for her response. She always put things into perspective, found an up to his down, and made a soft place for him to land. He needed her magic tonight.

"I'm reeling too, Tom. I can't believe we're starting over. The worst part is that this time, we're not filled with hopes and dreams. How do we carry on? I'm not sure I can find my footing to do what you want me to." She lifted her head from his shoulder and looked up.

"Don't worry. I'm glad you're seeing Ellen and Julie tomorrow. They'll help you find your way back to what you did so well before." Tom tried, but he knew he was failing dreadfully at this reversal of roles. Even he, the one who relished being on the receiving end of comforting words, found his own words annoying.

"We'll see. I'm not sure they can help me find enough energy." Lucy dropped back onto his shoulder. "Do you think Angela would come back? Do you know what she's doing these days?"

Tom remembered his former office manager. Maybe Angela was the better choice. If Lucy felt even remotely like Tom, being pressured to do something you weren't one hundred percent committed to wouldn't work. Hiring Angela might make it easier for them, and their relationship.

Tom scratched his head with his free hand, "I don't really know what she's doing. Last I knew, she worked for a one-doctor office outside of Portland. I can't remember where. I'll see if I can track her down. Is that what you want? Would you rather not help me?"

"Oh Tom, you know I always want to help you. I'm just tired, so tired. I need time for myself." Lucy rolled away from him.

He regretted his last question and followed her roll to spoon her stiffened back. "Relax, I've got you. Don't worry about a thing."

Tom prayed that this time, his words were adequate.

# CHAPTER 25

---

# ELLEN

ELLEN CREAKED OPEN THE HEAVY DOOR, RELIEVED that her non-barking dog wouldn't wake her three sons. She snapped on Random's leash and paused on the concrete porch to fill her lungs with the crisp, moist morning air. Today, all things were possible. How different life feels with a good night's sleep. Of course, her idea of a good night's sleep differed from most. For Ellen, waking up uninterrupted after five hours was something to be thankful for.

Yesterday, her meeting with Tom filled her terror-ridden knowledge gaps with reality. She always advised distraught or overwhelmed clients to first look at the facts. Without concrete facts, imaginations run wild. With clear data, the path forward opens, and solutions appear. Too bad she didn't listen to her own advice. Last night, with her painful assumptions and speculations traded in for facts, her nonproductive circular thinking finally stopped, and she slept.

Ellen bounced down the porch steps into a gray morning still waiting for the rising sun. Random trotted right, their usual route. Ellen's musings turned to today's meeting with Lucy. It would be delicate at best. The last thing she wanted was to add to Lucy's pain, but she suspected Lucy's speculation about Ben's death was just that. Speculation. Ellen couldn't imagine a link between Ben's death and Tom's firing other than the obvious. They both were incredibly painful experiences. She'd have to work to keep an open mind and see what Lucy offered Julie and her for consideration.

As she walked through the unlit streets, the rhythm of her feet started a parade of numbers marching through her mind. Numbers often resurrected spontaneously during her walking reveries. She didn't notice their beginning but wasn't surprised when a three-quarter time waltz of numbers surfaced.

22 23 24

25 26 27

To the steady beat of her feet, she wondered if Lucy was simply blinded by her grief. Was it a desperate attempt to make sense of the senseless? That was the obvious answer. It was the easy answer. Ellen resisted both.

46 47 48

49 50 51

She must not write Lucy off quickly. Had Ellen forgotten that her best option in times like this was to slow down, open up, and be curious? Without those three, doors slam shut before sneaking a peek inside. Prematurely closed doors never revealed secrets, much less opportunities.

94 95 96

97 98 99

The pattern continued its rhythmic waltz to 100 and started again.

Lucy wasn't one to jump to conclusions; Ellen knew that. Her faith in the intangible grounded her decisions. She didn't clutch at straws. Ellen discovered that years ago when she watched Lucy struggle to pay Tom's medical school debt while waiting for patient referrals to jumpstart his new practice. Most wives of new doctors, exhausted from supporting the family through medical school and residencies, fell into deep despair, wondering when their rewards would come in. Not Lucy. She knew their lives were held in the hands of a greater being.

13 14 15

16 17 18

Ellen's inner rhythm continued, and she turned down the same farm road she circumvented the night before. She looked across the rows of freshly tilled rows. Soon they'd be sprouting strawberry plants promising luscious end-of-June berries. She watched the morning sky slowly shift from gray to a soft, purplish pink. Random stopped and sniffed the pungent compost tilled into the soil. Ellen may not have the deep faith of Lucy and Tom, but she knew the universe always delivered. All she needed was to listen. Both backward and forward.

Forward was the easy part. She'd let Julie take the lead in their meeting with Lucy. Julie told Ellen she was going to J's Oyster Bar to clear her head and indulge in her favorite cocktail napkin investigating. Ellen knew how it worked and could trust Julie to be overflowing with cogent questions. Her job was to sit back with an open and curious mind, listen carefully, and sleuth out the path forward. Focused listening would lead Ellen to a path forged without judgment or assumptions, one free of preconceived notions. If there was one.

48 49 50

51 52 53

Backward listening took more effort. Ellen let her mind drift back in time. She walked and willed her mind to empty as the counting continued. She waited for something to appear.

85 86 87

88 89 90

Angela's out-of-the-blue dismissal a year ago popped into her mind. Ellen was usually party to major decisions, but that time, she was not. She learned of it after the fact when Dr. Green called to report that he was now Managing Physician and that Daniel had replaced Angela as Practice Manager. In hindsight, Ellen should have asked more questions, but she was caught off guard. Now, she wondered if that was exactly what was intended.

Did she miss something back then? Was Angela's dismissal the first step in letting Tom go? Angela was highly competent, and Ellen doubted that job performance was why she was dismissed, but when she asked Dr. Green what happened, he deftly changed the subject. Why didn't he want to discuss it? Was there something Angela knew that forced them to get rid of her? Was there something they were keeping from Tom? And, from Ellen?

Ellen climbed the half-dozen steps to her home. With a quick shake of her head, she cleared the final remnants of her guesswork. She intentionally dropped her slowly rising, tension-ridden shoulders. She packed away her accountant's mind.

She placed her hand on the latch just as the door swung open. "Mom, Jack is being a jerk!"

Her day had begun.

# CHAPTER 26

# JULIE

JULIE GATHERED HER PAPERS FROM YESTERDAY'S last client meeting. She carefully highlighted the client's name, slipped them into a plastic folder, and placed them in the to-be-filed basket on the wooden bookcase outside her office. They needed to make it into their final resting place correctly. There was nothing more frustrating than trying to find misfiled papers. Why was it so difficult for the staff to understand that these number-filled papers were the lifeblood of their business, that a simple-looking letter represented fifteen hundred dollars' worth of advice? Losing them was tantamount to misplacing blood tests or X-rays. No one was happy to recreate them.

She looked across the office. Ellen's door was open, a sign that she was free to be interrupted. Julie decided to take advantage of it. Ellen would help her refocus and get ready for their meeting with Lucy. She was sitting at her desk, a yellow-lined pad and her favorite .7-millimeter black Pentel mechanical pencil rested on the desk's dust-free surface.

Julie leaned on the doorframe. "Looks like you're ready for Lucy. I just need a few minutes to transfer my thinking to a notepad. I don't think Lucy would be impressed with my napkin notes."

Ellen was uncharacteristically slow to respond. She must not have seen her walk in.

"Probably not," Ellen murmured before her voice got louder, "or at least she wouldn't want to be billed for them." Ellen was sitting stiffly. Her back barely touched her chair. "It feels like days since I set up this meeting, not less than twenty-four hours ago. But I'm glad it is this morning. If it had been this afternoon, I would've tied myself into knots with foolish overthinking. It's hard to keep an open mind."

Julie noticed the tension in Ellen's hands clasping the arms of her chair. Changing the subject could help them both relax. "I was lucky. Good news, the CEO of Hampton Industries is folding."

Ellen released her grip and folded her hands before placing them on her desk. "You got him to give some raises?"

"I did, but it took some convincing. They'll get five percent. Better than nothing. Possibly five percent more in six months. I tried to convince him to do the full ten now because I'm not sure five will keep the CFO from bolting. I hate to be selfish, but if he leaves, my job gets tougher!"

"Mine too," Ellen commiserated, "when I try to explain the increase in their accounting bill. They don't seem to understand that it takes extra time to train a new CFO, no matter how qualified they are. In small companies, there's no one to do the training but us, their friendly accountants. And they forget that we don't do this out of the goodness of our heart."

"Well, I'm not too sure about that. Tell me again why we're meeting with Lucy?" Julie teased to try to get Ellen out of the funk she was in.

Ellen didn't bite. "One more thing. What about Angela's firing a year ago? Remember how surprised we were? And, when we asked why, Dr. Green just stonewalled us. I think it's connected somehow. Am I off base?" Ellen looked at Julie.

"Yeah, that was really weird." Julie played with her hair while she thought. "I never understood it; Angela seemed so competent. I forgot about that. You really think we need to go back that far? I only focused on the conferences last night. Never gave a second thought to Angela's dismissal. I'll look at it again and try to keep an open mind."

*Try* was the operative word. Julie's mind ricocheted back to the questionable international conferences, and Angela slipped out of her mind before she was back to her office.

# CHAPTER 27

# LUCY

LUCY PULLED HER WHITE SUBARU INTO THE LAST remaining client parking spot on the pier and exhaled with relief. She didn't realize how uptight she was until she arrived outside Ellen's office. She silently thanked the parking gods for making it unnecessary to backtrack and search for parking on congested Commercial Street. Once again, the universe delivered.

She turned off the ignition and rested her head on the steering wheel. Thank you, she prayed, for helping me be my best, most logical self today. After a few moments, she lifted her head and stared at the sailboats filling up the marina at the next pier. She loved Ellen's office and always said it was the best in the world. What could be better than being on a pier next to a busy marina, with power and sailboats bobbing in the water? Today, those boats brought her only pain. But she found it hard to look away.

Lucy picked up the Cordovan portfolio that carried the papers she had prepared the afternoon before. She needed to concentrate. She flipped through her notes and tried to collect herself. Her mind pulled her back to the marina. She was drifting into a no-man's land of angst and confusion. She squeezed her eyes shut and shook her head. Stop it. Not now.

She took one last glimpse and opened the car door. As she placed her left foot on the thick, weathered planking of the pier, her attention was diverted by a woman stepping off a large powerboat. Was that Angela? She hadn't seen her in over a year and never understood why the practice had fired her. She was so helpful to Tom and Lucy over the years as Tom's practice grew from one doctor to a large group practice. Angela was the logical choice to help Tom set up his new office.

If that woman getting out of that boat was Angela, she had changed. No, she must be mistaken. This woman was too thin, too intense looking. She didn't have the welcoming smile that always filled Angela's face. And as far as Lucy knew, Angela didn't boat, either sailing or otherwise. Lucy squeezed her eyes shut. She opened them. The woman was gone. Stop it Lucy, you're seeing things.

With one deep breath, she gathered her resolve, clutched her folder to her chest, and pivoted out of the car. Fake it until you make it. Lucy planted her right foot on the decking, squared her shoulders, and strode confidently towards the door with Fifty Portland Pier stenciled on its glass. It was time to present her case.

# CHAPTER 28

# TOM

TOM WOKE MOST MORNINGS TO THE SMELL OF brewing coffee and his wife peacefully gazing out to the morning's nothingness from her ocean-colored, tufted easy chair. It was her early morning refuge. They both were reverently grateful for the abundant life that gave them this incredible, everchanging, saltwater view of Casco Bay. He wrapped his frigid hands around a mug of tea and sat in Lucy's chair. He hoped it could magically transfer her grounded morning reverie to him. He was jagged and jangled from the upheaval of his life. Nothing was the same. Ben was gone. His practice was gone. Even Lucy, at this moment, was gone.

Tom focused on the view he indulged in on rare occasions. It always gave him so much pleasure and peace. Today, neither Lucy's osmotic calm nor his own prayers were working. He couldn't concentrate. The seagulls floating in the grayish-green ocean drifted by unseen. Cumulus clouds, heavy with moisture, started to gather. It was another damp, gray morning in Maine's mud season. Tom sighed.

His drifting mind settled on his aloneness. Is this the first time I've been alone? It's the first since Ben's death, but is this really the first ever? Lucy was always here at home. At the office or in the operating room, others picked up the reins to lead his life forward. When did he hand his life over for others to orchestrate? He didn't have the answer. He took a sip of tea.

He watched a lone sailboat courageously, or foolishly, brave the early spring waters. Had he ever been the master of his own life? Was it his own unspoken desire that fueled his excitement over Ben's journey? Had he unconsciously pushed Ben to fulfill his own dreams? A flush of guilt and shame rose to his face. He took another sip of tea to calm his uncomfortable introspection.

Tom needed, no wanted, Lucy. She would talk him down from this cliff of despair. But today she was gone. A meeting with Ellen. He regretted that he didn't bring her with him yesterday. Maybe if he had included her, she'd understand why she had to handle the next step of his career. If he had, she would be here now, with him. An unfamiliar, deep-seated irritation brewed inside of him. He felt deserted. He dismissed both emotions before he claimed them as his own.

Before Lucy left, she asked Tom to call Angela and ask for her help setting up his new practice. He heard the fatigue and anxiety in Lucy's soft voice. In the moment, it overshadowed the angry abandonment that now swirled in his gut. Of course I will, he told her. But now, a bubble of resentment blended with his emotionally toxic brew. His skin tingled with droplets of sweat, and he set the hot tea on the small table beside Lucy's chair.

Tom stood up, annoyed that he couldn't usurp Lucy's peace. He twisted his torso from side to side. He wasn't accustomed to this lack of movement except when standing in the OR during a complex surgery. But his mind was fully engaged in the operating room, and he barely noticed his body. Being immobile with an unfocused mind was new. Now, his body fairly shouted its discomfort. It was time to move; sitting was not helping his anxiety. He procrastinated long enough.

It was time to make the call. He justified putting it off until after Lucy was gone. Now, time was running out, and he needed to follow through with his promise before she returned. Tom wished he had been more available to Angela when she lost her position. After her fateful meeting with Dr. Green that day, her usual open and available self was locked behind an impenetrable door. Not knowing what happened, Tom asked Angela what was going on. Not now, was all she said. He complied, respecting their ten years together. Angela left that day. The next day, they replaced Tom as Managing Physician. He and the practice moved on. He was ashamed that Angela's *not now* had morphed into his *never*.

Lucy didn't appreciate how tough it was for him to make this call. How could he ask Angela to help when he had abandoned her? Tom's bitterness surfaced when the sting of his own rejection threatened to erupt.

Don't get ahead of yourself. First things first. Find out where Angela is. Bonnie, his nurse, rather former nurse, would know. After working together for years, Bonnie and Angela were close friends, and it was safe to assume they were still in contact. *Stop overthinking; just do it.* Tom picked up the phone.

"Good afternoon. Portland Surgical. How can I help you?" The voice on the other end was unfamiliar but cordial. Another change.

"This is Dr. Reynolds. May I speak with Bonnie?"

"Hold, please. I'll try her line."

Tom felt the new receptionist's aloofness. Was it imagined? Maybe there'd be an iota of his former practice camaraderie when he spoke with Bonnie.

"Dr. Reynolds, how can I help?" Bonnie's clipped greeting said it all. Their usual warm and playful banter was gone. He switched gears from connecting with an old friend to simply asking a stranger for information, ignoring his overwhelming sadness.

"Thanks, Bonnie. I won't take up your time; I'm sure you're busy. I'm trying to track down Angela. Do you know where she's working? I tried to call her personal number, but I guess it's disconnected." All his uncomfortable feelings spilled out in a regurgitated request.

"I'll ask Angela to contact you. I don't feel comfortable giving out that information. What number shall I have her call?" Bonnie wasted no time to end the call quickly. Once again, Tom wondered where the Bonnie he knew had gone.

"Thank you. Please have her call my home number, 207-846-1584."

"I will." And with that, she hung up—no goodbye. Tom was shocked by Bonnie's abruptness but stopped from reading too much into it. He was the one violating Daniel's instructions not to engage with anyone from the practice, while Bonnie was simply complying.

Tom laid the disconnected receiver next to one of the many drug salesman's freebie notepads they used for phone messages at home. He was ready to capture Angela's contact information. He returned to his seat by the window. The ocean spread before him, a great gray expanse of nothingness.

He had no choice. He would have to wait.

# CHAPTER 29

# DANIEL

DANIEL LISTENED TO THE SQUISH, SQUISH, SQUISH of someone's sneakers coming down the hall. Good, a distraction. He flipped over the financial statements laid out across his desk. When the footsteps slowed, he called, "Come in." Bonnie's tap, tap, tap on the door was unnecessary.

There was a deep furrow between her brows, and Daniel sensed her trepidation. She looked just like his five-year-old when he had done something wrong and was waiting to be punished.

"What's up?" He tried to make it easier for her by keeping it light.

"I hope I did the right thing," Bonnie shoved her hands into her pockets. "I took a call from Dr. Reynolds. He was looking for Angela's contact information. I wasn't sure what to say, so I told him I'd have her call him. I know Dr. Green doesn't want any of us to talk with him, but I didn't know what else to do. Can I call Angela to pass on the message, or will I get in trouble?" Bonnie moved her hands to her stomach as if she might be sick.

"I'm sure it'll be fine. Dr. Green just didn't want anyone discussing the practice with Tom. You handled it perfectly. You didn't give away Angela's personal information, and it sounds like you didn't invite a lengthy conversation. Angela can decide what to do." Daniel didn't want to add to Bonnie's stress.

"Oh, thank you. That's a relief. I was so worried." Bonnie's face relaxed, and her easygoing demeanor returned. "It was tough not to talk with him. He was, and still is, one of my favorite doctors. But I know Dr. Green wants us to cut all ties."

Daniel nodded. "I know how difficult this is for you. I appreciate that you followed management's wishes. It's a tough situation at best." He noticed the crease reappear between her eyes. "I don't see any reason to even mention it to Dr. Green, do you?" That should do the trick. He didn't want Bonnie to lose her focus. He relied on her to continue the smooth transition of Dr. Reynolds' patients to their newest physician.

"Thanks. That helps. I feel much better. I'll call Angela and tell her that Dr. Reynolds is trying to contact her. My guess is he wants help setting up his new office. I heard from the OR scheduling office that he's contacted the hospital. He's moving his credentialling from here to his new practice."

"I'm not surprised to hear he's starting again. He's a great surgeon. Anything else?" Daniel turned over the financial statements he'd rather avoid to hint that their meeting was over.

She shook her head no and walked out. Daniel listened to the squish, squish, squish of her sneakers fading down the hallway.

# CHAPTER 30

# LUCY

LUCY LAID HER PORTFOLIO ON ELLEN'S DESK AND lowered herself into the orange and gold geometrically patterned armchair, meant more for a living room than an office. Ellen circled behind the desk and smiled at her. Lucy appreciated how Ellen used every means possible to put her clients at ease. She peered out the sliding glass doors that led to the triangle-shaped deck overlooking the harbor, another perk of meetings with Ellen. She turned away when Julie slipped into the matching chair beside Lucy and across from Ellen.

"Thanks for meeting with me on such short notice." Lucy had dispensed with small talk on the endless walk from the front desk, past the conference room filled with someone else's client meeting, to Ellen's office. Lucy was ready now. Yesterday, she opened Pandora's box. Last night, she organized her misgivings. Today, she needed to know she was not alone with her fears. Today, she'd ask Ellen and Julie for help.

"Of course, no problem." Ellen's soft, warm tone calmed her. "After tax season I have a lot of openings. And to be honest, you piqued my interest yesterday. I want to hear more about what you're thinking." Ellen's unblinking eyes gave Lucy permission to spill.

"You probably think I'm crazy. Believe me, there are times I think so too. But as much as I try to put this out of my mind, it keeps coming back. I've learned to pay attention to ideas that won't let me go. You two are the only ones I can think of to talk with." Lucy looked away from Ellen and over to Julie.

"Ellen filled me in when she told me we were meeting." Julie grabbed her long curls into a makeshift ponytail. She knotted it around itself to hold it briefly in place before it untied to unleash the unruly curls again. "We don't think you're crazy at all. I'm glad you decided to let us help you sort through all this. Where do you want to start?"

"I tried to pull my thinking together so you can see where I'm coming from." Lucy opened her leather portfolio. She retrieved three one-sided sheets of paper. "I made a copy for both of you. Why don't you take a minute to look at my notes? It'll save some time." She slid one sheet across to Ellen, handed another to Julie on her left, and placed hers on the closed portfolio.

Lucy regarded her work judgingly. Last night, she was confident this would be enough to garner their support. This morning, it seemed pitiful. Did this one sheet of paper really capture everything?

As they read, Lucy reviewed the main points she had made. How she questioned the timing of Tom's firing right after Ben's death. How no one would discuss what happened. How their longtime friends and colleagues at the practice had cut them out of their lives. The coldness of everyone's reaction at Ben's funeral felt less like discomfort over a child's death and more like avoidance of what really happened or would be happening. And then, there was that box, the one Gary passed to Ben on the dock. Something about that box pierced her heart.

Julie was the first to speak. "Thanks, Lucy. This helps a lot. I'm only speaking for myself, but it gives me some new angles to consider. I didn't think about how the practice might be complicit in all of this. What do you think, Ellen?"

"I agree. Nice job, Lucy. It's important to gather as many perspectives as possible before choosing the next step. Two heads are better than one, and with the three of us, we can't go wrong." Ellen nodded her head and looked back to Julie to continue.

"I spent time last night putting together some questions, too. You might not have the answers, but do you mind if we start there?" Julie was looking at Ellen but tilted her head toward Lucy.

Lucy thought the question was for both of them, but the lengthening pause told Lucy they were waiting for her answer, not Ellen's. "Go for it. I'll answer what I can." Lucy put her copy back in the portfolio for now. She didn't want them to ignore it.

Julie repositioned her chair and looked directly at Lucy. "One thing that has been bothering me was the expensive international conferences. Do you know anything about those?"

Lucy paused. She was surprised by this topic. It was not on her list, but she was curious where it might lead. "Not really. Only a few comments from Tom about Gary being gone again. He was a little miffed that they replaced him as managing physician with someone who was gone so much."

"How often did he go? Do you know what the conferences were about?" Julie looked down at the pad of paper in her lap and slipped Lucy's sheet under its first page, which was filled with notes. Ellen picked up her mechanical pencil and wrote something on her own yellow pad in front of her.

"I'm not really sure. Two or three. Maybe four times a year. But the travel was so long that he was always gone at least two or three weeks each time. And his wife always went with him." Lucy's face tightened as she thought about Dr. Green's new wife and how his first wife, her dear friend Patty, was never included on any trips.

Julie interrupted Lucy's derailed thoughts. "Really, that's kind of odd, isn't it?"

"Not really. My guess is they were conferences on sports medicine and the latest drugs available in countries other than the US. Most conference sponsors are large drug companies that make sure there's enough on the agenda to attract the spouses. I fell for a few of those conferences in the early days." Lucy brushed her bangs to the side. "They were always a waste of time and money."

"Smart," Julie smirked. "Entice the spouses with a trip to China, and attendance is sure to go up. Everyone likes a trip made cheaper with some hefty tax deductions."

Ellen broke in. "Do you know if Dr. Green was the only doctor who went?"

"That I do know. He was. Tom said there was static from the other doctors about the excessive cost of these trips. Daniel suggested they increase the discretionary funds each doctor was allocated to help equalize compensation and benefits. Tom ended up with a hefty bonus because he didn't use much of his." Lucy's heart pumped faster. Was Ellen on to something?

"I remember that. I was worried that the practice couldn't absorb the big increase in doctor compensation. I cautioned against it. But the other doctors were more than happy to get more money. They voted it through."

Ellen stared at her notes. Lucy decided to jump back in.

"Look at number five on my list. Do you think the box Gary gave Ben had anything to do with those conferences? There was something weird about it. But I couldn't figure out what. Your questions about Gary's trip to China make me wonder. Do you think there's a connection?" Lucy sputtered with excitement.

"Tell me more. I'm not sure I'm following you." Ellen set her pencil down and rested her arm on the desk. Lucy had Ellen's full attention.

"I hadn't considered any of those trips Gary made over the years. Your questions are bringing back memories of more conversations with Tom." Lucy's words flowed with excitement. "He was concerned that Gary was too focused on the drugs that Chinese athletes were using. They're difficult to trace, and they're illegal here in America. Gary knew the Chinese had an unfair advantage over the elite athletes that Gary had as patients, and Tom worried that Gary's competitive side might stretch the bounds of his ethics." Lucy stopped for a deep inhale.

"What if Gary was using Ben as a drug mule?" Lucy stumbled over her choice of words. "Have I been watching too much TV?" Lucy laughed, then collected herself. This was too serious to joke about.

Julie ignored Lucy's nervous laugh. "You might be on to something. I do remember meeting with Dr. Green once about his personal finances. He liked to brag about his patients' careers. He said they only lost because his athletes didn't have access to the performance-enhancing drugs of other countries. He was angry that current drug testing at competitions

didn't detect their use." Julie's face beamed with newfound excitement. Lucy wondered if her own face appeared the same.

"Ellen, what do you think?" Lucy eyed Ellen.

"It's possible," Ellen said. If it was possible to see someone thinking, Lucy could see it now. "But how do we get more information? We aren't privy to practice finances anymore. We're cut off. I doubt your workpapers have the details we'll need to track down those conferences. Am I right?" Ellen tossed the question to Julie. Lucy was confused but didn't interrupt.

"You could be right. I'll check the files to be sure. I have some ideas on how to get the information. We'll talk later."

Julie was speaking directly to Ellen, and Lucy wondered what those ideas were. Obviously, she wasn't going to be part of that conversation, but maybe Tom would know. Ellen's slight nod to Julie was enough for Lucy to know they were approaching the end of the meeting. She didn't care that they had glossed over her first four points. This was a start. A good start.

Ellen picked up Lucy's prepared presentation. "Lucy. Thanks for taking the time to put this together. It's immensely helpful. Let Julie and me see what we can come up with. We'll be in touch, I promise. I'm not saying it'll go anywhere, but we'll investigate further."

Ellen might be downplaying her response, but Lucy knew her well. Ellen's efficient self never wasted time pursuing dead ends; even this tiny comment helped Lucy feel hopeful.

She was almost speechless with Ellen's promise, but not quite. "Thank you. I don't know what else to say. I came in today prepared to do anything to get your help, but I wasn't sure where to start. You not only listened to what I had to say, you connected the dots. You found the missing link that could make sense of all this. How can I ever thank you?"

"Let's not get too far ahead of ourselves. Remember, this may not go anywhere. But I promise we'll do what we can to check into those conferences."

Ellen walked around her desk to Lucy's chair, and she rose to accept Ellen's always comforting hug.

Julie waited for them to finish. "I'll walk Lucy to the front desk for her coat, I'm going that way anyway."

Lucy followed Julie out of the office, turned back one last time, and whispered, "Thank you."

Ellen didn't hear her. Her head was bent down, and she was studying her notes.

# CHAPTER 31

## LUCY

"ARE YOU GOING TO HELP ME? NOW THAT YOU'VE met with Ellen, I'm sure you can see it's the best way to get my new office going." Tom's interruption exasperated Lucy.

Earlier, when she arrived home after her meeting and running some errands, she pretended not to see Tom splitting wood. When she rounded the final curve on the twisting driveway that ended with an expansive scene of the ocean surrounding their home, she feigned being caught up in the spectacular view and scooted into the house. Sarah wasn't home from school yet, and Lucy needed alone time before facing Tom over dinner.

Lucy thought she had gotten away with it. She filled her favorite mug, a gift from Ben, with hot water and placed it in the microwave. She pushed the +30 button twice. Her hands warming around a cup of Bengal Spice was just what she needed to unwind. She collapsed into her favorite chair overlooking the water. Cinnamon and other inviting spices wafted from the honey-sweetened tea. Her mind slowed as it responded to the ebb and flow of the peaceful afternoon waves outside her window.

Lucy's nerves were starting to recover from her meeting with Ellen when Tom interrupted her quiet contemplation. She looked over her right shoulder at him. His red plaid woolen shirt, perfect for cool spring days like this, lay on the floor where it had fallen after he had thrown it on the kitchen stool. "Oh Tom," she repeated for one too many times, "I told you how I felt. I'm not going back to the office."

Lucy saw his smile disappear, and she was saddened to see Ben's face reflecting back. Both Tom and Ben's excitement could fade with only a few words from Lucy. She supposed it was the bane of every wife or mother who tried to coax the men in their lives back to reality.

"I know what you said, but I was hoping Ellen would persuade you that it would be best for us to do this together." Tom's right eyebrow lifted.

Lucy ignored the familiar pleading voice that too often resulted in her giving in to Ben. This was not going to be one of those times. Tom was an adult.

"She did not." She talked as if to a child. "I'm not going to change my mind." She turned back to the solace of the sea.

Tom stood behind her chair. He put his hands on her shoulders and began to massage them. She knew this tactic and was not going to fall under its spell. "Did you call Angela today like you promised?" Lucy wanted her weary assumption to be wrong.

Tom's hands dropped from her unresponsive shoulders. He moved in front of her chair, oblivious that he was obstructing her view and reverie. "I tried her home phone number. It said it was disconnected."

Lucy waited for him to say more, though she fully expected that would be the end of his report. She'd been here before and let an uneasy silence fill the space between them.

Tom paused. When Lucy didn't speak, he continued. "I decided to call Bonnie at the office to see if she could connect with Angela. It was so odd. I felt like a stranger." Lucy said nothing. His voice faltered. "Bonnie said she'd have Angela get in touch with me."

"Did she? I mean, did Angela call you?" Lucy knew this game. She'd have to drag every bit of information from him.

"No, she didn't. I'm still waiting." Tom hovered over her, insensitive to her needs.

"Please stay on it. I'm sure if you ask around the hospital, someone will know where she's working." Lucy inhaled deeply and exhaled with an extended, audible sigh. "Now, I'd like a little time to myself. Can I be alone for a while?" Lucy avoided his eyes.

She was shocked by her choice of unregretful words and couldn't believe she uttered them. Is this what grief does to a person? Was pain eclipsing the kind and caring part of herself, covering it with clouds of bitterness, despair, and resentment? Or was it simply revealing her dark side because her hope and faith were slowly slipping away? She was drained, depleted, and grieving just as much as Tom. But one of them had to make sense of what happened, and she didn't want the distraction of taking care of Tom to sap what little energy she had left. She sighed.

"Of course, sorry for the intrusion," he pouted. Lucy didn't react. She was too exhausted to engage.

# CHAPTER 32

# JULIE

JULIE WATCHED THE MAN IN THE DARK GRAY SUIT from her large, side-by-side office windows. He tossed his briefcase over the sailboat's railing and climbed aboard his boat tied up at the marina next door. She couldn't imagine living on a boat year-round, even if it was a luxurious sixty-five-footer with a brand name any sailor would swoon over. Every day, this man, obviously with a decent job, left his boat at 8:00 a.m. and returned no later than 5:30 at night. No overtime for him; he must be a banker.

During tax season, she observed his daily routine. For the ten weeks of their busy season, she was at the office before and after the stranger's business day started and ended. But now that tax season, with its long sixty to seventy-hour work weeks, was over, his marine lifestyle was mostly out of sight, out of mind. But tonight, for good reason, she stayed late enough to see the man's comings and goings to speculate about life on a sailboat.

Julie was waiting for Bobby and listened for the sound of the creaky wheels of the office cleaner's trash barrel as he pushed it down the hallway. Everyone had gone home for the night, and there would be no competition for his attention when he stopped at each desk to empty wastebaskets. Her thoughts circled back to why she needed Bobby's help in the first place. He could get her into Portland Surgical's office. She never heard Bobby's approach until he spoke.

"What're you doing here again? I thought the other night was an anomaly. Are you turning this into a habit?"

Julie spun around in her chair to greet him. Bobby was a breath of fresh air amid the endless march of stale and musty tax returns. He was not what you expected in a cleaning person. Well-educated, engaged in life, and a hopeless gossip, Bobby was everyone's favorite. When you were lucky to run into him on a late work night, you could always count on an extended conversation. Even in the middle of tax season, everyone was happy for the diversion of their good-looking janitor.

"Just the man I was waiting for." Her broad smile was intentional.

"Oh yeah? Need help moving something?" Bobby doubled as the office handyman whenever they needed him. Whether scraping the mahogany exterior of the building's saltwater-weathered door, painting out an office, or carrying old files to offsite storage, he was always available.

"Not this time. This is something special, something only you can help me with. And it doesn't involve your muscles." There it was again, something Julie barely admitted to herself and worked even harder to discount. Like it or not, there was something about Bobby. She tried to ignore it.

"Really? And what might that be?" he flirted. "Do tell."

Julie flipped her long hair over her left shoulder. Damn unconscious behaviors.

"First, you can't tell Ellen about this." Julie's delivery switched gears. She needed to stop her unruly subconscious in its tracks. This was serious business.

"Really? You've got my attention now." Bobby slumped into Julie's client chair. He had been there many times before. "What's up?"

"Ellen doesn't know all the details about this, just enough to keep her honest. I'll tell her about the product, not the process, so she can say she knew nothing about this." Julie lowered her voice. "You know how it is with CPAs and their code of ethics. Gotta live by the book. Ellen sometimes pushes the boundaries, but I know her well enough that this is something she'd rather not be party to. That's where I come in. Sometimes, it pays not to have those initials behind my name."

"I always wondered why you weren't a CPA." Bobbie clasped his hands behind his neck.

Julie tried not to stare at his abs. "I was going to study for the exam, but once I saw that it didn't matter to my clients or Ellen, I figured, why make my life miserable? I know I'm a great tax accountant, and the CPA exam and those three initials are mostly about auditing and financial statements. Not much about taxes. It didn't take much to convince me to forget about trying to pass a grueling sixteen-hour test."

"Aah, that explains it." Bobby's voice dropped. "Okay, Ms. Non-CPA, spill. What do you have for me?"

Julie watched the flex of his biceps as he folded his arms on her desk and leaned forward.

"You're the only person I could think of to help me. I'm sure you heard that Tom Reynolds was fired from his practice." Bobby nodded his head. "You're still cleaning the offices over there, right?"

"Yes, to both. I heard all about his first and last day back when it happened. Everyone was worked up, and because they weren't supposed to discuss it with anyone, they let loose when I showed up earlier than usual that day. I guess I don't count as anyone!" Bobby laughed. Julie knew Bobby was a pro at fading into the woodwork. She'd fallen prey to it many times and unloaded things on him that afterward made her wonder why.

"Good. I'm glad you're still cleaning there." She slowed the pace of her words. "This has to stay absolutely confidential, and I know that can be a stretch for both of us. This time, I really mean it. Not a soul can find out."

Bobby's close proximity made her sit back in her chair. Having long ago kicked off her heels, she pushed her shoeless toe into the carpet. She wheeled her chair back a few inches.

"Got it." Bobby looked into her eyes for emphasis, and Julie looked down, thankful that her French-Canadian ancestry had helped hide the blush that was rising.

"I need to get some stuff from their offices. After hours." Julie lifted her eyes to meet his. He nodded his assent. Julie kept talking.

"Unfortunately, Ellen and I were fired too, and we don't have access to their office records anymore." She had his attention. "Lucy, Tom's wife, was in today. Have you met her?

She thinks their son Ben's death wasn't an accident and that somehow Tom's firing is connected. We don't know if she's right, but Ellen and I agreed to check some things out."

"I don't know Lucy, other than she was a favorite of everyone at Tom's office," he said. "When their son died, everyone was more concerned for her than Tom. They loved the whole family and knew Lucy would carry the family's healing. She must be a great woman."

Julie's mind drifted. Maybe that's why I'm attracted to Bobby; he has a healthy reverence for women and isn't afraid to show it.

"Anyway…" Julie rubbed her cheek to bring herself back. "We don't have the detailed financial records that we need to investigate further. I told Ellen I thought I could find a way to get them and that she wouldn't want to know how. She should just leave things to me."

"So, where do I come in?" Bobby leaned in further. "Do you need me to find something or get something you missed? Just tell me what you're looking for."

"I wish it were that easy. I won't know what I need until I see it. I need you to let me into their office to search for past invoices in the accounting files. Luckily, I've been there so many times over the years I won't have any problem retrieving them. I need a backup of their QuickBooks files, too. We delete the files as soon as we finish the tax return." Julie tried to give him only as much information as was needed. She may not be a CPA, but she still tried to respect a client's confidentiality.

"So, how are we going to do this?" Bobby sat back in his chair. "I'm sure you've got it all worked out." A familiar shit-eating grin spread across his face. Julie breathed easier now that his biceps were no longer a distraction.

"I need to get in there as soon as possible before they change passwords. As long as they didn't change them yet, I can still get into the computer. They've always been slow to do that. When Angela left, it took months and a lot of nagging from me before they finally took care of it." Julie looked up at Bobby and hoped the fluttering of her eyelashes wasn't real.

"I'm there every night," he said. "When I finish here, I do the law offices upstairs. Then I take a quick dinner break and finish the night cleaning over there."

Julie knew that Bobby had found a way to have a robust personal life by only working five or six hours, five nights a week. His days were filled with his ex-girlfriend's six-year-old. The highlight of his week was going to kindergarten to read books to the boy's class. Even though the relationship with the boy's mother had ended, Bobby was the only father this child had known for five years. Bobby did not abandon the child. Another reason for Julie's heart to flip-flop.

"Can you get me in? Can I meet you there some night?" Julie's mind hiccupped when she said *night*.

"How about later tonight?" he said. "No time like the present."

Julie wanted to jump across the desk and plant a big one on him. She restrained herself.

"Where do I meet you?" is all she said.

# CHAPTER 33

# BOBBY

BOBBY RAN THE LIGHTWEIGHT ORECK VACUUM up the center of the law firm's hallway. Good enough. If he varied the path taken by his one push each night, most nooks and crannies would be sucked clean by the end of the week. No one was the wiser that the entire hallway was not perfectly vacuumed every night. On nights that he didn't run into an interesting conversation, he could easily finish most offices in under an hour. Good thing he was paid by the job.

He locked the third-floor law offices occupying the top two floors of 50 Portland Pier. He silently thanked Ellen for referring the entire building to him as clients. It made his workday that much easier. He checked his watch: 8:45. Plenty of time to grab a quick beer and burger at the Old Port Tavern before meeting Julie. Bobby double-checked the office building's front door to ensure it was locked tightly. No matter what he did, the moist salty air swelled the wooden doorjamb, and a secure closure was almost impossible unless you threw a hip into it.

He pushed the door tight and glanced up at Julie's window. She was hunched over her desk. He watched her fingers run through her thick dark curls, then stop to massage her scalp. Has she been there since they talked? Should he ask her to join him?

The sound of a lone car rumbling down the old, heavy, loose planks of the pier caught his attention. It passed him and slammed to a stop at the end of the pier. Another driver duped by the city's misleading *Scenic Drive* sign. Not even close to a drive, it ended abruptly with an unobstructed view across the harbor to South Portland. Bobby shook his head at the misguided wisdom of tourism politics.

When he looked back up at Julie's window, she was gone. Some other time then. He was surprised to find himself disappointed.

# CHAPTER 34

# JULIE

JULIE ROTATED THE SECOND-FLOOR ELEVATOR key up to the left, its on position. Only those from Hartmann and Associates and Bobby, of course, knew that the lock was installed upside down. On meant off, and off meant on. She tested it by selecting the second-floor button. It didn't light up. It was locked. She pushed number 1 to get to the lobby and the garage.

It was probably foolish to go home to change, and maybe she was influenced by too many detective shows. Still, for the task at hand, business clothes and high heels, even if they were only accountant heels, not come-fuck-me stilettos, needed to be shed. She hadn't planned to work late or set up a stealth operation with Bobby tonight, and the outdoor light of her townhouse was off. With her car lights from her designated parking spot illuminating the back door, she unlocked it and went in. She'd be quick.

Five minutes later, she emerged from her walk-in closet wearing black skinny jeans, a black turtleneck, and her favorite black leather jacket. A pair of Van's black high-tops comforted her feet. She admired herself in the full-length mirror; not bad, not bad at all. Enough already. She strode out of her bedroom, across the cluttered living room, and after a quick stop in the kitchen for a protein bar, she locked the door behind her.

She drove through the quiet streets of Portland. For a city of 100,000 people, it sure did shut down early. Of course, not as early as her hometown of 2,000. She remembered how terrified she was of coming to Maine's biggest city. Now, twelve years later and eight hours from the Aroostook County potato farm she loved, she marveled at how naive she had been and how terrified she was when Ellen called her for an interview.

Julie's first job as an accountant was working for an unscrupulous lawyer who called himself an accountant. He took advantage of Julie's naivete by asking her to do things an experienced accountant would have questioned. He was masterful at manipulating both Julie and his clients with big words and convoluted language. Not wanting to sound stupid, the deep-pocketed doctors he targeted would nod their heads, pretend they understood, and sign on any dotted line he presented them with. He easily convinced them to write hefty checks that he promised to turn into huge profits and used his legal background to set up his own small-time Ponzi scheme. With Julie in the dark keeping their clients happy by taking care of routine accounting work and tax returns, no one was the wiser. Then, one day, he was gone, and Julie was left holding the bag. Her naivete disappeared with him that day.

By the time she met Ellen, Julie had shared her limited knowledge of her boss's doings with the police. She then started looking for a home for the clients she loved. One of those clients mentioned her to Ellen. During Julie's interview, Ellen said what most impressed her was how Julie's clients still trusted her despite being swindled by her boss. Ellen hired her on the spot, and Julie's clients were more than willing to be added to Ellen's growing practice. Their mutual commitment to stellar client service bonded Julie and Ellen over their ten years together.

Julie didn't want to lose Ellen's respect over tonight's escapade. She, like Julie, would do anything for her and might've joined in on the caper if it helped them. But unlike Julie's first boss, who was only motivated by money, Ellen was driven to do the right thing and hinted that sometimes you do things because they are morally right, even if it means breaking some rules. She would understand if push came to shove, but Julie wanted Ellen to put her credentials at risk only if necessary. Best to keep this caper under wraps.

Julie pulled her car under a flickering light on the narrow street home to a row of medical office buildings. Both sides of the road were filled with overflow cars from the tiny parking lot at the train station one block over. No one had expected the success of commuting to Boston by rail, and ten years later, it showed. Her car wouldn't be noticed among the others forced to park there. It was the best alternative tonight; there was no excuse for being in a medical office parking lot that should be empty at ten o'clock at night.

She locked the car door and moved out of the streetlamp's glow to meet Bobby.

# CHAPTER 35

## JULIE

JULIE STEPPED OUT OF THE DARKNESS ONTO THE short driveway that led to the well-lit medical building. Bobby's truck should be in the staff parking lot. With luck, he'd be the only one there. She moved with purpose, not wanting to look suspicious. She laughed. A lone female in tight black pants, black turtleneck, and black leather jacket, out for a stroll on a dead-end street? How could she not look suspect?

She rounded the back corner of the building and headed to the lone turquoise door. No windows in or around it, just like Bobby said. Everyone's idea of a staff entrance. She stayed in the shadows and glanced at her watch: 9:55. Five minutes early, a long wait when you're breaking and entering. Technically though, she was only entering—not breaking.

At 9:58, the door opened, and Bobby stepped out. He glanced up at the half-moon partially obstructed by fast-moving clouds. She moved out of the shadows. Without lowering his gaze, he asked, "Ready for this?"

"As ready as I'll ever be." She edged closer, trying to soak up some of the assurance she detected in his voice. Her confidence was flagging. "Let's get this over with. I'll be quick. In and out as fast as I can." She hesitated. "Does anyone ever show up this late?" She was afraid to know the answer.

"Rarely. Most nights it's only me." His voice remained calm and steady. "We'll be fine."

"We need a signal just in case; I don't want to be caught red-handed." Her voice was froggy, and she cleared her throat.

"I've got you covered. I'll stay in the hallway with my vacuum cleaner. If I hear anyone, I'll start it up. It'll be your signal to hide and my alibi for being there."

Julie followed him through the door and into the administrative wing of the large medical practice. She let him take the lead so she wouldn't get lost in the maze of offices and exam rooms. The view from behind wasn't bad either.

She grabbed the doorknob when they arrived. It didn't turn. "Damn, it's locked. Now what?"

Bobby placed his warm hand on her trembling shoulder. "Oh ye of little faith. Do you think I wear these hip-clanging keys to look sexy? Step back."

She melted under the touch of his hand and dreamt about other places it could explore. She moved away quickly. Stay focused, you fool. You can't afford any mistakes.

The key to the filing cabinet was in its usual place: on top, in the bluish-green pottery cup with the whale's tail handle. Another piece of advice not followed. Why lock something if everyone knows where to find the key? She remembered her own welcome mat and smirked. C'est la Vie. Do as I say, not as I do.

She pulled five thick folders from the filing cabinet's third drawer and sorted through the invoices. Bobby's vacuum started to roar. She dove behind the outward-facing desk, crawled underneath, and curled into a tight fetal position. It was an old desk with a modesty panel and side drawers, not one of those modern table things with four legs and no privacy. She was well hidden.

The vacuum stopped. She heard Bobby's voice. "Dr. Green, what're you doing here this time of night?"

Julie tucked further into herself and tried to breathe quietly. Her heart pounded.

"I could say the same for you. Shouldn't you be finished by now?" His reply was short and gruff. Dr. Green was annoyed.

"Late start," Bobby said. "I took a break for dinner. Guess the time got away from me. Old Port Tavern can do that to you."

Julie envisioned him flashing his pearly whites. His grin could melt anyone, male or female.

"I haven't been in that place for years. Has it changed?" The desk shifted slightly as Dr. Green perched on the corner of Julie's hiding place. His well-polished, designer shoe dangled into her field of vision.

"Never does. You should try it again. A nice mix of ordinary people who don't bother you with their stupidity."

Bobby hinted that Dr. Green was one of those ordinary people. Julie knew he was not.

"Ordinary people; I'll have to think about that." His laugh sounded forced. Julie never liked the guy or anyone else who needed to hide behind their credentials.

Bobby cut him off. "I still have an hour or so before I get outta here. I promise I won't get in your way."

"No problem." Dr. Green's dangling shoe showed no sign of leaving. Why was he here?

"I was just finishing up, and I don't like leaving this office unlocked. Do you mind?" Julie watched the bottom of the door partially close and heard Bobby set the doorknob's lock.

"Right, I'm leaving. This can wait." Dr. Green's two feet hit the floor and walked out of Julie's view. The room went dark, and the door closed.

Bobby jiggled the doorknob as his last signal that Dr. Green was gone. His dirt-sucking alarm retreated down the hall.

Julie was left alone in the dark with her questions.

# CHAPTER 36

## BOBBY

BOBBY WATCHED JULIE UNFOLD HER BODY FROM her cramped hiding place. She stretched her arms over her head, and her black turtleneck lifted to reveal a bit of skin. When she bent over to stretch and touch her toes, her flexibility and well-muscled backside caught his attention. How had he never noticed?

"Sorry it took so long to get back." Bobby reined in his wayward thoughts. "I thought he'd never leave. He kept following me and babbling about the good old days at the Old Port. I got paranoid thinking he suspected something. Ended up redoing most of my cleaning before he finally got bored and left."

He looked into Julie's eyes to resist the urge to do an up-and-down scan of her body. "I double-checked to make sure his car was gone. You're safe."

Julie rolled her shoulders and swiveled her hips in a slow circle. "You weren't the only one paranoid. If I hadn't been so keyed up, I would have fallen asleep waiting."

She tossed her long hair over her shoulder, something he watched her do hundreds of times in the office. This time was different. It must be the intrigue of doing something dangerous together. Or seeing her as something other than an accountant. Or maybe it was more.

"It's almost midnight. Let's get this over with. How can I help?" He leaned over the desk where Julie was sorting papers and recognized the distinctive vanilla smell of her office. "Just tell me what to look for, and I'll set them aside. Or do you want me to start copying?"

"Good idea. I'm almost done, and then I'll back up the computer. Here, start with these." She handed him a bunch of invoices. "Front and back. Both sides unless they're blank. Try to keep them in the same order." Her fingers lightly brushed the palm of his hand as he retrieved them from her grasp.

"Yes, boss," he mocked, thinking it best to keep things light. His other thoughts did not need to see the light of day. Or, for that matter…. night.

# CHAPTER 37

# DR. GREEN

"WHERE WERE YOU LAST NIGHT? IT MUST HAVE been awfully late. I tried to stay awake but finally gave up and went to bed. Were you at the hospital? I hate that you won't let me call or text you. How am I not supposed to worry?"

Dr. Green was annoyed by his wife's interrogation. Couldn't she just trust him? It was the curse of having a second wife. Why should she trust him if his first wife couldn't? He breathed in the comforting aroma of his favorite roasted garlic, lightly toasted bagel that she placed in front of him.

"I'm sorry. I should've called. I got hung up at the hospital doing patient rounds, and I forgot to call you. It was no big deal. I came straight home after." He picked up the bagel and took a big bite. It had the right amount of veggie cream cheese, just like he liked it.

"It would be so much easier if you'd let me send a quick text. I promise I won't abuse it."

He hated the way she tried to use a sexy, whiny voice to manipulate him. He dropped his bagel on her latest Pottery Barn purchase.

"I've told you a thousand times. I ignore text messages. Interruptions slow me down. Remember the last time you convinced me to let you text? I missed them, and you were frantic. Trust me, this is much better." Dr. Green took another bite of his bagel and tried to end the conversation.

"You never used to mind my interruptions. A text from me, and you'd be right at my side."

He knew this tactic and decided this time to fall for it. He wanted her to stop questioning last night. "No need for texts. Just say the word, and I'll be more than at your side."

He grabbed her wrist as she turned away. "Come on, let's go."

She tittered and followed him upstairs.

# CHAPTER 38

# ELLEN

ELLEN LOOKED AT HER WATCH: 9:30. JULIE STILL wasn't in. She was never this late. Was it time to worry? Not yet. Like her mother, Ellen never wasted time worrying. The right time to worry was later, not now. When her first baby slept straight through his afternoon nap to the following morning, she told herself to wait. If he was dead, he'd still be dead the next morning. Waiting to worry was her way of forestalling an agonizing experience that might never materialize.

Still, she wondered what Julie was thinking yesterday when she told her to stay out of it and leave it up to her. Hopefully, Julie hadn't done anything stupid. She picked up her desk phone and buzzed the front desk. "Katie, do you know when Julie is coming in? Was she at a client's office this morning?"

"I don't think so. I haven't heard anything from her." Ellen heard a faint elevator ding as it arrived at their floor. "Wait a minute, this might be her." Katie paused. "It is. Should I send her to your office?"

"Yes, please. Thanks, Katie." Ellen hung up the phone. As she waited, her faithful seagull landed on her deck and began pecking at her sliding door like clockwork. Julie interrupted her with a light tap on her door.

"Come in and close the door."

Julie sat down. No matter how sweetly Ellen made that request, Julie was one of the few on staff who didn't freak out when she said it. Julie didn't skip a beat.

"I worked on this until three this morning." She spread an Excel spreadsheet on the desk and flipped it around for Ellen to analyze. "It's just preliminary. I'm not done yet, but I started organizing the conference information."

Julie had told Ellen during their post-Lucy meeting that she would retrieve the detailed information that they needed. Obviously, she followed through.

Ellen studied the gridlines. "The first column has the dates from oldest to newest, the next is the cost, and the third is the conference sponsor. Interesting, don't you think?"

"Same two weeks every year. Cost increases some each year, but the sponsor is different. Odd, don't you think?" Ellen was quick to pick up on what Julie had already noticed.

"I think so. When a conference locks in a date, they stick with it year after year. Participants like regularity, something they can count on. That's not unusual. But a different sponsoring organization each year is weird. They'd never give it up to a competitor. Financial sponsors come and go, but not the underlying organization. I'm not sure how important that is, but it's something to think about." Julie gathered up the paper and placed another spreadsheet in front of Ellen.

"This one tracks other international travel. There's one formal conference yearly, but three or four other trips each year, all to the same area in China. No rhyme nor reason for the timing of those. Or at least I haven't figured out the pattern yet."

Ellen ran her finger down the long column of numbers. "Wow, that's a lot of trips in the last five years. Who did all the traveling?" Ellen looked up to see a sly grin on Julie's face.

"Just as Lucy said, it's all Dr. Green."

# CHAPTER 39

# TOM

TOM STEELED HIS SHAKING HANDS ON THE unforgiving granite surrounding the kitchen sink. The ordinarily soothing view of the ocean didn't help him find solace. He was alone again, and he hated it. When busy, he could ignore the running commentary looping through his subconscious. But deserted with no distractions, he relived all the horrors of three months ago. He wished Lucy had skipped her early morning yoga class to be with him.

With Lucy gone, he could not block the imagined scenes of Ben alone and dying on the deck of their beloved *Ocean Potion*. In the movie of his mind, he saw Ben confused and struggling, trying to rouse himself from the noxious fumes that filled the boat's cabin. He was at Ben's side as his son fought rung by rung to climb up to fresh air. He heard Ben's rapid breathing and tasted his despair as he was dizzied from lack of oxygen. The smell of salty air, once a comfort to Tom, now the harbinger of danger, surrounded him.

Tom was a man of facts and science, strong, capable, and confident. But now, grief and imagination took over and shoved aside logic. Life became blurry, difficult to pin down, impossible to move forward. Where was Lucy to help him?

A persistent and rhythmic sound pulled his attention. Tom prayed that he was still in bed and that it was the alarm clock putting an end to his nightmare. He shook his head slowly from side to side, wishing for a different reality. On the sixth ring, he accepted that it was the ringing of the family phone. It was rarely used these days, and the caller ID was blank. He reached for the receiver. It might not be the end of his nightmare, but it would be a diversion.

"Tom Reynolds," his unused voice was croaky.

"Dr. Reynolds, it's Angela."

The sun broke through the clouds outside the window. He brightened. "I'd know that voice anywhere. Angela, how are you?"

"More importantly, how are *you*?" Her soft voice soothed him. "How's Lucy? And Sarah? I've missed you all so much."

"It's been tough for sure. It's the proverbial one day at a time. All we can do is keep moving forward."

"I'm so, so sorry, Dr. Reynolds. I should've reached out to you before this. It was so awkward when I left that I wasn't sure if you'd appreciate hearing from me."

"You know you've always been appreciated, Angela. I'm the one who should apologize for not being there for you. It was a shock to both of us that day, and I guess I thought it was my fault. I was so ashamed that I hadn't seen it coming." He could not share his feelings a year ago but had no choice now. Things were different. He needed her.

"Why would you think it was your fault? You did nothing wrong."

Angela had a knack for putting him at ease. "That's exactly it. I did nothing. I was demoted as managing doc at the same time, and I only focused on what was happening to me. I forgot that your life was turned upside down too."

"I guess so," her voice was quiet for a split second. "But in hindsight, it was the best thing that ever happened to me. Since I left, I've used all the skills and knowledge I learned in your office to help new doctors set up their practices. I'm working with four different offices now. So, no hard feelings on my part. It's all good. I promise. Life's too short to hang onto petty grievances."

He let out a quiet sigh of relief. Here was the Angela he knew and loved, the assistant ready to manage and control everything in the mutually shared corners of their lives. He turned around from the kitchen sink and lightly leaned his body on the edge of the black and white mottled counter.

"I'm glad you feel that way." Tom unwound as he listened to the cadence of this pleasant conversation. He sensed that she might be amenable to his proposition. "It sounds like you've been doing exactly what I'm hoping you can help me with."

"Really? What's that?"

He perked up at the eagerness he heard in her voice. "I assume you're calling because Bonnie asked you to. She must have told you I'm no longer at the practice. As you might guess, I need help setting up a new office. I knew you'd be the best person to do it."

"Really? I would've thought Lucy was. I remember when you first hired me. It was so easy because of the great job she did setting things up."

She called him out on his white lie. He wondered if it

was on purpose and thought it best to be honest. "Well, I suggested it to her, but she needs more time. It's been tough on us. She just wasn't up for it." Lucy would want him to tell the truth.

"I can only imagine. I mean, really, I don't want to imagine the hell you've been through." Her voice was gentle and caring. His tense shoulders dropped a notch.

"Thanks for saying that; I knew you'd understand. You've always been at my side. Remember how I called you my office wife? I was used to having Lucy at my side, and you replaced her so well. I had the best of all worlds back then, a wife at home and one at the office." He felt different, almost happy. He might be lucky enough to have it again.

There was a pause, and he wondered if he'd gone too far with the joke. Lucy was irritated when he once let this slip out at home, and she scolded him for treating them both like indentured servants. His shoulders crept back up towards his ears.

"Yes, I remember." Angela laughed. Tom relaxed again, but he'd watch what he said. He needed her. "You were the perfect boss, never interfering with my office admin. You stayed with what you do best—medicine. I took care of the rest. A match made in heaven, as far as I'm concerned."

"What do you think? Do you have it in you to help me again?" If Angela said yes, Tom could go back to how it used to be. He'd leave all the paperwork to her, and she'd only involve him when she needed his signature.

"I assumed that's why you're trying to reach me." Her voice slowed, and his stomach churned at the thought that she might say no. "As luck would have it, I just settled my newest client into his office and hired his staff. I'll have time to help. So yes, Dr. Reynolds, I'm available. I would love to recreate what we had before. Where do we start?" Angela didn't waste time getting started.

He relaxed to hear the promise in her voice. "The truth is, calling you is all I've done, So I'll ask you the same question. Where do we start?"

"There's nothing I love more than a clean slate." Tom settled into her take-charge attitude. He'd be well cared for. He'd let her take control.

"There's a lot to do behind the scenes. First, do you know what entity you'll be using? Sole proprietor, corporation? I'd suggest setting up an LLC. I can take care of that for you. Then, we'll confer with Ellen to see how you want to file your tax return. I assume Ellen is still your accountant?"

"Of course. Ellen's been with me since day one, and like you, I wouldn't want to do this without her. We won't have to worry about any conflict of interest either because her firm was fired at the same time I was. She'll be available to help whenever we need her." It felt good to contribute his two cents. Angela's enthusiasm was contagious.

"Good to hear. I'll bring her into the process when I think necessary." She paused, and he heard the rustle of papers. Prepared as always, he guessed.

"What about office space? Do you have a place yet?" she asked. "We need to nail that down before we order office stationery and forms. Do you want me to start looking? Maybe contact a realtor to show us what's available?"

"Yes, please." Tom strolled over to Lucy's plush chair to relax and enjoy the view. "Just do what you think and let me know when you need my input. I fully trust you. You did this for me for ten years, and you know me better than anyone else." Then he caught himself and added, "Except Lucy, of course."

"Alright then. I'll be in touch. I'm in my glory. This is what I love to do."

Tom wanted her passion to travel through the phone line to him. Now that he had turned over his responsibilities, he could admit that he was not looking forward to this new beginning. But with Angela there to carry most of the burden, a tiny spark of excitement resurfaced.

"You've made my day, Angela. Thank you so much." His own powerful exhale surprised him. He hadn't realized the level of apprehension he was carrying.

"Thanks for remembering me, Tom. I really appreciate that you want me to help. Everyone likes to feel needed."

Tom loved the combination of compassion and confidence he heard in her voice. He collapsed willingly into her care.

"I'll wait to hear from you, then." He heard the call disconnect and was a little bereft that she was gone. Then he remembered he had forgotten Lucy's only request. He hadn't discussed salary arrangements.

Too bad. It was his show now. If Lucy didn't want to be part of this, she had no say. A bead of sweat rolled down his brow, and he swiped it away.

# CHAPTER 40

# JULIE

JULIE WALKED TO HER DESK AFTER HER BRIEF morning meeting with Ellen. She was eager to resume her investigation. She did a cursory shuffle through the invoices Bobby had copied for her the night before. The faint smell of Old Spice threatened her concentration and tugged her back to the goodbye hug they shared at the end of last night's escapade. Was it wishful thinking, or was their embrace more than that of old friends and co-conspirators?

She slid her computer mouse to clear away the generic screen saver. The monitor came to life and pushed Bobby to the back of her mind. She plugged the flash drive into the USB port, and, voila, the medical practice's entire financial life was at her fingertips. She wasn't old enough to remember the antiquated computer programs that Ellen once worked with, but she heard the stories. Those programs allowed untrained staff to fill them with entries that didn't make sense and produced out-of-balance books. It was an accountant's nightmare.

Then everything changed. Inexpensive and robust in its financial data collection program, QuickBooks was an accountant's dream come true. The books always balanced even if the client's staff messed things up. And as long as the raw data was entered, everything was at Julie's fingertips and could be easily fixed. She could find all of her own solutions. The days of waiting for clients to answer questions they didn't understand, much less find answers to, were over.

She double-clicked *International Conferences and Travel* from the Chart of Accounts. Ctr + Q gave her the report she was looking for. She filtered for *all transactions*, and the account history appeared. Just as she had remembered, there were barely any transactions until about five years ago.

She ping-ponged between the numbers on this report and those on her preliminary spreadsheet from the night before. She compared the amounts. They matched perfectly in the early years. But then, about three years ago, those recorded in QuickBooks began a separate journey from the amounts found on the invoices.

She ran her fingers through the drape of her long, tangled curls. The numbers on the computer screen were substantially more than those on the spreadsheet before her. Ellen's teaching voice whispered in her ear as she focused on the discrepancies. "Double-check everything. Don't forget to trace numbers back to the original documents. It's the only way to verify their, and your, accuracy."

She zeroed in on the three years when their paths diverged to confirm that last night's analysis supported what was in QuickBooks. She grabbed the invoices for those years' conferences. Bobby had copied them exactly as he found them, including stapling a copy of the glossy marketing brochures to the receipts. She's not sure she would have bothered with these brochures and was thankful and impressed with the thorough job he had done. She started to drift away and then caught herself. It was time for doing, not dreaming.

The copied brochures were now only in black and white, but the pictures of the Great Wall, Buddhist temples, and playful pandas still would capture the attention of co-traveling spouses. Inside was the list of mundane and innovative medical presentations that transformed an exotic vacation into a deductible business expense. The back panel gave her what she was looking for: cost.

She verified that the amount in the brochure agreed with the paid invoice stapled to it. No problems. She looked up at her computer screen to compare those with the numbers recorded in QuickBooks. Problems. Big problems. There were large differences between the two and no apparent rhyme or reason as to why. What was going on?

She swiveled away from her desk to look out the window. At her last eye appointment, the doctor said to take an hourly break to change her focus. Her investigating brain could hook her for hours at a time, and when she finally tore herself away, she was stiff, sore, half-blind, and, in the official language of accountants, brain-dead. She set a computer alarm to remind herself but was a pro at ignoring it. Today, it wasn't necessary. Her mind needed a change of focus as much as her eyes did. Not seeing the forest for the trees was every bit as dangerous as forgoing the trees for the forest.

Julie counted to sixty to extend her long-distance gazing. She needed to stay sharp to find clues linking Lucy's notions to actual facts. She looked back at her screen and studied the numbers for the conference three years ago. The amount in QuickBooks was five thousand dollars greater than the brochure she held in her hands. Julie's inner Sam Spade went into full alert. She looked at the following two years. It was off too, but the differences had grown. What the hell?

She planted her elbows on the desk, rested her chin in her hands, and closed her eyes. Her brain's hamster wheel began to whir, and Julie circled over, around, and through all the possibilities.

Hours later, Julie's eyes burned from staring at the numbers on her computer screen. If there had been a competition for the last to blink, she would've won hands down. She'd been sitting at her desk all day and desperately needed a break. Not even the urge of bodily functions could interrupt her concentration. She raced through the office to the bathroom. Not for the first time, she wished the office designer hadn't placed it right next to the reception area where everyone knew what you were up to.

"You did it again, didn't you?" Katie's joking followed Julie into the bathroom. "Glad you made it in time!"

Julie didn't slow down; she knew better.

Afterward, she leaned against the highly polished cherry counter surrounding the reception desk. Katie teased, "Occupational hazard. Investing in a box of Depends might be a lot easier."

Julie stared out the reception area's bank of windows. It looked out at the same scene as her two windows, but the third window made it more panoramic. With a view like this, clients didn't complain if they had to wait. And when clients weren't waiting, it was Julie's first choice for stretching her legs and refocusing her attention. Her vacant staring let the internal landscape of her thinking broaden. Katie returned to her work, and Julie appreciated the lack of mindless chatter. The slightest intrusion could snip the thread of truth stitched within the numbers Julie was examining.

Without another word, she walked back to her office. She may have been there physically, but mentally, she had never left her desk.

# CHAPTER 41

# ELLEN

ELLEN SPENT THE AFTERNOON DOING HER SECOND job: running a small business. Billing, budgeting, and branding all took a back seat during tax season. Before April 15th, none of those were a priority. Moving twelve hundred tax returns through their office was. Everyone, from the owner to the administrative staff, had one common focus: processing the endless bits of information flooding their office. Lost or mislaid information was verboten.

Over the years, Ellen's team had developed an organized and efficient process for gathering, compiling, and transforming all the relevant pieces of a client's tax life into accurate federal and state returns. Every bit of paper was meticulously tracked, whether arriving by snail mail, email, or carrier pigeon. Although client-specific *Organizers* were sent to them in early January, most clients failed to take advantage of this effortless way to compile their information. Instead, they returned the unused packets along with their unopened tax mail. Others mailed their information one piece at a time with little or no explanation and, on occasion, no identification. Once it arrived at Hartmann and Associates, it became Ellen's problem, not theirs.

Unlike some tax preparers, Ellen and her team were thorough. They didn't take what clients sent and just fill in the blanks of the return. Their job was to look for gaps in information and find missed opportunities to help lower the client's tax. It was like solving a puzzle. The ultimate goal was finding enough tax savings to justify the bills Ellen was now drafting.

Ellen dropped the last invoice onto the growing pile waiting to go to the billing office, when she noticed Julie gliding trancelike to her office.

"Julie," she called out. "Do you have a minute?" By the downward cast of Julie's eyes and the tilt of her head, it was apparent she had been working on the Reynolds' project all day and was trapped in analysis paralysis. Julie pivoted and backtracked to Ellen's office. She sank into the pillowy comfort of the client chair and rested her head on its soft back.

"Did you find anything?" There was no need for Ellen to specify the topic of her question. Julie closed her eyes and hesitated as if she was hauling the answer up from a deep, dark well.

"Something's definitely off." Julie gazed above Ellen's head, lost in the big beckoning eyes of three purple-hued Holsteins staring back from the fine art print hanging behind Ellen. It paid homage to Ellen's Wisconsin Dairyland heritage. She waited for Julie to continue.

"I haven't gotten to the bottom of it yet." She dropped her eyes to look at Ellen. "I have no idea what's going on. I need time to find the why, as well as the who, behind the what. Give me a few more days. I need to do more digging."

"Got it." Ellen understood the process. "Any chance you found a link to Ben? I still find it hard to believe that there's a connection between the practice and Ben's death. Lucy thinks there is, and I'm trying to keep an open mind."

Julie shook her head no before Ellen had finished speaking. "Not a thing. But I haven't really looked. I've been focusing on the international travel aspect. Maybe when I'm deep and dirty into things." Julie's voice trailed off, and Ellen knew she was disappearing into a private interior place.

"Of course," Ellen said. "I wouldn't even know what to look for. I think another meeting with Lucy is in order. I want more details about the investigation into Ben's supposedly accidental death. What was the malfunction, why did it happen, those kinds of things. Too many gaps for me."

"Do you need me for that? To meet with Lucy?" Julie stood up.

Despite her offer, Ellen guessed that her mind had already left the meeting and that her body was anxious to follow. "I've got it. You stick with what you're doing."

Julie mumbled something unintelligible and walked away.

# CHAPTER 42

# LUCY

"LUCY, IT'S ELLEN, ELLEN HARTMANN. I'M GLAD I caught you at home." Lucy was in the middle of making Tom dinner when the phone rang. She was uncomfortable with the cold shoulder she gave him yesterday. He didn't recognize this new side of her, and neither did she. And, although she hated the cliché of it, simple lobster rolls were still his favorite.

Like most Mainers who hated the stench of boiling lobsters in their kitchen, she had picked up three cooked lobsters at the local grocery store. She mixed them with just enough Hellman's mayonnaise, never Miracle Whip, to hold the chopped lobster meat she pulled from the shells. The mixture would rest on a few strips of thinly sliced, crunchy iceberg lettuce in the bottom of a butter-slathered, lightly toasted, top-split hot dog roll. An ample serving of his favorite Cape Cod kettle chips would bring back Tom's smile.

"Hi Ellen, what's up? I didn't expect to hear from you so soon." Lucy buried her excitement under a cordial greeting.

"Nothing to report, but Julie's on it. She still thinks there may be discrepancies with international travel, but she needs more time. I told her to keep going."

If Ellen's choice of *may* instead of *is* was her way of not letting Lucy get too hopeful, it wasn't helping. "Tell me more. What did she find?" Lucy probed gently.

"She wouldn't even tell me." Ellen's words drained her anticipation. "But that's not why I called. Can we meet again? I need to pick your brain for details, and tomorrow is supposed to be gorgeous. I'd love to get away from my desk for a walk and talk. Are you up for it?"

"Of course I am. Where and when?" Lucy tried to appear amenable, not impatient.

"Nine o'clock? At the Mackworth Island parking lot?"

"Sounds good. See you then." It would be tough to wait until nine, but Lucy could linger over coffee with Tom. "Is there anything special I should bring?"

"Just yourself," Ellen said. "Everything I need you already have with you. See you tomorrow."

"Nine o'clock sharp. I'll be there." Lucy hung up the receiver and turned on the griddle.

She opened the door and called to Tom at his woodpile again. "Dinner's ready in about ten minutes. Time to quit and wash up."

Tom threw the split log he was holding onto the woodpile. Lucy quietly waited for him to look up. When he did, they locked eyes, and she flipped her hair with a come-hither look. She stopped herself before falling into more foolishness and walked inside.

# CHAPTER 43

# ELLEN

ELLEN SURREPTITIOUSLY CALLED THE SCHOOL TO say her sons would be a little late. She had a surprise for them. She knew she had been preoccupied and was all too aware of the unpredictability of life. Time with her sons would help restore her lagging spirit. As the three headed out to walk to school, she told them to get in the car and she'd drop them there. School was only two blocks away, too short for the bus, and they were always happy to trade the walk for a ride with their mother.

On the way to the car, the boys battled again over whose turn it was to ride shotgun. Kevin's logic eventually won without intervention from their mother, and he settled into the place of honor. Jack and Ethan sat behind him. An empty seat between those two kept the ride peaceful. She understood the value of mommy vans with four bucket seats that separated sparring siblings. She swore she'd never go there. Her sporty sedan was more her style, and the boys loved her trendier set of wheels.

"Hey, you forgot to drop us off," the trio sang when their mother turned left instead of going straight.

"I did?" She feigned innocence. "As long as we're going this way, what do you say we go out for a big breakfast?"

"But Mom, we'll be late for school!" Kevin never liked to break any rules, but the other two found no fault with her suggestion.

"Surprise! I already called them and said you'd be a little late, that we had a family matter. I think breakfast qualifies, don't you? Are you in?" she teased.

"We're not stupid. Of course, we're in." Jack glared at his brothers, daring them to say otherwise.

Ellen's scheduled walk with Lucy gave her the perfect opportunity to spend extra time with her sons. But when she recalled the topic of their meeting, bitter bile from her empty stomach rose to burn her throat. How does one recover from losing a child? Was it even possible?

She glanced in the rearview mirror. Both boys' grins confirmed she had made the right choice. She turned to look at Kevin. Worry etched the furrow between his intense blue eyes. "Lighten up, it'll be alright. I'm the parent here, remember?"

She reached over and took his small hand in hers. Ellen wished her overly responsible middle child would give up trying to fill the too-big, man-of-the-house shoes left by his father.

Cirrus clouds, delicate and wispy, wafted through the cornflower blue sky as Ellen drove across the not-quite half-mile causeway between Mackworth Island and the mainland. The road ended at an unoccupied guardhouse displaying a sign that cautioned walkers to watch for aggressive turkeys. It was spring mating season again. She read the sign each spring for years and had yet to see even one turkey, aggressive or not.

The mile-and-a-half trail circling the one-hundred-acre island was one of her favorite walks. It was beautiful any time of day, any day of the year. The path followed spectacular views of Casco Bay and looked across the water to Portland, Falmouth, and Yarmouth waterfronts. The mythically named Calendar Islands, in truth, one hundred and thirty-six, not three hundred and sixty-five, dotted the panoramic view. Ellen pulled into one of the last two spots in the tiny parking lot. She sat on the hood of her car and waited for Lucy.

A few minutes later, Lucy pulled her white Subaru into the last spot in the lot, one car over from Ellen's. She looked lost in thought and didn't notice Ellen sitting there. Ellen slid off of her car and walked closer. She waited. It was a minute or more before Lucy opened the car's door. She must've been pulling herself together in anticipation of a difficult conversation. At least, that's what Ellen would be doing if she were in Lucy's shoes.

Ellen didn't let on that she had been watching. Instead, she widened her arms and invited her friend in for a comforting hug. Lucy's body was hard and stiff. But as she relaxed into the wrap of Ellen's arms, she softened a bit. Together, they drew in long, deep inhales, and when their synchronized exhales loosened their pent-up emotions, they did it again.

"Thanks, I needed that," Lucy confessed.

"I guess I did too; it felt good." The contrast of a raucous breakfast with her three very alive sons and the pending discussion with a heartbroken mother weighed on Ellen. It certainly wasn't anything her accounting classes had taught her. She was thankful that years of therapy gave her the tools to manage challenging situations. *If only I could've deducted all that therapy as a business expense.* She smiled.

Lucy bent over to tie a loose shoestring. She stood up and stepped forward. "Ready?"

"Right behind you. Lead the way." Ellen followed three steps back. The start of the gravel trail was narrow, one person wide. Neither of them talked. Both knew the trail would open up soon enough. Ellen would speak when the path widened.

"What a gorgeous day," Ellen said. "I love spring mornings like this. A little warmer than usual. It's just enough to remind me why I live in Maine. Winter can make me doubt my sanity."

"That's for sure. Winter gloom and doom can get to you—too many days with no sun. I used to dream about sailing away to the Bahamas forever. Now, not so much."

Lucy tiptoed close to the topic at hand. It offered Ellen the opening she was waiting for.

"How are you doing, Lucy? I mean, woman to woman, how are you coping." Ellen tried to connect personally first. She cared about Lucy. Professional motives could wait.

"What's there to say? It's a nightmare. We try hard when our kids are small to keep them physically and emotionally safe. We dupe ourselves into thinking once they reach adulthood, they've made it. But we're wrong." Lucy walked rhythmically and robotically, as if on autopilot. Ellen listened quietly.

"It's awful. That's about all I can say. It changes you. I barely recognize myself. Sometimes I feel strong, sometimes weak. I never know what to expect. I feel like that little silver ball in a pinball machine. I bounce from one bumper to another, trying to stay in play, to keep it together. Then I just lose it and go down the tubes." Lucy seemed to want to share. Ellen let her.

"Tom and I are having a tough time connecting. We know what the other is thinking and don't want to go there. Anything else feels too frivolous and unimportant. So, we pass on information like 'I'm going to yoga now' or 'dinner will be at six.'" Lucy coughed and covered her mouth with the inside of her left elbow.

"Must be lonely," Ellen said as they turned off the trail onto an old concrete dock. They sat beside each other and dangled their feet over the water. It was low tide, and the dark water flowed twenty feet beneath them.

"I hadn't really thought about that." Lucy's voice hushed before she added. "But you're right. It is lonely. And there's nothing worse than feeling alone with someone right next to you. I know Tom feels it too, but we can't seem to find a way to bridge the gap."

"It might be too soon, but have you considered a support group? I know the Center for Grieving Children works with parents too. You might want to check them out. It's free, not that it matters," Ellen offered.

"Thanks, you're not the first to suggest that. Tom's not ready, and I think we should go with Sarah—all of us. We're stuck in this nightmare together, and I'm afraid if we don't deal with it at the same time, we won't make it. We owe it to Ben."

Ellen nodded, then looked down at her feet. The salty water swirled over and through the slimy green rocks below. Lucy was opening up more and more. Ellen hated that she noticed, but Lucy was exactly where she wanted her. It was time to dig deeper.

# CHAPTER 44

# LUCY

LUCY PUSHED HERSELF UP FROM THE DOCK AND touched her toes to stretch out her back. She rotated her hips to get out the kinks and looked down at Ellen, gazing across the undulating waves to the Portland skyline. The only high-rise condominium towered solitarily over the Eastern Promenade's century-old Victorian homes. Who allowed that? She hated how it dominated the skyline.

"Shall we move on? I know you have questions. I'm ready for them now." Lucy was thankful that Ellen had given her time to unload. Too many emotions were crowding out facts that she suspected were hidden underneath her anxiety and grief. But together, they might draw back the heavy curtain and shed some light on Ben's death.

Ellen sprang up. "Sorry. Lost in another world. This place does that to me. My brain takes a back seat to my feelings when I'm out here. Doesn't happen too often in my line of work."

"Happens more than you think. Why do you think we

all love you? You're a lot more than numbers." Lucy locked elbows with her as they walked in silent solidarity.

"I want to talk about Ben's death," Ellen said.

Lucy had been waiting for Ellen to push open the door that she hesitated to walk through herself. Her knack for finding the right time to broach difficult subjects during difficult meetings was a talent Lucy often marveled at.

"Tell me what you know from the official reports. Tom shared bits and pieces when we first met, but didn't go into the details."

Lucy found herself morphing from a grieving mom to her former journalistic persona. It had been decades since her dream of being an investigative reporter was set aside to support Tom's dreams, but it was still there. "Because the death was in international waters, there were actually two autopsies, one in Eleuthera, or rather Nassau. Once again, in Miami after the body was shipped to the US."

"Was there anything unusual?" Ellen asked. "Were both reports the same? Tom said his death was due to accidental carbon monoxide poisoning."

Lucy dropped Ellen's arm and looked briefly towards her before staring at her feet again. They were walking through a wooded section of the trail, and it was rife with tripping hazards like exposed roots, broken branches, or Maine's eternally erupting crop of spring rocks.

"Not really. Miami's autopsy mirrored the other. It read like a cursory review of the original findings. At least, that's what it looked like to me. I looked again at everything last night in anticipation of our meeting." Lucy started her fact-checking the night before, allowing her to finally sleep.

Staying in her head as if the subject was unrelated to her kept her out of her body and away from her emotions.

"Did either report say why there was carbon monoxide in the cabin? I assume it was from the heater," Ellen said. "Any speculation as to why it was even on?"

Lucy slowed to put a little more distance between herself and her friend. Ellen's probing was beginning to shake her up, and she wondered if Ellen sensed this too when she started walking a little faster. Lucy picked up her pace and shouldered her grief like a heavy backpack.

"I don't think so. I'm not sure they even examined the boat. Just the body." Lucy stayed with generic terms. It didn't make sense that Ben used the heater on a hot Caribbean night, but she couldn't go there right now. Both Ben and the *Ocean Potion* were stuffed full of too many nightmares. If she was going to help Ellen find a link to Ben's death, she had to stay logical and unemotional.

"They released the boat a while ago. We had it transported back to the Miami Beach Marina where it sailed from. It's waiting for us to decide what to do with it. Tom's not sure he wants it back, and I can't seem to leave it behind." Lucy's grief began to slip from her shoulders. She yanked it back under her control.

"Is there anyone down there who could inspect the sailboat or give us an idea of what may have gone wrong? The police, or a private investigator?" Ellen stopped to question her.

"Not that I can think of. I don't know anyone down there." Lucy again considered her days as a journalist. Maybe if she could ignore the weight on her back, she could turn this into someone else's story to unravel.

Lucy gasped and grabbed Ellen's arm. "I have an idea!" she squeezed it to get Ellen's full attention. "What if we went down to Miami Beach? We could inspect the boat ourselves and keep searching until we found answers to all our questions. We wouldn't have to worry that a stranger who doesn't really care will miss something." Ellen was listening intently, and Lucy hoped that Ellen was taking her suggestion seriously.

"Who knows? Since Ben sailed from the same marina, someone might remember him." Lucy pushed back her bangs and rubbed her forehead. "I don't know what we'll find, but if I don't go, I'll never know." She might actually find answers to her son's death. Her backpack of grief shifted a bit. "When I followed a lead for the paper, I paid attention to everything. Sometimes, the smallest comment would unlock a story."

"Wait, you were a journalist?" Lucy nodded. "When? I never knew that about you."

"A long time ago. In Boston, before I met Tom. Hopefully, my former skills aren't too rusty." Lucy's shoulders broadened to carry this new task alongside the old. "I can do this. It'll give me something to do, help me cope."

"Count me in. An accountant likes nothing better than a little warm weather after slogging through too many tax returns during the winter doldrums. Let's do it."

Ellen's lack of hesitation filled Lucy with hope and excitement about what lay ahead. She hooked her arms into Ellen's, and together, they circled back to the parking lot.

# CHAPTER 45

# ELLEN

"I'LL BE GONE TWO OR THREE NIGHTS. FOUR, AT most. I won't know for sure until we get there." Ellen had called her boys' father when she returned from her walk to fill him in on her trip to Miami Beach. An unexpected benefit of divorce was having another parent to leave your kids with when you couldn't be there. Hopefully, she could reap this benefit again. She didn't count on much from her ex, except this. Having held down few or no jobs for most of their marriage (and most of his lifetime), he was readily available. At the same time, it meant that all things financial fell on her shoulders. Today, she was happy to accept his always-available side.

"I'll leave tomorrow morning after the boys leave for school. You can move in here again." Another benefit. His nomadic lifestyle meant he didn't hesitate to spend time in a real house. She still cringed at her oldest son's question when he was almost six, "Is it against the law for Daddy to sleep in his car?" It was all she could do to stop herself from inviting his father back into the house or giving him money to rent a place where he could safely stay with his sons. Instead, she set up a plan for him to spend his time with the kids at her house. At least she knew where her sons were. Before this arrangement, the boys would come home with stories of sketchy trailers with no heat and frozen pipes. They saw it as an adventure. She saw it as a testament to her bad choice of men.

But, and it was a big but, trumping everything else, he loved his children. She knew nothing would ever change that. He didn't walk away from his boys as many fathers did. He stayed close. His sole purpose as a father was to tell his sons how special they were and how much he loved them. Love was his specialty. Things could be worse.

She switched the receiver from her left ear to her right. One more thing he was good at—talking. She was equally good at slipping off into her own internal conversation. Another benefit of divorce, you don't have to listen.

"Well then," she slipped back into the conversation. "I'll let the boys know you'll be here when they get home from school tomorrow. I'll have plenty of food for you guys. Have a great time. The boys will be thrilled." She ended the call before he started on another topic.

She buzzed Katie at the front desk and asked her to make plane reservations and book a hotel close to the marina. From examining Google Maps for the Miami Beach Marina, they should be able to maneuver around the area easily. With luck, Ben left his mark. Good or bad, it didn't matter. Either way, she prayed that someone would have information about his movements that final night. With luck, they'd find a loose thread to help them unravel the truth of Ben's last chapter.

# CHAPTER 46

# JULIE

JULIE WAITED FOR THE SQUEAK OF BOBBY'S WHEELS. Again. She needed his help. She hadn't thought things through and failed to retrieve the practice's bank statements. She needed Bobby for another clandestine escapade.

Today's analysis of QuickBooks pointed out the one big problem with her favorite software program. Financial information entered could be manipulated by a savvy user wanting to transform that original data into alternative facts. As long as the total dollar amount of transactions in QuickBooks agreed with the total amounts running through the bank, the books balanced. Double-entry accounting had done its duty even if the details that made up those totals had been buried. Her work showed that payments for the conferences were combined with other transactions whose details had disappeared. Bank statements would reveal the truth behind the numbers.

She rose from her desk at the first distant squeal from Bobby's trash barrel. She never would have believed it possible for her heart to flip-flop at the sound of a wheel needing oil. She forced herself to walk slowly, casually toward Bobby and met him in the hallway as he left Ellen's office.

"Here I am again, waiting for you. I bet you can guess why." She touched her hair and began to push her spiraling curls over her shoulder. Damn! Maybe if she shaved her head, she'd stop all the flipping and flirting.

"Can't live without me?" Bobby winked. Julie hoped the trash barrel would diffuse the sexual tension sparking between them.

"Something like that." Her right hand started to rise to her hair again, but she caught it in time and slipped both hands into the back pockets of her black pants. Not the jeans of the other night, but just as formfitting.

"I need something else from Dr. Reynolds' old office. Can we go again?"

"Yes, ma'am. Tonight? It's usually empty by 6:30 or 7:00. How about we drive together after I finish the offices upstairs and get you to bed early?" The left side of his mouth lifted into a mischievous grin. She lifted her right eyebrow in response.

"The copies you made last night were perfect. I worked with them all day but hit a brick wall when I tried to trace things back to the invoices. I can't go any further until I get the bank statements. I need to see exactly what ran through the bank. That's why I need you again." Julie was babbling like a high schooler. Not again.

"Who knew I was such an expert?" Bobby laughed.

"Expert? Huh?" Julie had lost the thread of the conversation, and it unnerved her.

"Copying. An expert at copying." Bobby's smirk reappeared. He knew exactly what was happening, and she was every bit as good, if not better, at playing this cat-and-mouse game.

"Right. And illegal entry. I'll need both." She turned to go back to her office, opened the folder she was holding, and pretended to read as she walked.

"I'll come get you when I'm done upstairs. Should be less than an hour."

His words trailed her as she retreated. Julie felt his eyes following her well-toned ass down the hall.

"That was uneventful." Julie hugged the passenger door of Bobby's truck to keep from sliding too close as they rumbled down the wood planks of the pier. As he predicted, the trip to retrieve the bank statements was a quick in and out with no interruptions. Although it took time to copy five years of bank statements, there were no glitches, and in less than an hour, they were back at the office.

Julie jumped down from the truck and stood at the front door. Bobby stepped out and stood at her side. It was a warm night by Maine standards, a balmy 49 degrees. The South Portland skyline twinkled across the harbor.

"I'm hungry." Bobby turned and looked at her. "How about you? Want to get something to eat before we call it a night?"

Julie was waiting for Bobby to suggest a drink or something. She wasn't ready to call an end to the night and was psyched that he didn't either. "How about J's? I'm starving too. And I wouldn't say no to a beer." Julie didn't wait for a response. She turned away from the water and walked towards the bar they just passed. A full moon lit her way, and she was silent under its spectacular glow.

Bobby followed. He picked up his pace and was first to the door of J's. Used to fighting to lead in the male-driven financial world she competed in, she reminded herself that letting a man treat her like a woman was not a sign of weakness. She let him open the door for her.

She scanned the bar and was relieved to find two available barstools next to each other. She wasn't ready for an intimate dinner at one of the few tables surrounding the bar. Not yet.

The bar's owner put Julie's usual in front of her. Bobby nodded, and his own draft beer appeared. "You two know each other? I've never seen you in here together," J remarked.

Most nights, Julie was here alone after a long day of work. She didn't like to share her special place with just anyone. Tonight was the exception. "We work together, sort of. Our hours don't usually coincide though." She turned to see Bobby's reaction, not wanting him to feel less than her.

"That's a nice way of putting it," Bobby laughed. "She fills her wastebasket during the day, and I empty it at night. It's a match made in heaven."

Julie wasn't surprised that Bobby didn't care about their different work lives. He was as different as night and day from the egocentric lawyers, bankers, and other professionals she dealt with every day.

"And I do my best every day to make sure he has plenty of work at night." She turned to Bobby. "Do you need a menu or know what you want?"

J pulled out her order pad and waited. Julie ordered first. "I'll have my usual."

"Same here, make it a dozen tonight." Julie cringed at the oysters Bobby would be slurping next to her while she ate her beloved burger and fries. She cautioned herself to focus on the company, not the bivalves slipping down his throat.

Their first beers went down quickly, and J had delivered the food by the time the second arrived. Julie shifted her eyes away from his plate. Best to keep looking across the bar or down at her food. She didn't want to ruin the night by hurling in his lap.

They bantered as they ate. He was a die-hard Red Sox fan like most New Englanders. She was a fan of their nemesis, the Yankees. With the new season underway, there was plenty of fodder for intense conversation about the past and foolish speculation about the future of these two sparring teams.

"That's it for me," Bobby finished his third beer. "I've got some cleaning to do."

"You go, I'll pick up the tab. It's the least I can do for all you've done for me." Julie motioned to J to give her the bill.

"My pleasure. And if you need my help with anything else, let me know."

Julie wondered if a midnight booty call qualified and saw the guys across the bar watching them. They were wondering too.

# CHAPTER 47

## TOM

LUCY DROPPED HER BOMBSHELL, THEN conveniently left to get ready for bed. She closed the bathroom door before Tom could react. "What? What are you talking about?" He waited outside the door, but her lack of response made it clear this was not up for debate. It might not be, but there would be a discussion.

He slipped into his blue plaid pajama shorts and tossed on his old Bowdoin College t-shirt. It was decades old, well broken in, with the soft cotton comfort that comes from too many washings. His favorite shirt will end someday too. His thinking had changed since Ben's death. He didn't like it.

Tom sat on top of the bed instead of pulling back the covers. Lucy would see that he was not done with the conversation. He grabbed his book from the nightstand and leaned back against the pillows. He pretended to read. When the bathroom door opened, he put down the book and waited for Lucy to look at him.

"Sit down and explain." He patted the bed next to him and put out his left arm for her to snuggle into. He tried to soften the tone of the difficult conversation. Lucy rested her head on his shoulder, and he pulled her tight.

"I want to understand what you're thinking. You know I'll support you, whatever you decide." He kissed the top of her head and noticed a few gray hairs. They were her first. He needn't ask where they had come from; he had a few too.

"I lied about my meeting with Ellen. It wasn't to discuss helping you at the office."

He pulled away to look down at her. Her words were tough to hear. They'd always been honest with each other. Who was this Lucy? What had happened to his perfect wife? His perfect life? He prayed it wasn't another thing coming to an end.

"I'm not ready to accept that Ben's death was an accident," she said. "And why did they kick you out of the practice? I can't accept that either. What possible reason did they have to fire you? The two things must be connected. It's the only thing that makes sense to me."

She looked up at him as if searching for answers. He wished he could give them to her.

"Oh Lucy, I want answers too. But are you sure you're not clutching at straws?" He tried to be gentle by using an old cliche.

"I wondered that too, but when I talked with Ellen and Julie, I didn't feel as crazy. They're going to help me. Ellen didn't even hesitate to say she'd go with me to Miami to inspect the boat. Like me, she doesn't understand where the carbon monoxide came from. Why was the heater on at all?

It was Miami Beach and the Bahamas, not Maine. For God's sake, Maine is the only reason we even had heat in the boat!"

Lucy's body pulled away from Tom as she pleaded with him to understand. He gently pulled her back. "I hear you. It doesn't make sense, but does an accidental death ever make sense? I don't want you to get your hopes up. It's not going to change things."

"I know it won't change what happened, but it will change me. I'll be able to make some sense of my life again. Every day won't be an endless stream of what ifs and if onlys. I'm tired of constantly wondering, if not that, then what. Am I crazy?"

"You're not," Tom pulled her closer and kissed her head again, "if it helps, go. See what you can find. It can't do any harm. You can check on the boat. Maybe arrange for someone to bring it back to Maine. I know you're not ready to give up *Ocean Potion*. I won't fight you on bringing it back anymore. I'm done blaming the boat."

"Good. I'm glad we can agree on that. It was one night out of the hundreds that we spent as a family on her. I have so many happy memories, and oddly enough, I'm comforted by knowing Ben spent his final hours there." Lucy slid under the covers, signaling the conversation was ending.

Tom snuggled her under the cocooning warmth of the blankets. He wrapped his arms around her to spoon. Being the big spoon to her little one helped him feel like the strong, powerful man he wanted to be, a man capable of protecting his family, keeping them from harm, and supporting their every need. He knew he had failed them miserably.

# CHAPTER 48

# TOM

TOM SAW HIM BEFORE HE SAW TOM. ALTHOUGH the largest in the state, Maine Medical Center, was still small. It was bound to happen sooner or later. It might as well be now. He steeled himself for an uncomfortable encounter.

"Dr. Green. Nice to see you." Tom reached out his right hand. Today, his former colleague was Dr. Green, not Gary. Things had changed, and there was no reason to pretend otherwise.

"Tom, how are you? And Lucy? I worry about you two." Gary squeezed his hand.

Tom was stunned that his former colleague and friend acted as if nothing had happened. Gary had been such a big part of their family; how could he be so distant, so insensitive when his own godson had died? Tom knew he loved Ben; he had watched them together for years. Gary loved children, wanted some of his own, and even confided that he and his new wife were struggling with their inability to conceive. Surely, all of this, would have helped him understand the depth of Tom and Lucy's loss. Tom could almost forgive Gary for his emotional immaturity.

But asking Tom to leave his own practice, the one he had created from nothing, was something else. He would never understand, much less excuse him for doing such a thing. And he would not give Gary the satisfaction of seeing the depth of his suffering, whether from Ben's death or the death of his former practice.

"We're as good as can be expected, given the situation." Tom pointed his chin and looked straight at his one-time buddy. Gary glanced down at the dark green rubber tile floor and coughed.

"We're slowly learning to move on from both terrible tragedies." Tom accentuated *both* to subtly attack the man standing across from him. "Lucy and I are looking forward to practicing medicine my way." He emphasized *my* and waited for Gary to make eye contact before continuing. "Angela will be working for me again, and I'm about to lease a new office."

"Angela? Really? Are you sure that's a good choice?"

Gary's wide-eyed sputtering strengthened Tom's resolve to keep him uninformed and at a distance. What a jerk. He wished he was more comfortable with swearing. Only a four-letter word could express what he was really feeling.

"Not that it's your business, but yes, I'm sure. You're benefiting from the practice she helped me build, and I have no doubt that she will do it for me again." Tom was amazed at how easily these passive-aggressive comments surfaced. Where were they coming from? He wasn't sure he liked it.

"Sorry, of course it's none of my business. Just trying to help." Gary put out his hand, and Tom wasn't sure if it was for a goodbye or an apology. It didn't matter. There was no way he was extending his own. Gary studied the floor as if he had lost something.

Tom turned and walked away. He remembered his mother singing *Que sera sera*. This time, it wasn't his job to fix things. Whatever will be, will be.

# CHAPTER 49

---

# BEN

SLEEP WOULDN'T COME. EACH TIME HE STARTED to nod off, Ben relived last night's shocking encounter, and his body jerked him awake. The events of the night looped through his befuddled brain.

It was after midnight when Ben left Monty's Sunset Bar and Grille, the quintessential tiki bar in the middle of the Miami Beach Marina. There were five hours left before the bar would legally close, but he was wise enough to know that it was best to turn over his barstool to someone else. As he carefully circumvented the strange swimming pool separating the bar from the restaurant, he whispered thanks to his dad for choosing this marina as one of the places to celebrate his liberation from school. This bar and South Beach, with its art deco architecture, raucous bars, and nude beaches, met everyone's expectations, no matter what age.

He had strolled back to Pier J, where the *Ocean Potion* waited, and noticed how the thirty-six-foot sailboat was dwarfed by the boats surrounding it. It was one of the few sailing vessels in the marina. Most other slips were filled with gigantic ocean-going yachts, making Maine's boating community look pathetic. He felt lost among these giants and was ready for the two-day voyage ahead of him. His confidence was boosted by a fun night filled with stories of others' successful journeys.

He looked up at the sky and noticed how the bright lights of the well-lit marina belied the night's new moon phase. Tomorrow night, he'd have an authentic dark sky experience. Even in under-inhabited Maine, it was tough to get the real deal. Ben's classes in astronomy and comparative religion boosted his interest. Ancient spiritual communities believed that this phase of the moon was for introspection as well as planting seeds for the future. They were worthy tasks for tomorrow night.

He remembered putting the temporary guest card into the lock of the pier's white metal gate for the third time. It finally worked. As he fumbled to return the card to his right pocket, two beefy men lifted him off his feet. His feet dangled and kicked, and he struggled to find the wooden planks beneath him. The men must have followed him, waiting to push through the gate as soon as it opened. Last night's speechless panic from being silently dragged to the *Ocean Potion* filled him.

Ben bolted upright, and his scream jolted him awake with the same dumbstruck terror he felt when the two men tossed him on his boat. He didn't want to relive any more of that night. He was dizzy from fright and begged his brain to stop toying with him. Enough, no more, not tonight. He staggered out of bed, grasped the ladder's railing to steady himself, and struggled up the ladder toward the beautiful night sky.

# CHAPTER 50

---

# LUCY

LUCY INHALED THE HOT, HUMID AIR BREEZING IN from the Uber driver's window. Katie from Ellen's office had booked everything perfectly, and their flights from Portland to Miami went smoothly. Because the Miami Beach Marina was a short walk from South Beach, where the hotel was booked, Katie wisely suggested keeping things simple and skipping renting a car.

Ellen was texting her boys, and Lucy used the break in conversation to relax and enjoy the view. She drifted back to the tasks ahead, and her chest constricted. What would they find? Was she doing the right thing? Lucy stared out as if she'd find clues on one of the many billboards they passed. The sky was the same cloudless blue she had left back home, and neither did much to lift her cloudy disposition.

As they got closer to the hotel, their driver-turned-tour-guide showed them unusual sights along their route.

His banter smoothed out the wrinkles of her anxiety. Her interest was piqued when they passed the massive Topgolf facility with three stories of tee boxes for hitting golf balls into a massive net. Ben told her about these places where food, drinks, and golf were served up as outdoor recreation, mostly for non-golfers. Ben's laughter, now gone, surrounded her as she recalled how he whiffed a big drive and almost fell off the third story at one of these places in Myrtle Beach during spring break last year.

Lucy smiled, but it didn't last. It was too soon. Memories like this could sink her into despair, and she was relieved when their driver pointed to the parade of cruise ships in Port Miami. She appreciated the diversion of gargantuan ocean liners marching by her window. Royal Caribbean, Norwegian, and other cruise lines flanked the highway as they neared South Beach and the adjacent Miami Beach Marina. Interesting to look at from afar, but she was grateful that her family enjoyed the sea from their own ocean-going vessel. Being hauled like cattle to company-owned shopping areas designed to keep away the natives living on their island destinations was not her idea of fun.

"Are you ready for this?" Ellen put down her phone and covered Lucy's hand with hers. She gave it a tiny squeeze.

"I am. I need answers, and I know we'll find them here. I know it."

"Well, I can promise you this, Lucy. If there are answers to be found, we won't leave until we find them."

Their driver pulled into the porte-cochere behind two palm trees that framed the historic tan travertine face of the Stanton South Beach Hotel. Architects restored the 1939 Art

Deco building and hid the fully renovated, modern facility behind its familiar facade. It was the best of both worlds. The hotel paid homage to the 1930s party town of the rich and famous while indulging today's guests with twenty-first-century comfort.

Her appreciation of its beauty faded. She wouldn't have been at this hotel if Tom had met Ben in Miami Beach.

They could have sailed overnight to Eleuthera together. But then again, she might have lost both. She craved a different conclusion and a do-over. Another chance, another time, fate might be kinder.

# CHAPTER 51

## ANGELA

ANGELA PICKED UP HER LAVENDER-LINED NOTEPAD and favorite purple pen and scanned the lengthy list of the day's labors. With the four existing practices she managed and the addition of Tom's, there was much to stay focused on. She didn't want to trip herself up by letting something slip through her control. She leaned back in her Aeron chair and studied the list.

Long ago, she learned to handle things once. Deal with the issue and move on to the next. It kept her efficient and effective. Angela studied her list to look for anything that could be ticked off quickly, or that fell into the category of urgent. Her existing practices typically ran on autopilot because she personally hired their in-house staff. They were trained to follow her instructions explicitly and to contact her if anything unusual surfaced. She praised them for following daily routines and encouraged them to let her be the troubleshooter for everything else.

Nothing looked pressing or inviting, and she flipped to the next page of her legal pad, filled with to-dos specifically for Tom Reynolds. She was searching for something quick and easy. She wasn't ready for long phone calls with the hospitals and health insurers. The conversations themselves were usually short, but getting there meant following the maze of instructions to get to the right department and finally talk to a real person. She lost a lot of time to calls like that and needed something else to jump-start her day.

1. Update credentials with both hospitals.
2. Notify all health insurance companies for billing registration.
3. Post ad for medical assistant at Jobs in Maine and ZipRecruiter.
4. Setup LLC with state.
5. Get new Employer ID for LLC.
6. Finalize office lease.
7. Order office furniture and medical equipment.
8. Order office stationery, etc.

She ticked number six. Finalizing the office lease would be quick, easy, and mostly tolerable. She had nodded a perfunctory greeting to the building's owner and landlord when she passed him in the hallway earlier this morning and knew he was in, just down the hall, in the office suite next to hers. The building was filling up slowly, and she knew there was space available for Tom. Her other practices filled over half of the space in this newly renovated office building.

Having all of them close by made managing their practices much easier.

Angela's office was on its top third floor and looked out into a nature conservancy crisscrossed with walking trails that most city-dwellers didn't know existed. The building was further from the hospital than a lot of medical buildings, but luckily, the younger generation of doctors wasn't spoiled by decades of being able to walk across the street to the hospital to deliver babies, do surgery, or do rounds. Those buildings, with their luxury of closeness, had slowly disappeared as the expanding medical center bought them up and tore them down.

There were three rooms in her suite, more than she needed, but it gave her room to grow when, and if, she chose to add an assistant. The rooms were furnished sparingly. One had her desk, another office copier and supplies, and the third sat empty. She preferred to meet with clients on their own turf, and there was no need to impress anyone with lavish furnishings that bragged of success. Instead, her minimalist vibe reeked of efficiency, effectiveness, and a touch of secrecy. A shared bathroom down the hall gave her the occasional opportunity to overhear conversations not necessarily meant for her ears.

Before going to speak to the landlord, she closed her private office's interior door to peer into a small oval mirror discreetly mounted on its back. She liked what she saw. The highlights she added to her mousy brown hair and new half-bangs did exactly what her new hairdresser said they would. The golden strands accentuated the natural wave of her shoulder-length hair and made her look bouncier, younger, and even fun. The half bang softened her face and erased her former severe, schoolmarm looks with her forehead exposed by a pulled-tight ponytail. Her foray into the world of makeup with just a touch of mascara and blush seemed to be working. Am I pretty? She heard her dead mother's words: *pretty is as pretty does.*

Satisfied for now, she left her office suite after double-checking that the exterior digital lock was set. She didn't trust easily duplicated keys that multiplied without one's knowledge. With a digital lock, she could change the code anytime she wanted. She did it regularly, just as she did her passwords.

She headed down the hall to Medical Offices of Maine, or MOM, as the leasing agent liked to call it. She lightly knocked three times, opened the door, and walked in. A handsome thirtysomething dressed in khakis and a polo shirt looked up from his computer. The smoky and spicy smell of his perfume, rather cologne, threatened to choke her. With lips tightly locked, she returned his foolish grin.

"Angela, how are you? I didn't get to say a proper hello this morning; you seemed in a hurry when I saw you earlier. Must have a lot on your plate today." His hand slicked back the top of his dark hair.

Angela had no reason to let him into the workings of her life and no intention of engaging in mindless small talk. "I do. I always do. I have a new practice I'm working with, and I'm hoping we can have fifteen hundred square feet on the second floor. It's for Tom Reynolds, the surgeon? You know, the one whose son died at sea?"

"I don't really know him, but no one missed that tragedy. Listening to the stories after he died was like driving past a bad car accident. You try not to stare, but you can't stop yourself. The speculation and assumptions about it were phenomenal." He leaned in. He wanted her to spill the gory details.

"Yeah, it was awful." Angela heard the whispers about a drug deal gone wrong, but there was no need to wallow in Ben's death now, and if there ever were, it wouldn't be with this guy.

She lowered herself into the only chair in the small room, one of Walmart's hard white plastic chairs that stack up when summer starts to bloom. "To add insult to injury, Tom's surgical practice pushed him out. I'm helping him set up a new practice, hopefully here. If you have room."

"Whoa, that's hardcore," he slicked his hair back again and then wiped his hands on his trousers. "That never made the news. Unbelievable. I'm sure his colleagues are keeping that under wraps."

"For sure." Angela refused to dissect that either. "What do you think? Can I get a lease for him under the same arrangement as the others?" A sly smile leaked across her face as she worked to corral his attention.

"Sure thing. I'll get the lease to you by the end of the day. Easy peasy. I'll just insert a new name and the appropriate square footage." He leaned back in his chair like men do when trying to feel important. She wasn't impressed.

Angela slid a piece of paper across the desk with the correct name and numbers for the lease. "I'll get you the first and last month's rent and the security deposit within the week. I need to set up bank accounts and have Tom put some initial money in." Her internal monitor buzzed TMI. Keep him close but at a distance.

"Sounds good. I'll just add it to your other payments? That's working for you, isn't it?" He looked at her hopefully. She looked away. He was fully onboard. She was smart enough to know that the best way to keep him hooked wasn't with the personal relationship he hinted at but simply to fill up his empty building.

"It is. We've got a good thing here, so I see no reason not to keep it going. It's always a pleasure to work with you, MOM." She laughed, pretending this was a moment of mirth with a good friend, which he was not.

"You know what they say, MOM knows best! Or was it father knows best?" His laugh annoyed her. She said nothing. His face blossomed pink, then red. "Before my time. Yours too." He cleared his throat, "Doesn't matter, I guess. It's working for both of us."

Angela wasn't going to give him an inch. She pushed herself up from the uncomfortable chair. She was done here. She headed for the door.

"Hey, what do you say we go out on my boat again? It's ready whenever you are. Next sunny day that's reasonably warm?" His eagerness irritated her. She said yes before and had no desire to say it again.

Her hand was already on the doorknob, but she turned back, smiled, and reached across the desk to shake his hand. When he squeezed it, she hesitated, then reciprocated. Best to leave him wondering if she meant yes or was just sealing the deal.

She closed the door without a goodbye and went back to her office. She punched the code, opened the door, and circled around her desk. She returned to the cozy comfort of her Aeron chair. No doctor she ever worked for thought about sore backs from ill-fitting desk chairs; they simply bought the next cheap chair available. This chair was the first of her many secret indulgences. She smiled and pictured the rest hidden from the judgment of others.

She lifted her lilac pad and leaned back in luxury. A broad smile reserved for only herself melted her face into a semblance of softness. Grabbing her favorite purple ink pen, she ticked off number 6 on today's list and added *9: Open bank account.*

# CHAPTER 52

# GARY GREEN

IT WAS TIME TO GO HOME, BUT HE WASN'T READY. Gary Green sat in his jet black, highly polished, impeccably clean Mercedes sports coupe in the hospital's now mostly vacant physician parking lot. He needed to pull himself together. There was too much on his mind, and from past experience, he knew greeting his wife with a head devoid of space was not good. She craved attention, but he needed more time to prepare for her.

He was stunned. He didn't think Tom was capable of being so cold, and he was still chilled by their verbal exchange this morning. It was not what he expected. Nothing about it spoke of the man he loved.

He was confused. Why would Tom treat him that way? And what was he doing, starting a new practice? Gary gave him the golden opportunity to call it quits. Why wouldn't Tom want to spend more time with Lucy and Sarah? He needed to move on to a quieter, less stressful life.

Ironic to think Tom would be better at home with his wife while he sat in a car in an empty parking lot, avoiding his own. But Tom and Lucy's relationship was built on longevity and trust, something he no longer had. Gary allowed himself a moment to dream about the life he'd be living had he not chosen to go into that closet with his current wife.

*Water over the dam. You made your bed; now lie in it.* Damn you, Dad. His father's criticism infiltrated his already crowded headspace. Would he ever be rid of his father's unkind voice?

Tom's words, a guilt and shame cocktail intended for him to drown in, reminded him of his father. It was not what he expected from the man he admired, the one who mentored him. Tom always treated him respectfully and was kind to everyone. He welcomed Gary into his practice and his family, and Gary willingly accepted Tom as a replacement for his father.

Now, he was terrified of being overcome with sadness. How had things gotten to this place? He only did what was best for Tom. Why didn't he see it? He was actually happy to see Tom walking towards him and expected him to thank him, take him out for lunch, or invite Gary and his wife over for dinner. He hoped to hear stories about how retirement was just what Tom needed. Instead, his former friend was encased in a rock-hard cube of ice that Gary doubted would ever melt. Never would he have guessed that Tom would brush him off.

And working with Angela. What was that about? Gary changed his internal conversation to avoid the rush of feelings threatening to overtake him. It was easier to focus on someone else's failings. Another lesson from his father, and as much as he tried to avoid being anything like him, this was one trait he used too often.

Gary thought Angela was over and done, forever out of the picture, when he put an end to things a year ago. He thought she would stay clear of anything or anyone close to him. They both knew what was at stake. Did she think he wouldn't find out? Why would she put either or both of them at risk? Word must've spread about Tom leaving the practice, and she had assumed Gary's relationship with Tom was over. Was he the only one who thought otherwise?

He leaned his forehead on the black leather steering wheel and let his body melt into the heated seat. He had to let go of all this before he headed home. He wished there was someone he could talk to, someone to help him make sense of it all. If he'd been honest with Daniel when he first hired him and told him why he was replacing Angela, he would have had someone to help sort it out. Discussing things with his wife was out of the question. She'd never understand and was too lost in her own world. He didn't want to slip in her eyes as the man who would protect and support her.

He shook his head, stiffened his spine, and started the car. The roar of the well-engineered and fine-tuned engine revved him up enough to push away his mental machinations. *Suck it up, buttercup.* His father's words echoed in his ears. He shifted the car into first gear and slowly let out the clutch.

# CHAPTER 53

## ELLEN

THE SUN WAS SETTING WHEN ELLEN AND LUCY checked into their hotel. They both agreed that a good dinner and a stiff drink would be enough for today. They'd start fresh in the morning.

Ellen was pleased to discover the hotel had its own Michelin-starred restaurant and suggested they indulge themselves. Portland, Maine's restaurant scene was rising as one of the country's top food cities, and she was used to dining excellence. Too often, in too many cities, places were recommended as the best in the area, and she quickly learned that *best in the area* didn't mean much. The ambiance and food at some of those places would've made diner food seem ready for Michelin status.

Here at the hotel, the award-winning *Den at Azabu* was hidden within the bigger restaurant. It was booked months in advance, but Ellen assumed the main restaurant enveloping it couldn't be too far removed from that prize winner. They sat at the spacious bar, separate from the sushi bar. She needed a warm drink to thaw her cold, stiff fingers from the overly air-conditioned hotel and asked for a saké. Lucy seemed impervious to the cold and ordered a glass of rich, oaky Chardonnay.

"Glad you suggested this Ellen." Lucy picked up her stemless wineglass.

"A fresh mind on a new day is always a good thing." Ellen sipped her saké, and her body relaxed. "Things are much clearer and less intimidating after a good night's sleep and an even better cup of coffee." She savored the drink's effect.

"I'm sure we'll find that good cup of coffee, but I'm not too sure about a good night's sleep."

Lucy was right, and strange hotel rooms only made it worse. Ellen took another sip. Excellent. She'd ask for the name of it so she could order it at Benkay in Portland.

"I hear you. But I'm hoping a light Japanese dinner with a couple of drinks will help us both drift off to sleep. At the very least, it won't hurt. Tomorrow, we'll begin searching for some answers. You made the right decision bringing us down here, Lucy."

"I can't thank you enough for coming along to help me, help *us*, really. Tom thought we were crazy when I first told him, but he finally came around. He's starting to see things my way. He even agreed to bring the *Ocean Potion* back to Maine. That was a huge shift for him." Lucy set down her glass.

"Really? He didn't want to bring it back? Sounds like a man's solution to an uncomfortable situation. If you don't see it, it can't get you."

Ellen looked over the bar's bottles to find Lucy's reflection in the mirror. It was awkward trying to converse with someone sitting so close. And, like elevator riding, there seemed to be an unspoken rule to just look straight ahead.

"Amen to that," Lucy said. "But I've learned that what you can't see doesn't go away. It's still there waiting to ambush you at the worst time. I'd rather look anything in the eye. Then I know what I'm dealing with.

"All kidding aside though, there are just too many family memories to let it go. I'm choosing to remember Ben alive on it." Lucy's voice trailed off. "But then again, I didn't have to see what seven days on the open sea had done to him. Tom did. I'm sure he'll never forget."

Ellen filled her tiny cup with the last drops of saké from the exquisite porcelain tokkuri. She watched Lucy pick up her glass and take a long, slow sip of wine.

"You're right," Ellen said. "I shouldn't have been so harsh. I'd want to turn my back on that too. It must have been horrible." Ellen watched Lucy's mirrored eyes slowly squeeze shut.

"He never said much about it. As a doctor, I suppose he knew how devastating the sight was for families, and he kept the details from me. That was fine; knowing the specifics wasn't going to change the outcome. And I think this time, my imagination was my friend."

Things were getting too deep, too fast. This was supposed to be a light evening. Ellen motioned to the bartender that they were ready for menus. He quietly slipped her two, and she passed one to Lucy. "What are you up for? Should we go all out and order a Sushi boat?"

"Too much for me, and it doesn't look like they have one anyway. Too bastardized for this place, I guess," Lucy laughed. "But we still have time for the happy hour specials. It goes from 6 to 8."

Ellen looked at her Fitbit, avoiding today's step count. She knew there had been too much sitting. "Plenty of time, it's only 7:30."

Lucy pointed to the Kanpai Hour specials in her menu. Ellen flipped to that page. She had never seen that term before and made note to look up the meaning later. "These are perfect. I don't need a lot of food either. Or leftovers. A doggy bag filled with surplus sushi sounds ghastly."

They laughed in agreement, then ordered. Ellen's distraction had worked.

Ellen woke at sunrise. Hotel drapes never prevented slivers of sunlight from infiltrating the room, and even the latest hack of using hanger clips to hold them shut didn't work. On top of that, she forgot her sleep mask. She used to think they were a luxury for hoity-toity celebrities until they became her saving grace on sleepless nights.

She pushed back both layers of drapes to take in the view. How different, she thought, from the shores of Maine. No islands in the distance, no granite cliffs, just smooth, sandy beaches brushing up against miles and miles of open ocean. Hard to believe it was the same ocean that crashed on her rocky coast.

She turned from the window to listen at the door connecting her room to Lucy's. No movement, nothing. If

Lucy had a sleepless night, Ellen was not going to wake her. She understood the importance of one more hour of sleep.

Ellen decided to scope out the area on her own. According to Google Maps, the marina was only a half mile away. She might as well kill two birds with one stone and get in her daily walk at the same time. She pulled her t-shirt and shorts from her suitcase, appreciative of warm weather packing. When she traveled in winter, walking clothes took up half the suitcase with her warm, thick socks, hiking boots, long silk underwear, and heavy sweaters. Pulling out summer walking clothes somehow lightened the task ahead.

Her mind drifted to her boys back home. They were probably trying to convince their father that now that the snow was gone, it was time to wear shorts even though it wasn't even fifty degrees. She missed them but didn't call. She knew this was their time with their father (or his with them) and respected that their father-son relationships deserved time and space without her interference. If she were being truthful, she'd admit it was nice to let go of her responsibility for a day or two and forget about them a bit. They are fine, she chanted to lessen her mother's guilt. But Lucy would never be fine without Ben, not even for a split second. Ellen repeated her mantra two more times.

It was another brilliantly blue day, a cloudless sky with a gentle tropical breeze. She was in love and wondered, not for the first time, why am I in Maine? Then she remembered. Summers down here were hot and humid, and her claustrophobia would erupt, making her withdrawn and cranky as the heavy air surrounded her. No, this clime was for vacations only.

It was a short block to connect with the walkway between South Beach and Miami Beach Marina. She had no problem finding her way and was thankful she didn't need to use Google Maps. No matter how she tried, she always went in the wrong direction. It was the same when her sister used east or west when giving directions. Left and right were the only things that made sense to her. She must have direction dyslexia, if there was such a thing.

After passing an artist's rendition of a black and white lighthouse, a far cry from those in Maine, she arrived at the end of the sprawling marina. According to the map, the public walkway continued from Dock A through Dock J. All the slips seemed filled, and she noted as she passed them that there were only a few sailboats among the many yachts. The land side of the walkway was built up with what she guessed to be private condos. There wasn't a hotel in sight, and her financial mind speculated what these perfectly placed residences would be worth.

At Dock E, there was a two-toned blue sign announcing the Dockmaster's office. *Visitors Welcome* was prominently highlighted in gold, and she wondered if they meant it. She walked through the unlocked white metal gate and headed toward the water to find out. The office was in an octagonal or hexagonal building (she didn't stop to count) with heavily tinted windows. She couldn't see inside. It felt foreboding and off-limits. So much for the big welcome. She'd wait to see if they needed it; if they did, she'd let Lucy lead the way. Lucy was the boat person. She'd know what to say and do.

Ellen breathed in the warming Florida morning before retracing her steps back to the walkway. She turned left towards the far boundary of this large, exclusive marina.

While the yachts continued to fill the docks, each one larger than the last, the shore-hugging condos ended abruptly. In their place, alone and in the middle of opulence, she found *Monty's Sunset Bar and Grille.* An ungodly valuable piece of real estate for a bar, it must have preceded the current marina. Or, someone with a clear vision and a lot of money, knew tourists would love the location with its proximity to yachts they'd never own, while real boaters would make good use of

its tiki bar. She thought it looked like the perfect place to find someone who would remember Ben.

It was closed, of course, and she looked for a sign posting the hours that it would reopen.

"They open at 11." Ellen heard a rough and raspy voice behind her. Startled, she turned to face a salty, leather-skinned old hippy.

"Hi, I'm Marley Roberts. Call me Bob. Yeah, I know. My parents had a sense of humor." He offered Ellen a rough, calloused hand. She extended hers warily.

"What can I do to make your day better?" he said.

# CHAPTER 54

# LUCY

LUCY'S FOOTSTEPS ECHOED OFF THE WOODEN planking as she walked down Dock J. Although filled with boats, it was empty of humans except for one tall, well-built, but not overly muscular man in baggy blue shorts and a tattered t-shirt. He stood with his back to her. She was heading to the *Ocean Potion* moored in slip 77, close to where the guy stood. Her family's boat was dwarfed on its portside by a huge, three-story yacht that had backed into its designated berth. An expansive party deck spread across its stern. It was overflowing with boisterous boys and bikini-clad partiers. Blood-red, parasol-piercing, cherry-laden drinks were hoisted in a group toast, and she guessed they must be college students on spring break.

On the *Ocean Potion's* starboard side was another yacht, just as massive but more foreboding than the first. It was gunmetal gray, long and low, with sleek lines that oozed intrigue. There was no evident party deck; instead, she saw a narrow passageway circling its first story. Three people stood on it watching the other yacht's partying crowd. As she walked closer, her mind catapulted from contented recognition to complete confusion. Standing there, on the ominous vessel, was her own Tom. Gary Green and Angela were at his side.

The young man turned slightly. He reminded her of Ben except with longish, blond-streaked sailor's hair. Was it his haphazard way of dressing or his confident stance that brought Ben to mind? He was looking across the bow of the *Ocean Potion* from one boat to the other as if deciding which one to choose. As she approached, he turned to face her.

"Ben," she whispered.

"Ben," her voice intensified until she cried out, "Ben! You're here!"

A frantic knocking jarred her awake.

"Lucy! Lucy, are you alright?"

Through a shadowy and hushed haze, her ears opened to Ellen's worried voice coming through their adjoining door. Lucy was still in the hotel, not on a wharf. Ben was still dead.

"I thought I heard you scream," Ellen said.

Lucy struggled to pull back the veil that separated her dream world from reality. She rubbed her eyes to erase the scene. She massaged, then scratched her head to dislodge the confusing thoughts. She cleared her throat of the giant lump threatening to strangle her and found her words.

"I'm fine, Ellen. It's just a bad dream." She swallowed again. "My head's spinning. It was so weird."

She turned the alarm clock upright to read the red numbers that kept her awake until she finally flipped it over at 3:17. It was now 8:12.

"Thanks for waking me up. I can't believe I slept this late; it's not like me." She crawled out of bed, happy to leave her bewilderment behind, and opened the door between them.

Ellen's face was serious, and the worry lines on her forehead were deep. "I just got back from my walk. I figured you might've had a rough night of it, so I tried to leave quietly so you could sleep."

"Thanks, you were right. The extra sleep was nice, but I could've done without the nightmare. Don't worry yourself; I'm fine now." Lucy wrapped both arms around her torso to ground herself.

"Okay. I believe you." Ellen didn't push her. "I'm going to jump in the shower. We have a meeting at nine. I found someone who's willing to help us. Can you be ready?"

"If there's coffee, I'll be early. Just knock when you're ready, and I'll be good to go."

Lucy closed the door, walked to the window, and slid back the drapes to focus on the ocean. She looked for the same peace she found at home when her hands wrapped around a cup of tea, and she sat in her favorite chair. Ben's physical presence, even in a dream, had stripped away the defenses surrounding her tucked-away grief. Now, it waited for her acknowledgment. Her eyes filled with tears, and she swallowed the sob waiting behind them.

Ben shouldn't be dead, she cried to the silent room. Ben should be here with me. He should be crushing me in his young man's embrace and lifting me off my feet as he loved to do once he outgrew me. She choked down her grief and moved away from the ocean view. Today, there was no solace washing over this shore to help her.

She crossed the room to the bathroom; she needed a shower too. Not the one Ellen needed to wash away her hot and humid morning walk, but one to rinse clean the remnants of Lucy's ruminations that still struggled to decipher exactly what that dream meant. A shower might bring her back to reality.

Lucy trailed behind Ellen as they headed to the South Beach Café where Ellen had arranged to meet their new and still unnamed assistant. She didn't offer Lucy any details, only that they could get breakfast and coffee at the same time. Lucy was confused but trusted that Ellen had her reasons. The biggest thing on her mind right now was food. She was starving after last night's light dinner.

Lucy picked up her pace to walk side by side with Ellen. She was still unsettled from the dream and needed to fill the uncomfortable silence with something else.

"I plotted out our whole investigation last night when I couldn't sleep. Not that it makes any sense this morning." Lucy laughed. "I don't think going yacht to yacht is going to get us too far. Unless, of course, we want to spend a few weeks down here."

"Hmmm, let me think," Ellen locked arms with her. "Nope, wrong time of year. Now, if it was freezing in February and I could get out of tax season, I might say yes. But with spring erupting in Maine and humidity looming down here, I'd say it's an emphatic no."

"I'm with you. So, what's our plan? Do you really think you've found the right person to help us?" Lucy tried to pry.

Ellen dropped Lucy's arm and slowed down as they approached the cafe. Tables of four decorated with Florida flowers and colorful coffee cups waiting to be filled were spread around the sidewalk. Ellen scanned the tables and customers, probably looking for the person they were meeting. Lucy searched too, even though she didn't know who she was looking for. Then she saw him.

Her gaping mouth was an in-person version of Edvard Munch's *Silent Scream*. She ran towards the familiar face.

"Bob, is it really you? Ellen, Ellen! Come here! I want you to meet someone."

Lucy peeked over her shoulder. Ellen was grinning and stepped closer to squeeze Lucy in a playful hug.

"I already know him. Can you believe our luck? My morning walks never disappoint, and the universe never fails to deliver."

Flabbergasted was an understatement for all that stirred in Lucy's gut. She grabbed Bob in a bear hug. Speechless was an understatement too, and she was glad the waitress didn't ask but simply filled the coffee mugs already on the table.

"Wow…wow." She drew out the words long and slow and took her first draught of coffee. "I can't believe it." She looked at Ellen, and her words finally broke loose.

"Did I tell you about Bob, our savior on Eleuthera? His kindness, persistence, and professionalism kept us going. Without him, Tom and I would be rotting in a Bahamian prison. We could've killed the authorities for their lack of urgency. Bob's the one behind Ben's rescue efforts. We owe him so much."

Lucy's appreciation tumbled out, leaving room for her churning stomach to fill with hope. She glanced at Ellen. Her beatific delight said it all.

"I learned as much from Bob this morning when we met." Ellen smiled at Bob. "When he asked how he could help me, I jumped right in. I knew we'd need some local talent to help us. As soon as I mentioned Ben by name, we discovered we were in this together. I agree. Bob's a gift from heaven. Someone up there definitely loves us."

"Ladies, ladies, you're making me blush." A blush could never penetrate that overly tanned, overly wind-kissed, overly smoked face. Lucy loved every bit of it.

"But why are you here, in Miami Beach?" she asked.

"I just brought over a boat from the island. Another sideline, you know." Bob swept back the straggly blonde bangs shading his eyes. "It takes a few of those to make a living on Eleuthera, even with a lifestyle as modest as mine. And there's nothing better than a cruise on a big-ass sailboat that you don't have to maintain or make payments on. It's my idea of getting paid for an all-inclusive vacation. Can't be beat."

His guffaw reminded Lucy of her first meetings with him. Despite the horror of that time, his free-flowing laughter lowered the temperature of her burning anxiety and scorching grief. She remembered how he orchestrated the search for Ben and how his fellow volunteers rallied at his and their side. They put the official Bahamian rescue to shame.

"I can't believe you're here. We need your organizational talents." Lucy was still in awe. "Can you help us get started? My mind is spinning with all I want to do. I'm not sure where to start."

She looked into Bob's gorgeous green eyes. She had never forgotten their endless pools of comfort and often returned to their memory when feeling overwhelmed. She fully trusted him and hoped, no prayed, that she could turn all of this over to his competent hands.

Lucy saw Bob turn to look at Ellen. She nodded slightly as if giving him permission to take the lead.

"We talked a bit this morning when we first met," he began. "It seems we have two separate issues to investigate. One, trace Ben's movements on his last night here. And two, search the *Ocean Potion* for what caused the leak or anything else that tells us what really happened."

He looked directly at Lucy. She recognized his conviction and, from experience, knew that he would be brutally honest. "I agree with you, Lucy. The authorities only did a cursory review of the boat. They were convinced it was an accidental death and wouldn't consider anything that said otherwise. You did the right thing coming down here. It all seemed too open and shut."

Bob took the helm, and Lucy let him. His disgusted look mirrored what erupted in Lucy's stomach whenever she thought of that incompetent inquiry. She looked across to Ellen, who nodded slowly and soberly. Lucy was finally validated for pushing to know more.

"And I think we'd be smart to do both parts of this investigation together," Bob scratched his head. "If two heads are better than one, we can't go wrong with all three. With my marine knowledge, Ellen's analytical mind, and your intuition, Lucy, we've got it all covered. And, best of all, from what I can tell, we're all persistent and not afraid to speak up. I know we won't let anything fall through the cracks."

"I feel better about this minute by minute," Ellen said, turning first to Lucy and then Bob. "Your understanding of what's up is amazing. I can see why Lucy was so happy to see you."

Lucy watched Ellen's excitement mix with the telltale signs of impatience. Her fingers started to drum on the table. Lucy's impatience was also stirring, but unlike Ellen's, hers was mostly invisible to others. She breathed deeply and rolled her creeping shoulders back to a more relaxed position.

"Where do we start?" She shifted in her chair as her eyes moved across Ellen's face before settling on Bob's.

"Let's start by searching the boat." His coffee cup clanged on the table. "We can see if we turn up anything unusual or worthy of pursuit. From there, we can decide if we need to talk with the medical examiner and set up an appointment if necessary. Then, if we still have time today, we can talk with the Dockmaster. See if he remembers Ben and the *Ocean Potion*."

Lucy relaxed into the oddly comfortable metal bistro chair. She usually found them too stiff with hard round seats that were always too small. Maybe it was Bob's voice, not the chair, that was so comfortable.

"Tonight, I'm going to send you guys off to bed while I go to the bar. I can blend in with the locals and the regulars and see if there are any stories I can dredge up about that night. I'll fit in better alone. Much easier to get the inside scoop. No offense."

Bob peered through the fringe of his uncombed, sun-bleached hair draping over his forehead. He looked at her, then Ellen. Lucy assumed he was giving them time to absorb what he had just laid out.

"What do you think? Sound like a plan?" he asked after a few seconds.

Ellen probably had time to think about it earlier this morning and responded first. "Sounds like my kind of plan. Fluid, flexible, and freeing. Fluid enough to get us started, flexible enough to let us pivot with whatever we find, and freeing when we find answers to what's been worrying us the most. What do you think, Lucy?"

Lucy was still a little off-kilter, first with the dream and now finding Bob. She was thinking and didn't want to leave any stone unturned, any sleeping dog lying, or in this case, any bubble, whether salty or fresh, unburst. Lucy was silent a few seconds longer as she finished checking her internal list.

"Sounds good to me."

Lucy heard a collective, or to be exact, a dual exhalation, and all three of them shook their heads in unison. They were off and running.

# CHAPTER 55

## ELLEN

ELLEN TRAILED BEHIND LUCY AND BOB AS THEY headed through South Pointe Park to connect with the walkway to the marina. The two chatted like old friends lost in their own world. It was obvious that Bob had been an enormous support and ally for Lucy and Tom during the horrors of Eleuthera.

Ellen was thankful the universe dropped Bob into her lap. Truth be told, she had doubted she could help Lucy find the answers she was searching for. At the time, she wanted to support Lucy in any way she could. Now, she was more than happy to turn the investigation over to Bob. His knowledge of all things marine far surpassed any Ellen possessed.

The trio walked past the artistic rendering of a lighthouse that Ellen had studied that morning. She was beginning to see how it mixed the ancient ritual of a seafarer's beacon with modern-day aesthetics. Her initial rebuff gave way to curiosity, and she was able to see that the design represented both Miami Beach's Art Deco past and today's modern art.

It wasn't what she saw in New England, but she would accept it. Not that anyone asked or even cared. She thought of her sons back in Maine and the framed picture in her office taken at the Portland Lighthouse. Her heart softened as she saw her sons' arms around each other on Maine's rocky shore with the lighthouse in the background. She hated being away from her boys, even when safely taken care of by their father. How does someone live without their child forever? She looked at Lucy. Can you ever fill the emptiness left by their death?

Ellen's heartbeat accelerated, and her breathing shallowed. Anxiety would only make the search more difficult. There was no room for her own emotions. She breathed deeper to calm herself as they approached the marina. Best to stick with an accountant's brain and leave motherhood behind. Thankfully, Bob was here to help support Lucy. There was room for Ellen to take care of herself.

"Pier J is where we'll find the *Ocean Potion*," Bob explained to them when the path widened and Ellen could walk beside them. "It's the dock for transient vessels and the same pier, but not the same slip Ben was in before. Most of the boats come and go, but a few are berthed there permanently. While you two begin looking around on board, I'm going to look for someone who might remember Ben."

Ellen didn't argue. Boat people had their own language and idiosyncrasies. Her midwestern upbringing made her a landlubber, and she was smart enough to leave any boat conversations to Bob. The last thing she wanted was to set someone off because she wore the wrong shoes or grabbed the wrong thing for balance. She looked at her feet and trusted that her new Sperry deck shoes were acceptable.

Access to Pier J was locked. Its restricted access sign stated only owners and their guests were welcome. Ellen waited for Bob to solve the problem. He pulled the necessary keycard from his pocket and unlocked the gate. She figured his credentials as head of BASRA, the Bahamian volunteer rescue organization, coupled with Ben's tragic story, must have been good enough to gain access.

Just how secure was the area? She turned around and looked at her surroundings. Nothing but multi-million-dollar condos and yachts. Then again, it was probably more secure than it looked. Her brain blipped. Don't be lulled by money and what it can buy. Ben is dead after only one night here. Things are not always as they seem.

# CHAPTER 56

# LUCY

LUCY STOPPED CHATTING. HER PACE SLOWED AS they approached the *Ocean Potion*. She stood and stared at the boat. This is where Ben's body was found. She froze, then prayed. She asked the *Ocean Potion* to give up her secrets and reveal the truth. She begged God to help her make sense of this tragedy. Her faith told her that Ben was at peace. She was only asking for the same. She stood silently for a few minutes, Bob on one side of her, Ellen on the other.

"Ready?" Bob's question brought her back to the present.

"I just need to catch my breath. I think I forgot to breathe somewhere along the way." She grabbed Ellen's arm.

"I hear you, I did the same." She patted Lucy's hand. "Take your time. This is the tough part. We're ready when you are."

Lucy gathered her courage before taking her first step on the *Ocean Potion*. She needed to shake loose the image of Ben's body and replace it with happy pictures. Memories of Tom teaching Ben to sail, of family trips to Maine's many islands, of fair winds and following seas. Anything, no matter how trite, to diffuse her anxiety at being here, the scene of Ben's death.

She drew in a long, deep breath and exhaled slowly. She knew breath would calm her; it always did. She looked up at the cornflower blue sky, the same one she remembered on her walk with Ellen. A slight breeze blew back her hair. She knew it revealed the graying hair at her temples. She didn't care; it was the least of her worries.

One more breath, and she was ready. She stepped aboard.

"Care to join me?" Lucy smiled and motioned them on board.

Bob stepped quickly onto the boat and offered his calloused hand to Ellen. She gingerly placed one foot on the deck, then gasped and grabbed the railing when the boat dipped. Obviously, Ellen wasn't as comfortable with boats as she was. Lucy appreciated Ellen even more for stepping outside of her comfort zone to be here with her.

"I'm going to let you two poke around now. See if you notice anything unusual." He took Lucy's hand, "You'll have the best idea if anything seems out of order. I'm going to start by nosing around the neighbors. See if they remember anything out of the ordinary the day Ben was here. Sound good?"

He dropped her hand and waited for her consent. She nodded and turned to Ellen.

"Are you up for this? I can tell you'd rather be on dry land." A little humor might diffuse Ellen's discomfort and Lucy's uneasiness. "We'll start below deck. Come on, Ellen. I'll help you climb the steps below. Just turn around like this, grip both railings and slowly step down. I'll be here to catch you."

Lucy waited at the bottom of the ladder for Ellen. Luckily, it was a calm day with little movement in the marina. There were no big boats with bigger wakes to knock Ellen off her feet. When Ellen was safely below deck, Lucy moved to the back of the cabin.

She spied a thin blanket crumpled atop the berth. This was where Ben slept. Was the blanket wrinkled from his last sleep or a messy investigator? She sat down and clutched the blanket to her throat. Her imagination took her to a place where nothing good had ever happened. She squeezed her eyes shut and tried to stop it. She began to lose control.

Ellen rested her hands on Lucy's trembling knees. She was kneeling in front of Lucy. "I'm here with you, Lucy. Take your time; we have all day."

"I can smell Ben. After three months, I can still smell him." Lucy started to sob. "It's crazy, but I smell all his scents from infancy through adolescence. All of it. I can feel him here with me, but I'll never see him again." She shook her head from side to side, then buried her face in her hands. She unleashed her grief.

Eventually, her sobbing subsided, and she patted the berth for Ellen to sit beside her. She was uncomfortable with Ellen silently kneeling at her feet. Ellen sat, and Lucy leaned her head on her shoulder. After wiping away her own tears, Ellen cupped Lucy's head with her hand.

Lucy dried her eyes and wiped her nose on the untucked end of her t-shirt. She stood up and looked down at Ellen. It was time to find some answers. "Okay, I'm ready. Let's do this."

Ellen stood up too. "This is your boat, Lucy. Tell me

where to begin. I don't know boats, and it's too invasive just to start digging around. What do you want me to do? Where should I start?"

Lucy needed Ellen here but wanted to be the one to go through Ben's personal things. Ellen could start with something generic, somewhere innocuous and unrevealing.

"Why don't you start in the galley, I mean the kitchen," Lucy suggested. "Pretty standard stuff in those few cabinets, and even a landlubber like you would spot anything that shouldn't be there. I'll start going through his personal belongings."

Ellen turned toward the tiny kitchen. She rested her hand lightly on the stovetop to pull open the oven door, and an ear-piercing scream sliced through the devastating tension.

"I should have warned you," Lucy laughed, grateful for the relief. The stove slowed its back-and-forth swing and settled into its illusory stationary position. "That's a swinging stove; it moves with the waves. Helps keep the pots from overflowing in rough seas."

Their tears turned to laughter just like that. Tears and laughter, like love and hate, were alternate sides of the same coin. Today, Lucy was happy for both.

"It's time for true confessions." Ellen grew serious. "I'm terrified of boats and the ocean. All those creatures floating underneath, waiting to grab me. Ever since my dad made me dangle my feet in the lake to let the fish bite my toes, I've been terrified. I can only imagine what lurks in the ocean."

"I'll protect you." Lucy rode the fine edge of laughter, "And if I can't, Bob will. You're safe, I promise. We're not going anywhere, and I doubt whether there's much lurking in this marina except a floating beer can or two."

"Enough of this foolishness. I'm fine; I won't distract you any further." Ellen bypassed the stove and moved on to the refrigerator. She opened the door and wrinkled her nose at the rancid smells spreading through the cabin.

"Whoa, baby! You should have had a woman sail this back from the Bahamas," Ellen was howling. "I guarantee a woman would have emptied this out. Yuck, I can't even begin to guess what was in here."

Ellen made her way through the kitchen cabinets, and they settled into an easy flow. Lucy moved from the sleeping area and scanned the tiny bookshelves behind the narrow couch. She pulled out a bright yellow paperback book and held it up for Ellen to see.

"I bought this for Ben when he left for college. It was one of my favorites, and I hoped it would be his, too." *The Art of Possibility* was a classic, and although the author had fallen a bit from grace for exactly what she couldn't remember, its wisdom was still valid. Ben wasn't impressed at the time, or so Lucy thought.

"Your kids just roll their eyes and write you off, but then you find something like this and realize you've made a difference."

She held the book to her chest, closed her eyes, and pictured Ben soaking up its wisdom. She read her inscription from four years before: *Give yourself an A, and the world's possibilities will unfold before you. Love, Mom.* She placed it back on the shelf. So much had changed; so much had ended.

206

She opened the sliding door to the next shelf and peered inside. She reached in and pulled something out. "Ellen, come here. Look. I think I've found something."

Lucy's chest tightened, and her breath grew shallow and fast. She sat down on the couch to steady herself and motioned for Ellen to join her.

"Could this be the box? The one Gary Green gave Ben on the dock when he was leaving?" Lucy's questions came out in a torrent. "You know, the one that got me thinking something was wrong? I'm sure it's the same size. He told Ben not to open it until his first port. Do you think it's the same one?"

Lucy's words echoed off the walls of the cabin. Ellen joined her on the couch, and they studied the beautifully crafted wooden box in her hands. Its lid had a carved image of a sailboat, a delicate rendering of the *Ocean Potion*. Lucy shook it slightly. Nothing moved or rattled, but it was heavy, filled with something.

"I can't open it," Lucy whispered. "You do it." She handed the box to Ellen.

# CHAPTER 57

# TOM

TOM SCANNED THE BUILDING'S DIRECTORY AS HE waited for the elevator. Newly engraved brass nameplates filled some of the places on the tasteful mahogany sign. It wasn't the generic black and white placard with plastic letters that could be quickly changed with the arrival and departure of transient tenants. This sign spoke of permanence, long-term leases, and the ability to afford the expensive space. Angela wanted Tom to add his name to the list of those already committed to the building.

Tom didn't recognize any of the names on the sign, but most had MDs attached to their names or were at least in the medical field. He guessed they were fresh from residency physicians who weren't snapped up by large medical groups. They were taking the same scary step of opening their own practice that he had taken decades before. He remembered Lucy and him signing the lease for his first practice. They were excited and overwhelmed by the enormity of it all. The lease, practice loans, equipment purchases, hiring staff; the list of things to do seemed endless. But then they met Ellen, and she walked Lucy through it step by step. Lucy made it all happen.

But where was Lucy now? How did he end up here, alone, and starting over? He looked up at the ceiling as if the answer could be found in the iron chandelier, then down at the foyer's dappled gray wood floor tiles. Everything here was new and modern. He wished he felt the same.

Angela called Tom last night to ask him to meet her here. She wanted his approval for the office space she found. She said she liked the space because it was in the same building as her office, and she could easily keep an eye on things as he concentrated on his surgeries. The negotiated lease was ready for his signature. Tom was happy to visit the space but wasn't sure about making the final decision alone—without Lucy.

The elevator dinged, and the doors of the sluggish elevator crept open. Tom made a mental note to take the stairs in the future. Other than splitting wood, he didn't get much physical exercise, and Lucy nagged him to do more. A brief stair climb every day would do him good. He waited for the doors to finish their slow opening, then stepped in and pushed 2.

The elevator stopped with an exaggerated bump, and its doors cracked open. Angela was standing there. The warm, friendly smile that greeted him for ten-plus years brightened her familiar face. She stepped forward and wrapped her arms around him.

"Tom, it's so good to see you. I can't believe it's been over a year. You look great." Angela's overzealous hug and enthusiastic greeting jolted him. He didn't remember this side of her.

She must have noticed Tom's reaction because her voice was softer when she added, "All things considered."

"Great to see you too, Angela." He ignored *all things considered*. He didn't want to unleash his grief. Not here, not now. "I hope it's not insulting to comment that you look fantastic." Tom took a desperate stab at changing the subject.

Angela had lost significant weight since he last saw her. Where before she dressed in nondescript, bulging-at-the-seams office scrubs, with shapeless sneakers that propelled her from room to room, she wore red high heels today. Their tips peaked out from under sleek black trousers, and the silky, deep blue top with three buttons undone was hard to ignore. He mentally chastised himself for taking the time to count them. She was always frumpy and dumpy, and now he saw she was much younger than he had thought.

"Working for yourself must agree with you." He switched gears again. Tying his comment to work might save him a potential #metoo moment.

"It does. I've never been happier. Thanks for noticing. It means a lot to me."

Tom dodged her eyes. He was appalled by what tugged at his attention and knew avoidance would be his best friend.

"So, show me this place. What do you have in mind?" He moved into the empty space.

"I know it's tough to imagine with four bare walls, concrete floors, and an unfinished ceiling, but it has great light. With a good design, it'll be wonderful. Check out this great view."

Angela walked over to the windows. Tom focused on the clicking of her heels and watched her feet instead of her behind. This craziness had to end. Her tapping heels stopped. She stood at the window staring at the budding trees. When she didn't turn back, he joined her, making sure to keep a respectable distance between them.

"Patients won't mind waiting in the exam rooms if they can enjoy this view." Angela's voice was slow and eerily seductive. "I've drawn up preliminary ideas for the contractor I'll find to retrofit the space for us. I've penciled in a beautiful corner office for you. The plans are laid out on that table in the middle of the room. Come see." Her heels clicked back to the center of the room. Tom followed six paces behind.

Angela stood behind the table and leaned over the plans. Her blouse draped open to reveal things Tom never anticipated seeing. He blinked hard to erase the image and circled the table to stand at her side. He stared straight ahead. What is going on? This is not who I am.

"That looks wonderful." Tom leaned on the table to get a better look. When his hand landed a little too close to hers, he snatched it back, straightened up, and backed away. It was safer with a little distance between them. "I can see you know what you're doing. The design makes good use of the space. I'll be at the hospital most of the time and won't need a lot of room. This should work fine. Sign me up. What's the next step?"

He knew he was going too fast and didn't want to make decisions without thinking. He needed to finish this meeting and escape whatever was churning in his gut. Angela ambled toward him, hips swaying from the height of her sexy red heels. His wayward thoughts had to stop.

"The lease is in that envelope on the table." She pointed back to the center of the room. "You can sign it now, but I won't turn it in until you put money in the account I set up for you. Sign the bank signature cards next to it, too. I've already signed them. We'll need the rent for the first and last month and a security deposit. About $15,000 just for that. If you can deposit twenty-five, it'll be enough to get started. I'll give you a complete budget for the renovation in a few days."

Twenty-five grand! An alarm went off inside him. He didn't handle the money. Lucy did. With Ellen. Everything was happening too quickly now. He didn't like this pace, and neither would Lucy. Where was she when he needed her? Angela was a good manager. He knew that. He could see that, once again, she had everything handled. But with the red heels, the hips, he needed to slow down. This was all too unsettling.

He paused and took a breath. Lucy's distant, muffled whisper leaked into his subconscious. *Go slow.* He'd heard it before, and she was always right. He walked over to the table, grabbed the signature cards, and stuffed them into the envelope with his name on it.

"Thanks, Angela. I'll take these home so Lucy and I can review them together." He shot out his hand before she could hug him again. Angela smiled but said nothing when she shook it.

Tom walked to the elevator and punched the down button. He prayed it was still perched on this floor. If it wasn't, the stairs were calling his name. He urgently needed to retreat.

# CHAPTER 58

# LUCY

*DOCTOR, DOCTOR, GIVE ME THE NEWS, I'VE GOT A bad case of loving you.* Lucy was rattled by Tom's ringtone playing in her vibrating back pocket. The box slipped from her grasp and landed in Ellen's lap.

"It's Tom. Bad timing but I should answer it. I never checked in with him last night. He's probably wondering what's going on."

She reached for the irritating phone, unsure if her frustration was for Tom or the foolish ringtone he insisted she use as his only-for-her signature ringtone. Luckily, they didn't call each other much, or she would have deep-sixed the annoyance ages ago.

"Hi Tom. We've just started searching the boat. I have a lot to tell you."

Despite the frustrating ringtone, she couldn't wait to tell him their friend, Bahamian Bob, was helping them. She had never called Bob that before, but she loved how it rolled off her tongue and knew Bob would laugh when he heard her call him that.

"So do I," Tom barreled ahead. "I just met Angela at the new office. It's brand new and will take about four to six weeks to renovate. We need to decide quickly."

Lucy slammed the brakes on her line of thinking and detoured to Tom's. He rambled on.

"It's a blank slate right now, and we can design it however we want. Angela's office is also in the building. She'll be nearby to manage my practice since you won't do that."

Now she knew why the sound of Tom's incoming call exasperated her. It was his relentless whining. That ringtone was gone.

"Not again Tom. Stop blaming me for wanting to do something different with my life. I don't have to do everything you want. I'm sorry if I led you astray by fulfilling your every need over all these years." Would she ever get him to understand? It was starting to feel hopeless.

"I never asked you to do that. But you could've told me that you were changing our game plan. I'm left high and dry while you find yourself. Do you think that's fair to me?" He was off and running. She didn't think he heard a word of what she said.

"Stop Tom, right now. I don't want to go there again. Why did you call? I want to get back to what *I* want to do," Lucy let anger and sarcasm drip from her response. There was no holding back; her emotions were too raw.

"Never mind," he sputtered. "I just thought you'd want to know that I'm about to sign a ten-year lease and give Angela

$25,000 to start things rolling. I want my new office to open by June 1st. Not that you really care."

"I'm going to be the adult here and ignore that comment." Lucy skipped a beat. "Do you like it, the office, I mean? Is it what you want? It's just Angela's suggestion; you still get to say yes or no. You don't have to do everything she suggests. Putting all your eggs in the basket of one person isn't always a good idea."

Lucy didn't know where that last comment came from, but something was telling her to slow Tom down, to caution him to take some time before committing too much.

"To be honest, I feel like it's the only basket available to me. Angela has always been at my side, and I don't know why I wouldn't trust her again. I don't have another choice, do I?"

Lucy ignored the childish pleading she detected in his voice. She was not going to fall for it again.

"All I'm saying is you have time to think this through. It's Wednesday. I'm sure I'll be back on Friday. Things are going faster here than I expected. Can we go over things this weekend before you sign on the dotted line? Will a few days make any real difference?" She tried to be rational.

"I guess not. Sorry for disturbing you, it won't happen again." Lucy overlooked his sarcastic tone. Someone had to be an adult.

"Besides Tom, you won't believe who we met. It's unbelievable!"

Silence.

"Tom, are you still there?" More Silence. He had hung up, not even a tiny bit interested in what she had to say.

"Fuck you," Lucy whispered. She liked how Julie's words rolled so naturally out of her mouth. If Tom didn't change, he just might hear them again.

# CHAPTER 59

# JULIE

AFTER A BATHROOM BREAK, AN EXTENDED CONVO with Katie, and as many distractions as she could find before returning to her office, Julie planted her butt in the chair. She couldn't focus today. Give me the weekend, she begged. But she had two days to go. Damn.

She wished she was in Miami with Ellen and Lucy. They didn't need her, but Julie could use some warmth on her sun-starved skin. She was sick and tired of Maine's nonexistent spring. There were just too many days with gray clouds hiding blue skies that she couldn't even remember anymore. She was done with the browns and grays of mud season. Sure, a few yellow daffodils or red tulips helped, but what she really needed was green, any green. Next year, she was out of here. She deserved a warm weather, after-tax-season retreat. And hopefully, not alone.

She needed to get to work. Ellen was counting on her to have some answers when she returned, and she had wasted enough time. None of it would get her work done. Who knows, I might luck out and find a good excuse to work late. She shut down the thought as quickly as it surfaced. She didn't like the urges that seemed to come from nowhere whenever she thought about Bobby and she didn't have the time or inclination to figure out what the hell was going on. Not today.

Today, she needed to dig deeper into the bank statements they had retrieved together. Julie slipped into accounting mode and logged into QuickBooks to pick up where her earlier examination had stopped. She scanned her notes to remind herself of where she had left off. Checks written for international conferences were padded with extra dollars going to something or someone else.

The bank statements confirmed what she suspected. QuickBooks was jerry-rigged to include checks paid to the conference sponsor with dollars transferred elsewhere. The amounts weren't terribly large; they were small enough to slip by unnoticed, and it was safe to assume there were more hidden in the books. She flipped through five years of bank statements and highlighted similar transfers. There were many.

She used QuickBooks' *Find* function to filter for the dates and amounts in question. She traced them from the report to the fudged transactions. A lot were buried in *Office Expense,* a big catchall for paper, pens, coffee, water, and anything that didn't fit somewhere else. The yearly totals were usually pretty high, but if it didn't fluctuate much from year to year, she didn't bother analyzing the details when preparing the tax return. Now, she saw the account had been increasing for years but never large enough to attract her attention.

She examined the year-to-year growth in other accounts to find other creeping balances. Medical supplies and lab expenses were bloated too. She expanded her search from five years to ten. It was clear someone was screwing with the books. This wasn't sloppy bookkeeping or harmless errors made by a newbie bookkeeper. This was fucking embezzlement. Nothing more, nothing less.

She dropped her Number 2 Ticonderoga pencil on her desk. It rolled off to join the others on the floor. She pressed her palms to her eyes, brushed her hair back from her face, and circled her chair toward the window to clear her head. The numbers proved what she suspected, but what the hell was going on? She braced her left elbow on the chair's armrest and rested her chin in her hand. She let her curiosity wander through a wide range of explanations. She slid open the center pencil drawer and pulled out her bright orange highlighter. She folded under the filled pages of her lined yellow pad to a blank page and wrote at the top: **WHEN??? WHO???**

She was tired after a long day of sleuthing. Under her desk, her toe played with the shoes she had long ago kicked off. It was almost five. Time to call it a day, but she needed to see the big picture before leaving for the night. If she didn't wrap this up with a bow, she'd have a tough time falling asleep and didn't need Ellen's legendary lack of sleep. The whole office stayed clear of Ellen when she wasn't sleeping.

Julie listed the totals from a few significant accounts and tried to get a broader view. She wrapped her long hair around her fist and looped it into a loose ponytail. She examined it for split ends before dropping it down her back. It unfurled as she bent over her worksheet to stare at the detailed configuration of numbers. One account alone meandered from $10,000 to $50,000. When she added all the accounts together, what started as a mere trickle became a flood of cash pouring out of the practice.

She grasped the arms of her executive desk chair and leaned back. From a distance, she could physically see how the figures in the spreadsheet had grown from three to five to seven digits long. It reminded her of a sapling with new, spindly twigs slowly growing into longer and stronger branches. You can't see the tree's slow growth at first. Only later, when you look at the before and after pictures, can you see how it grew. Over ten years, embezzlement had spread its branches throughout the practice finances.

Julie knew she'd find more in the books, so she tried to gather enough data to answer who and when. The listed monies had gone to another account. Who owned that other bank account? The practice didn't. She checked that first. It wasn't on the Balance Sheet, the standard financial report that listed all practice assets and liabilities. If it wasn't on the balance sheet, it was owned outside the practice. But by who? Someone inside must be transferring it out.

The cooked books had been baking for at least ten years, a long time to go undetected. Who had access to the practice finances for those ten years? The obvious answer was a doctor. Admin and nursing staff tended to come and go, while doctors were apt to stay. There were a few doctors with ten years of longevity, but she doubted it was any of them. They had limited access to the books, and if they did, they wouldn't know what to do with it.

Except for one. He had experience with QuickBooks because he asked Julie to teach him so he could better understand practice finances. At the time, she was impressed that Dr. Green wanted to educate himself, but now she wondered. Had she trained the embezzler?

She already knew his connection to the inflated international travel expenses. He was also connected to the firing of both Hartmann Associates and Tom Reynolds. Was this why they had been let go? Were Lucy's suspicions correct? Was Dr. Green the embezzler, and behind Ben's death?

Julie's toes pushed against the carpet, and she turned her chair slowly around to gaze at the boats bobbing at the marina next door. She wanted some perspective. She paused her mind's rumblings to watch the resident businessman return to his floating home.

Gary Green seemed too easy an answer. This kind of embezzlement would've been tough, if not impossible, for Gary to pull off alone. He wouldn't have had enough access until he became Managing Physician. That was only a year ago. Did he have an accomplice?

Tom Reynolds managed things for at least the decade before. But Tom? As much as Gary Green seemed the easy answer, Julie couldn't see Tom as the right answer. Were there two embezzlers working together? Julie combed her mind for images of the folks who worked in that office. Who, other than Tom, was there for ten years with access to the books? Not many. But there was one. Tom's right-hand person since the beginning, the one Julie had worked side by side with for years. The easy and right answer surfaced.

Angela. Everything pointed to Angela. She had the longest tenure and the most continuous access to the books. She was the original bookkeeper until the practice grew large enough for her to hire staff to do the grunt work. But she still supervised and reviewed their work every day. Damn! Was it Angela? She slammed her hands on the desk. She was pissed off before, but if it was Angela?

Julie remembered how Angela's bookkeeping assistants changed frequently over the years. She always wondered why the position was so unstable. When she asked her, the answer was simple. Angela had exacting standards and was proud of it. The fired assistants made too many mistakes, were too slow, or missed too many days of work. She always had a reason for their departure, and Julie chalked up the staff turnover as the bane of a too-demanding boss. Goddamn, Angela! Could it be? Had they all been duped?

Julie heard the distant sound of a squeaky wheel. The deep furrow between her brows relaxed and smoothed. Either Bobby was early, or Julie was late. Or both. She listened for other sounds of an active office. Nothing. She was the last at her desk.

She slipped her feet into her heels, thanked a faraway god for rewarding her hard work, and walked down the hall to greet Bobby.

# CHAPTER 60

## BAHAMIAN BOB

THERE WASN'T MUCH ACTIVITY IN THE MARINA, never was on a weekday. The flashy yachts were for impressing, not boating. Bob was looking for someone berthed at Pier J who might remember Ben. All thirty-six slips were filled. The transient boats, only there for a night or two, wouldn't be helpful. But with any luck, industrious year-round owners or their crew would be doing minor repairs or washing decks.

He pulled a pair of sunglasses, free swag from a bank, from his pocket. They were left behind at the bar in Eleuthera, where he sometimes bartended. He rarely wore sunglasses, and there were deep crow's feet at the corners of his normally squinting eyes. Today, he needed the shades to hide his spying.

There was a guy and a girl on a large yacht kitty corner to the slip where Ben had been. They were exactly what he was looking for. Crew members, not owners. The two were tanned, athletic, and young. Owners were pale, out-of-shape, and old. These two seemed close to Ben's age and wore the telltale uniform of the crew: khaki shorts and midnight blue polo shirts emblazoned with the *Golden Hour*'s setting sun logo. The same sinking sun peppered the yacht's deep blue upholstery.

"Hey there, how you doing?" Bob called. "Nice boat. I'm docked in #23 near the end. A tiny little sailboat compared to this beauty." He pushed his sunglasses to the top of his head. He needed to connect as a fellow seafarer, not a tourist who had slipped in after someone left the gate open. The guy sheltered his brow with his right hand and peered at Bob.

"Do you like the powerboat?" Bob slipped his sunglasses down. "I'm thinking of giving up sailing and going for power." Asking for advice was a surefire way to open them up. Everyone loved to be an expert.

"It's a great boat, but it's not ours." The girl looked at the guy before saying more to Bob.

"We're the crew, the caretakers," the guy said. "We keep it ready for those rare times the owner wants to use it and take it out for a spin to keep it in shape. She's incredible."

"Hey, could I come aboard and check it out? Only if you think it's alright. I don't want to get you in trouble." Bob guessed the guy had a fragile ego that could be easily tweaked.

"The owner's not even here." Here it comes; Bob had called it. "He's off to one of his other homes, won't return until it starts to cool off in September or October. Until then, it's all ours. Come aboard. It'll give us something to do."

A lot of young couples thought crewing was the perfect job. They got to cruise to exotic places on out-of-their-reach yachts and live in some of the most exclusive marinas. It was the ideal opportunity for anyone, young or old, who wasn't ready to commit to adult life. It's how Bob got started and where he still was.

The guy slid the gangplank out to the dock so Bob could board in style. The girl met him with a plate of cookies and a beer. Not his usual libation this time of day, but who was he to refuse? He needed their help. He grabbed a cookie in his left hand and an icy Coors Light in his right. The mountains on the beer's label were the perfect shade of blue.

"Thanks. You guys are great. You didn't have to do this, but I do appreciate it. My kind of beer, and it looks like the cookies are homemade."

"Not much to do here, so I've taken up cooking." She had a pretty smile. "The galley on this thing is better than any kitchen I've ever had, and Jared tells me I'm getting pretty good."

Bob noted the guy's name.

"You're not ready for Food Network, but you're getting there fast." Jared kissed her on the cheek. Another couple living the dream.

"When we signed up for this gig, neither of us could boil water," Jared confessed. "We told them we could prepare meals, that Emily didn't have formal training, but that she had learned from her mother and grandmother."

Bob slid the name Emily into his memory.

"It wasn't too far from the truth. They preferred simple menus anyway, so it worked. Luckily, I had a few months to practice before I had to prove anything." She slid her arm into her partner's and offered him a cookie. He refused.

Bob didn't. He grabbed another warm chocolate chip cookie from the plate before Emily set it on the coffee table.

The cushy couch and lounge chairs surrounding it called him to sit and relax for a while, but he resisted the urge to sink into them. Today was not a party.

"I'm mostly a sailing man based out of the Bahamas. Eleuthera, to be exact." Bob took off his sunglasses again. Eye contact built trust. "Me and another guy brought a beauty over last week. Sixty feet long. Just the two of us. We waited for smooth sailing to make it easier to manage. It was a great sail. Couldn't have been any better. The other guy flew back, but I decided to stick around for a while. Needed a break from my volunteer job. I'm glad I did. I ran into some people who needed my help."

"Needed your help? To take a boat back to the Bahamas? Why pay for a plane ticket when you can get paid for your return trip, am I right?" Jared's sarcasm grated on Bob, but he kept it to himself.

"You've got my number, bro. When you're not on a schedule, you can fit into someone else's." Bob tipped up his bottle to get the last slug of the frigid brew before it was lukewarm and undrinkable. The day was turning into a scorcher.

"You're living the life we hope to have someday," Jared said. "Too many down days working for one boat. It gets boring." He turned to Emily and smiled. She glanced down at the deck.

"Well, if you make a change, let me know—lots of opportunities in the Bahamas. I run a volunteer rescue agency. Bahamian Air-Sea Rescue, BASRA for short. Officially, we assist the government rescue. Technically, they assist us. We're the one that gets things done.'

"Cool."

Bob was losing Jared's interest. Not many kids their age thought about anyone but themselves.

"Yeah. I get to meet people at some of the best and worst times of their lives." Bob steered the conversation towards Ben. "It's both sobering and uplifting. Right now, I'm staying to help a mother. Her son disappeared on his way to Eleuthera. She's trying to figure out what went wrong."

Bob looked down at the deck to give them time to absorb this. People were like flies on shit when it came to tragedy.

"If you don't mind, can I ask what happened?" Emily's smiling face faded to concern.

Bob ran his fingers through his straw-colored hair to dry off the bottle's condensation. "About three months ago, I helped search for a missing boat. A father was supposed to meet his son on a solo cruise from Maine to Eleuthera. The kid never made it. We found his boat circling aimlessly hundreds of miles off course. He was dead. That's the underbelly of my job. It's tough."

Bob rubbed the back of his neck and took off his sunglasses. He wanted them to feel the enormity of what he was saying. He knew it still showed on his face, and Bob watched a cloud of distress move across the young woman's face.

"That's awful. Do most of your rescues end like that?" The pitch of Emily's voice rose higher and louder. She looked at Jared, obviously bored with the story.

"Thankfully, it doesn't. Usually, we're rescuing tourists who couldn't handle their rental boat. Or a paddleboarder caught in a current that took them miles from shore. That kind of thing. This one was painful. He was dead seven days before we found him. It was ugly. No other way to describe it." Maybe if he gave Jared the gory details, he could keep him interested.

"Whoa man, that's hardcore," Jared was finally interested. "Maybe I do like this boring life."

"So here I am strolling along the boardwalk this morning and I come across a pale woman, obviously a tourist, checking out Monty's. I bet you know that place?" Bob tried to keep Jared engaged.

"Sure do." Jared's face lit up. "Once the gawkers turn in for the night, it's our favorite place to hang out. Short walk back to the boat, if you know what I mean." He grabbed another beer from Emily, who had a cold one ready for him. She was well trained.

"Anyway," Bob slowed his delivery for effect. "It turns out the woman is down here with the mother of the young guy who died. They're trying to figure out what went wrong on the *Ocean Potion*."

"Wait. What was the guy's name?" Jared's eyes searched for Emily's and then moved back to Bob. "The one who died? We hung out with a guy docked across the way. You said *Ocean Potion*. Wasn't that the name of his boat, Emily?" His eyes flicked back to Emily again and froze.

The horror on both faces told Bob he hit the jackpot.

"It couldn't have been him." Emily's voice bounced between a sputter and a stutter. "Not Ben, we loved Ben. What a great guy. We hung out with him but didn't get to say goodbye. He was gone by the time we got up. Jared slept in after being overserved. Oh God, it was him, I know it was him. He said he was from Maine, meeting his dad. Oh my god, it was Ben, wasn't it?"

She breathed fast and shallow, and Bob wished he had a bag to throw over her head. If she didn't slow down, she'd be hyperventilating soon. He'd seen it before when delivering bad news.

"Yes, it was Ben." He took Emily's hands in his and steered her to the couch. He motioned for Jared to join her. Jared held Emily as she cried.

Bob eased into one of the cushy lounge chairs and watched from across the coffee table. "I'm glad I found you guys."

It was time for storytelling. "Tell me what you know."

# CHAPTER 61

# ELLEN

THE BOX WAS WARM IN ELLEN'S HANDS. AS SHE waited for Lucy's phone call to end, she held it to her nose, smelled the sweet, fruity scent of cherry wood, and returned it to her lap. Her left thumb unconsciously rubbed its smooth surface. The deep, reddish-brown grain of its lid was highly polished and highlighted the bas-relief carving of a boat. Her right index finger traced the boat's outline in a continuous circling of its delicate lines.

Lucy stuffed her phone into her back pocket. Ellen didn't hear what Lucy whispered at its conclusion, but her disgusted grimace said it all.

"That man's whining will be the death of us. I am so sick of it. Will it ever end?" Lucy plopped down next to Ellen. "Don't answer that; I don't want to waste another second on his foolishness. We have more important things to do."

Ellen's fingers paused their gentle caress.

"It's exquisite, isn't it?" Lucy stared down at the box. "A real work of art. Someone went out of their way to find an artist to carve this for Ben. The polished wood alone is remarkable, but this is an actual carving of the *Ocean Potion*. It must've been made especially for Ben. It's really a treasure." Her hand hovered above the box in Ellen's lap.

"I thought it was your boat. It's amazing. It not only looks wonderful, but it feels wonderful too. I swear it's warm to the touch, and its soft, rounded edges call you to stroke it. I'm afraid I've been fondling it while you were on the phone."

Ellen offered the box to Lucy. "Here, see how great it feels in your hands. It's really something. It almost feels alive."

Lucy took the box from her outstretched hands. She watched Lucy's left thumb slowly rub the edge while her right index finger followed the same path hers had.

"Ben must have loved this," Lucy turned to Ellen. "I think I'm ready to open it myself. Tom's call wound me up. But it also screwed up my courage to see this thing through. He didn't even ask what was going on down here. It's so frustrating. All he talked about was his new office and Angela."

Ellen wasn't sure whether to weigh in on Lucy's comments or let them pass. She knew Tom and Lucy were dealing with things the only way they knew how. Tom was focusing on work, his comfort zone, while Lucy was slowly rebuilding herself back into the strong, independent woman both seemed to have forgotten. With tragedy clouding their senses, neither recognized they were exactly who they were when they first met and fell in love. But Ellen remembered. Best not to say a word.

"Okay, let's do this. I'm ready to see what's inside." Lucy shook the box from side to side. "Whatever is in it fits perfectly, like the box was made for it."

Was this mother, Ellen's friend, ready to open this Pandora's box? Whatever was inside, once revealed, whether good or bad, would be with Lucy forever.

The *Ocean Potion* rocked from side to side, and Ellen grabbed Lucy's knee. For a moment, she had forgotten her water-based surroundings.

"Hey, anyone down there?" Bob's voice boomed from above.

Ellen's fingers relaxed. He was back, hopefully with some clues.

# CHAPTER 62

# LUCY

BOB'S HUSKY VOICE ECHOED DOWN THE HATCH, and his right foot appeared on the ladder. Lucy smiled at Ellen as they watched him descend. Did he have news? Did he find someone who remembered Ben? Her heart thumped. The box could wait.

Bob sat across from them on the cabin's other sofa. "I met some kids that hung out with Ben." He started to talk, then stopped. He leaned towards them. "Wait, what's that? Did you find something?"

"We're not sure yet. We were about to open it. But you go first. I want to hear about Ben. What did they tell you?" Lucy set the box down next to her; it could wait. Bob's words were more important right now, and she could use another minute or two to bolster her courage.

"Unfortunately, not as much as I hoped for." Bob sat down on the opposite berth. "Jared and Emily are crewing on a big yacht down the pier. They live on it. It's pretty boring they say, since it isn't used much. So, when Ben showed up, they were happy to have someone their age to hang with. Sounds like the three of them really hit it off. They were devastated when I told them what happened."

"What do they remember? I want to hear everything." Lucy was well aware of the end to Ben's story, but she needed details to soften the blow and make it more palatable. She was like a child wishing for a different ending to their favorite book.

"It sounded like a typical twenty-something night. Drinks on the boat, shared a joint or two, and then they moved to Monty's when the night wore on and the tourists went to bed." Bob looked directly at Lucy, "Monty's is where I ran into Ellen this morning. It's a bar in the middle of the marina. Tourists during the day and locals at night. They hung out there, but Jared and Emily left without Ben. They said he was still at the bar talking with a seasoned sailor who's a regular. I think he was the last person to see Ben. I'm going to head over tonight to see if I can find him. They said I'd know him because he looks like me, whatever that means."

"Didn't they see Ben in the morning? Why was that guy the last?" Lucy's foot tapped the floor. She was impatient; she wanted more from Bob. She needed a reason, any reason, to explain why her only son's life was over.

"Jared was late getting up, and by the time Emily went to get Ben for breakfast, he was gone. They didn't think much of it because they knew he was anxious to get going. He told them he was ready for uninterrupted time with his dad."

Lucy's foot stopped. Her shoulders slumped forward. She dropped her head to her chest and willed herself not to cry.

Her sobs had already splashed the cabin floor once today.

"I wanted more too," Bob leaned across the narrow cabin and held Lucy's hands.

She lifted her head and looked into his steady green eyes. She trusted this man. There was no one else.

"I'll find out more tonight. I promise." Bob's voice was soothing, and it helped Lucy's hopes stay alive. "Bars reveal a lot of secrets as the night wears on. Tongues loosen, new friendships deepen, stories are woven. I'm sure I'll find out more."

Lucy was deflated. She looked down at the floor. She needed some news, any news to lift her lagging spirit. "Thanks Bob. I'm sorry if I sound disappointed. I'm grateful you found someone who remembered Ben. I trust you. I'll be patient. Or at least I'll try." She let go of his hands and tightened her grip on the box in her lap.

"What's that?" Bob asked. "Quite a work of art. That's a carving of the *Ocean Potion,* isn't it?" Lucy shifted from disappointment to curiosity when his hand lightly touched the cherrywood box.

"It is. See the tiny letters etched into its side?" She placed the box in Bob's hands. He held it about two inches from his face.

"I've never seen it before," Lucy explained. "I know Ben would have shown it to me if he had it in Maine. I think it was in the package his godfather Gary Green gave him at the dock. He told Ben not to open it until his first stop. It's what made me think something odd was going on. Now I wonder if the box was only a gift."

"Let's find out." He passed the box back to her. "Open it. No time like the present."

It still felt warm and alive, but now it seemed lighter and less ominous. She slid the tiny brass button on the box's lid to the left and opened its latch. Her thumbs lifted the lid. A leather book with gold-leaf trim was nestled inside. She turned the box over, and the book dropped out. She pressed it to her hammering heart.

"Do you think it's a journal? Maybe Gary understood Ben more than I gave him credit for?" It was a rhetorical question. Lucy didn't expect an answer.

She held the book in her quivering hands and studied it. A flap from the back cover wrapped around half of the front to hold the journal closed. Lucy slid her index finger under the flap and lightly lifted it. It opened, then snapped shut, secured by a magnet. She slipped her finger under it again and held open the cover. Inside was an inscription.

Lucy's voice, a few decibels above a whisper, trembled as she read.

> *"To travel is to take a journey into yourself."*
>
> *Fill this journal with your hopes and dreams.*
> *I'm so proud of the man you are becoming.*
>
> *Love,*
>
> *Your Godfather Gary*

# CHAPTER 63

## DANIEL

IT WAS THE FIRST FULL WEEK IN MAY, AND DANIEL had a full day ahead of him. April's financials were on his desk for final review before passing them on to the doctors. They rarely looked at them, but he liked to be fully prepared if someone asked him a question.

He flipped the light switches and limped down the labyrinthine hallways back to the admin offices. Last night's workout had done him in, and he woke with the throb of a pulled groin. It was six-thirty, and he was the first to arrive for the day. He turned down the final hall to his office. He slowed when he saw his office door open. The light was on. He was positive he locked it the night before. He never left it unlocked; he always double-checked it. There were too many confidential things in it to not keep it secure.

He moved quietly towards the open door so he wouldn't alert whoever was intruding. Dr. Green was staring out the window in one of the visitor chairs. Daniel cleared his throat to announce his arrival. Dr. Green turned at the sound of Daniel's cough.

"You're here. Hope you don't mind. I used my master key to let myself in. I needed to catch you to discuss something before I headed to the hospital for rounds." He nodded his head toward Daniel's empty desk chair.

Daniel sat down. Did he really give me permission to sit at my own desk? He pulled out a notepad that the drug companies freely dispensed and grabbed a pen from his desk's center drawer. This must be an important conversation.

"What's on your mind?" Daniel planted his elbows on the desk, clasped his hands together, and looked up. "What do you have for me?"

Dr. Green was not his usual put-together self today. He needed a haircut and had dark circles under his eyes. He raked his fingers through his uncombed hair, then looked up at Daniel. He opened his mouth, then closed it.

"What is it? Did I do something wrong? I don't like the looks of this." Daniel squirmed in his chair, and his groin recoiled.

Dr. Green interrupted, "No, no." Then he hesitated. "You did nothing wrong. I did."

His halting delivery worried Daniel. This wasn't going to be an easy conversation, and he needed to be careful not to step in until he had to.

"There's something I didn't tell you when I hired you." Dr. Green rubbed his eyes. "It's about to bite me. I need your advice on the best way forward."

Daniel didn't let his face and words reflect what he was thinking. Why me? Why am I your chosen dumping ground?

"Go on," he said instead. "What's this about?"

Dr. Green cleared his throat. He pinched the bridge of his nose, then fanned his fingers to rub his eyes and face. He cleared his throat again.

Daniel waited.

"I didn't give you all the details when we hired you to replace Angela. I should have told you the whole story. I thought it was best to keep quiet and put it behind us. The practice needed to move forward." He dropped his head into his hands and rubbed his temples.

Daniel couldn't imagine how replacing Angela could bring such angst to this powerful, talented surgeon. He needed to stay curious but didn't want to get caught up in Dr. Green's drama. "Tell me more."

"She'd been embezzling. For years. And Tom Reynolds never noticed. He was the Managing Physician and should have known. I caught it by accident. When I confronted her, she blackmailed me. I didn't know what to do. I did what I thought was best."

Daniel didn't react. He sensed he still wasn't getting the whole story. Was he being manipulated? "Wait, I don't get it. Blackmail? For what?"

"She called me out on my foreign travel."

Another vague answer. Daniel wasn't going to give up. He needed to hear the whole story. "Foreign travel? I know you were doing a lot of work in China. Is that what you're talking about? Did she think it was too expensive? I still don't know what you mean." Daniel pressed him harder. He didn't like this game of twenty-one questions. Any empathy or sympathy he might've had for this man was quickly drying up.

"That's part of it, but I slipped in some personal travel too. It was wrong; I see that now. When I confronted her about the missing money, she threatened to expose me. She knew the other doctors wouldn't be happy. She said they'd throw me out of the practice."

"As well they should have." Daniel slipped and let his judgment show. Too bad, there's no excuse for dishonesty.

"I took the coward's way out and said I wouldn't prosecute if she left quietly."

"And then you hired me and took over as Managing Physician. Nice. You made sure no one would ever find out." Daniel's voice dripped with sarcasm. He leaned back in his chair, his power position. He was not going to make this easy for him.

"I know. I'm sorry. I should have told you the truth."

"Yeah, you should have. But tell me this, Gary. Why did you make me fire Dr. Reynolds? And Ellen Hartmann. More dirty work for me to clean up?" Daniel wasn't going to give him an inch. As far as he was concerned, the man sitting across from him was no longer his boss. He was now Gary, not Dr. Green.

"I didn't know what to do. I didn't want Tom to get in trouble for missing Angela's embezzling, and frankly, Hartmann should have caught it."

Gary's accusatory tone angered Daniel, and his subtle switch from accused to accuser wasn't lost on Daniel. "Nice, pin it on someone else. I'm not impressed. Are you looking for me to say what you did was right? I'm not going to do that. Sorry, but I have a reputation to protect, and I won't let you take me down with you. You're on your own with this. I'll quit before I defend your actions. No job is that important." His unconscious indignation straightened his spine.

"Sorry, sorry. I didn't mean that," Gary dropped his head. "That came out wrong. It was all wrong, and I need to stop the cover-up now. I'm afraid Angela will dupe Tom again. She's helping him set up a new practice. I have to say something. I have to warn him. I owe him too much."

"You should have thought about that a year ago," Daniel twisted the knife. It felt good.

"I know exactly how much I need to reimburse the practice for my personal trips. I'm prepared to pay it all back. That's why I need your help."

"Oh no, Gary. I won't help you reimburse your way out of this." He was a fool if he thought Daniel would help cover it up. He gave up a perfectly decent job to come here. This man enticed him with a higher salary, more benefits, and the promise that this medical office was something to be proud of. Now Daniel wasn't so sure.

"I'm not the one you need to come clean to." Daniel's voice was cold and unforgiving. "It sounds to me that, at the very least, a meeting with your partners is in order. You need to set things straight. But you owe Tom Reynolds a whole lot more." He paused to let his next words sting. "How could you have done that to him? His son just died!"

"I wasn't thinking. I was trying to protect him, but I was only protecting myself. I see that now. It was inexcusable." Gary squirmed in his chair.

Daniel was on a roll. "Yes, it was, Gary." He had no problem being judge and jury to this man. The pulled muscle in his groin twinged, and he resisted the urge to shift in his chair. "Your partners need to know what you did. They are the ones who will decide if they want you as part of the practice. Not me."

Gary Green sat up straight. His hands gripped the arms of the chair. Daniel waited for his next pathetic excuse.

"You're right," Gary finally said. "I knew you were an honest man when I hired you. I'd be stupid if this wasn't what I expected from you. It's rough, but it's what I need to hear. I don't like who I have become."

Daniel said nothing. His groin tweaked again. He sat firm.

Gary Green stood up, leaned forward, and placed both hands on the desk. Daniel resisted the urge to push back from this man who invaded his personal space. He refused to be intimidated.

"Let me talk to my wife first," Gary offered into the silence. "It's Thursday. Can you give me until Monday morning? Then we'll set up a meeting with the partners. Will that work for you?"

Daniel nodded. He liked this newfound power. Finally, he'd be respected as the competent manager he was. He might not have a medical degree, but he knew who the better man was.

Daniel ignored Gary's tentative movement toward a handshake. He would not reciprocate. He picked up the financial statement from his desk and studied it.

This meeting was over.

# CHAPTER 64

# THE OCEAN POTION

THE TWO WOMEN CHATTERED AS THEY STEPPED onto the dock. Gone was the heaviness and fear they carried when first stepping aboard. Hope had replaced it. It seeped into her cabin when they first discovered the box with its hidden treasure. It oozed through her nooks and crannies when they opened his journal, the one he wrote in each night. Her ribs tingled with tears and wept with laughter as they paged through its revelations.

The seasoned sailor, the one who rescued her from the open sea, stayed behind. "Go enjoy Ben's stories," he told the women. "I'll see you in the morning with a report. Best I do this part alone."

She welcomed him into her hatches and hiding places. She too, wanted to find the culprit. She too, needed to know why. Why did her once-in-a-lifetime sail end so tragically? Why did she lose the special boy who named her, the one who learned to hoist her sails and rudder her, the child-turned-man who fulfilled her every dream? She creaked in frustration.

The man combed through ropes and riggings, tested hardware and heating, examined every nook and cranny, above and below her deck. She expanded with trust, as she had under the care of Ben and his family—the family who, like her, mourned their son.

# CHAPTER 65

# JULIE

JULIE PICTURED HER OFFICE THROUGH THE EYES of the new clients coming to meet with her. It needed a cleaning or, at the very least, some straightening up. She counted fifteen stacks of extended tax returns on the floor surrounding her. The same number of minutes before the clients arrived. Her floor filing system wouldn't get a vote of confidence even if they knew there was a system to her mess. Others would see it as incompetent. She grabbed the closest stack and straightened the pile before placing it on the shelf. It wasn't Ellen's pristine, all-edges lined-up standard, but it was good enough for Julie.

The front desk buzzed. The clients were early. She grabbed the remaining stacks and shoved them haphazardly into the bookcase. "Be right out, Katie. Can you get them a cup of coffee before I come out to get them?"

"Already done. They're enjoying the view."

Julie smoothed the wrinkles in her skirt and blouse. She'd invest in an iron someday, then laughed at the foolish thought. Or learn to pull warm clothes from the dryer like Ellen did. Yeah right. She laughed again. This will have to do. She combed her unruly curls with her fingers. She was good to go.

A perfect young couple, impeccably dressed, with great haircuts, was staring out the window. "Megan and Will, how nice to meet you. I'm Julie." She liked using first names to level the playing field. Too many doctors had superegos and thought their medical knowledge made them experts in finance. It did not.

"Julie, so nice to meet you. What fantastic offices you have. I could suffer with this view every day." Megan turned and shook Julie's outreached hand.

"Isn't that the truth." Julie extended her hand to Will. "If you have to sit at a desk all day, this isn't too shabby. I have a great view from my office too. Come on back."

Julie hated the long walk to her office. The initial client connection was severed, if only for a minute or two, and she could only guess what looks passed between clients when they followed behind her.

"Here we are. Have a seat." Julie ushered them into her office and closed the door. She sat behind her desk, picked up one of the pencils rolling around its surface, and carefully folded over the top page of her lined pad of paper to hide the notes from her last meeting.

"Thanks for coming in today. Let's start by talking about how you found me. It helps me know what you're looking for and what someone might've said about me." Julie picked up their earlier connection by laughing.

"Megan is setting up my practice for me." Will smiled

at Julie, then turned to his wife. "She's the financial wizard in the family, a banker, to be exact. She asked me to check around the hospital for the name of a good accountant. Tom Reynolds highly recommended you."

"We love Tom and Lucy." Megan took over for Will. "When they said they worked with you for years, I told Will, that's where we need to go." She smiled broadly, revealing perfectly aligned, snow-white teeth. "Angela Dunphy suggested someone else, but we decided to first see what they were raving about."

Julie swallowed hard at the sound of Angela's name. "That's wonderful. Tom and Lucy are the best. You won't find many people better than the Reynolds." She relaxed back into her chair. She needed this to sound like an offhand comment. "So, you're working with Angela? I worked with her for years when she was Tom's assistant."

"She worked for Tom? She never mentioned it to us, did she Will?" Megan looked at him. "But I guess that means she's professional and respects privacy. I know we both appreciate that in our professions."

"What brings you in today?" Julie pivoted the conversation away from Angela. She wanted to speak with Ellen first. If she was right, she could rescue these new clients another day.

"Will finished his residency this spring, and we decided he shouldn't join a group," Megan said. "He's a dermatologist, and they're in great demand. I didn't think he needed any help funneling patients to him. I was right. His appointments are filling up fast."

"Good thinking. With the graying of our population, dermatology is in demand. Too many Baby Boomers baked in the sun during their youth, and now it's taking its toll." Julie hoped Will would join the conversation, but he was staring out the window.

Megan nudged Will's arm. "Angela agreed too. She's been really great to work with. Her office is in the same building as ours, so she's always available to answer any questions. She's taking care of everything. She said the only thing we'd need is a tax accountant. That's why we're here."

What a convenient setup. But Julie couldn't blow the whistle just yet. She hadn't figured out yet if Angela was working alone or with someone else. "That's good to hear. Is Angela your only staff?"

"Oh, she's not on staff. She's just a consultant. She'll manage the office person she hired for us. And, of course, she'll supervise finances and other stuff. With Angela onboard, I've been able to get back to my own job." Megan rattled on. "She's been indispensable. I don't know what we would've done without her. Her monthly fee is pretty reasonable, isn't it Will?" he nodded.

Silent alarms clanged in Julie's head. Of course, her fee was reasonable. There were other ways to get paid.

Julie tried to sound innocent. "She's been in the business a long time and certainly knows her way around medical practices. I didn't realize she started her own medical management company. How did you find her?"

"We were looking for office space at that new building off Congress Street." Will finally opened his mouth. "The realtor introduced us to Angela, thought she'd be perfect to help us. He said she was the right person to handle all the things I have no interest in doing."

Like too many doctors Julie worked with, Will passed his office management to someone else. It made embezzlement easy for staff prone to dishonesty.

"How convenient." Julie was surprised that she said that out loud and added quickly, "For both of you. It sounds very efficient and effective."

"We think so. That's why we came in to get acquainted. We want to be a tax client. Angela has the rest under control." Megan began to close the meeting. Another efficient, effective woman. Just like Ellen. And Angela. "We trust Lucy and Tom's recommendation, and I like what I hear. What do you think Will?"

"If you have room for us, I'd like to work with you." He squeezed Megan's hand.

"Great, we're all in agreement," Julie said. "Consider yourselves clients and call me anytime you have a question. Remember, there's no such thing as a stupid question, only the one you don't ask. Call or email anytime. Accountants can be the liaison between all your professionals: landlords, investment people, consultants, and bankers like you Megan. I'm always ready to give a second opinion."

Julie stood up, circled her desk, and offered her hand. "Thanks so much for coming in. I look forward to working with both of you." She stepped through the doorway and pointed down the hall to the front desk. "Katie will be waiting to take your coffee cups, get your coats, and officially welcome you as members of the Hartmann Associates family."

Julie sat down at her desk and twirled toward the windows. A sly grin crept across her face. Things were progressing nicely.

# CHAPTER 66

# BAHAMIAN BOB

BOB WIPED HIS BROW ON THE HEM OF HIS T-SHIRT and squinted up at the blazing sun. Four o'clock, and still no break in the heat and humidity. Sunset was hours away. Lucy and Ellen followed his suggestion and returned to the air-conditioned hotel to pore over the discovered journal. He was alone and uninterrupted in his search of the *Ocean Potion*. He desperately wanted to find an answer to Lucy's question. What caused the propane leak that killed her only son? Until he found it, she would have no peace. Neither would he.

The original canisters that held the killing propane were still empty. Their deadly vapors long ago dissipated over the open sea, leaving death as their only witness. The boat's return trip to Miami Beach was utilitarian, not for pleasure. There was no need for heating or cooking, so there was no need for them to be filled. But they had to be full to test for gas leaks. He scrutinized the fittings before removal to assure himself that simple cross-threading hadn't been the culprit. It was not.

Bob couldn't believe that this glitzy, full-service marina didn't have a propane fill station. Too mundane a service for a high-end place like this, he guessed. The closest place was too far to walk, but he hitched a ride with another commonplace boater looking for the same. Bob let the guy fill first and told him to head back without him. He wanted to talk to the guy working there alone. Maybe he remembered Ben.

The service attendant listened to Bob's story and apologized. Ben did not ring a bell. He wasn't sure if he worked that day or if he just didn't remember. There were a lot of people coming and going in any one day. He was sorry he was no help but could give Bob a ride back to the marina because it was the end of the day. The place was closing in fifteen minutes. Bob rested while he waited. It was good to be away from the over-the-top marina with its overflowing sidewalks and fancy slips. He missed the easy flow of Eleuthera.

Back at the boat, he carefully threaded the fittings that connected the filled canisters to the propane lines. He partially turned them on, allowing only a slow flow of gas. He didn't want to recreate the disaster that ended Ben's life. Using a solution of soap and water, he coated the lines inch by inch from the canister to the cabin's heater. The tiniest pinprick in the line would cause a soap bubble to rise. It was a sweltering day, even by Miami standards, and the solution dried up quickly. Progress was slow and tedious, but he stuck with it.

An hour later, he was satisfied that the flow of gas from the propane tank to the boat's heater was intact. There was no leak, and he decided to take a break. He needed a cup of coffee to make up for not having lunch after his breakfast of cookies and beer with Emily and Jared. He faced a long night at Monty's and wanted to be on top of his game. He went below deck to the galley to fill the tea kettle and make himself a good enough cup of instant coffee from the red plastic jar of Folger's he had noticed earlier. Not his first choice, but it was better than Starbucks.

Bob heard about Ellen's uncomfortable introduction to seaworthy cooking, and he tried to keep the *Ocean Potion*'s swinging stove still. That kind of stove was a savior in rough seas, not so much on dry land. His hands were slow and steady as he struck a match from the box on the shelf over the stove and held the flickering flame over the burner.

Whoosh! A plume of blue fire erupted from the stove.

"Oomph!" Bob jumped back.

The acrid smell of burning flesh filled the cabin. He pushed back his hair and felt new burnt and crispy ends. He brushed his hands over his face, waiting for the pain to erupt. Nothing.

He peered at the gas control. It was still in the off position. He found the leak.

# CHAPTER 67

# ELLEN

ELLEN GENTLY CLOSED THE DOOR BETWEEN THEIR adjoining rooms. They both needed a break from reading Ben's journal, where they looked for something, anything that would help make sense of his death. Lucy insisted they start at the beginning of his journey to relive her son's epic trip from Maine to Miami. She was fully aware of how it ended but wasn't ready yet to read Ben's final words. Still, it was exhausting, and they could use a rest from the daily recaps of Ben's journey down the coast. Interspersed with mundane sailing facts were Ben's reflections on his life and the people in it. These were intense, deeply introspective, and were never meant to be shared.

Ellen looked at the red 4:24 p.m. blazing from the bedside clock. There was still time to catch Julie at the office. She pulled her cell phone from the back pocket of her shorts and dialed the familiar number. "Katie, how are things? I'd love to say I miss being there, but we'd both know I was lying."

"You're right about that. I've been checking Miami's weather. You're twice as warm as we are here. I'm jealous," Katie laughed. "Want me to connect you with Julie? She just finished with a new client."

"Thanks, I'd appreciate that." Ellen looked at the bed while she waited for Julie to answer. She longed to stretch out on its pristine white duvet, close her eyes, and let her subconscious process the day's events. Maybe if she took time now to relax, she'd sleep tonight.

"Ellen, how's life in the sun? I was hoping you'd call. I've been spending time analyzing the books. Found some pretty interesting stuff." Julie was on a roll and then stopped. "But you go first. Mine can wait. Miami Beach has to be more interesting or at least more fun."

"You're right about that. A lot more eventful than I expected. I thought this was going to be a wild goose chase." Ellen smiled, recalling Bob's rough and raspy voice. "You won't believe it, but I ran into this guy from the Bahamas who actually helped Tom and Lucy find Ben. Once again, the Universe delivers."

"What are the odds of that?" Julie's laugh sounded tired; she wasn't her usual bubbly self. "Let me guess, you were on one of your walks."

"You know me too well. No sleep makes me an early walker. Bob's an early riser too. He stopped to help me. Kismet, I guess."

"What's he doing to help?" Julie pushed the conversation forward.

"Right now, he's going over the *Ocean Potion* with kid gloves, looking for what caused the gas leak that killed Ben.

The official report said it was the cause of death, but it never said why there was a leak. Shoddy job if you ask me." Ellen struggled to keep her irritation in check.

"So, still no clue? Frustrating."

"Not yet. But he did find some kids that hung out with Ben before he took off for Eleuthera. They didn't have much to offer but suggested he go to Monty's Bar to find the guy they said was the last to see him. It's a local place, same place I ran into Bob. He's going there tonight."

"I won't even ask what you were doing at a bar in the morning. Getting coffee?" Julie's teasing helped Ellen relax a bit. Her shoulders dropped. Were they up around her ears all day? Now that she noticed their creep, she might actually relax.

"Nope, not open. Not even for coffee."

"Wish I was there to help. You know how I like my bars." The knots in Ellen's stomach untied with Julie's laughter, tired as it was.

"That I do." Ellen hesitated, then changed the subject. "Lucy and I found something else. Ben's journal. She's still reading it. It was a little too personal, so I gave her some space." Ellen's voice trailed off, thinking about the gut-wrenching confessions of a young man searching for himself. Gary Green's inscription was correct. The sail had been Ben's journey into himself.

"A journal, huh. Interesting. Didn't know college guys were into that thing."

"It was a gift from his godfather, Gary Green. Not what we expected. It was in a gorgeous wooden box made just to hold it. Lucy thinks it was in the package that he gave Ben at the dock, the one that made Lucy suspect him in the first place. She's changed her mind about Gary's involvement in Ben's death. I might have to agree with her." The bed was calling to Ellen, and her eyelids started to droop.

"Hmmm, maybe," Julie's response was unexpected, and Ellen listened for more. "I've been looking at the numbers, trying to figure out what the hell's been going on in the books. It's a lot more than international conferences, for sure. It looks like embezzlement, and a lot of it."

Ellen's neck muscles tightened. "Embezzlement, really? Not just cheating the government with exorbitant, nonbusiness travel? Are you sure?"

"Been going on for years, at least ten. Gary was definitely padding his expenses, but I think there's more. It started long before the China stuff. Tom and Gary were the only doctors there for all of those ten years, but I might be clutching at straws. Neither one had enough knowledge of the books to make it happen. I suppose they could have relied on Angela for that, but collusion between owner and staff seems awfully far-fetched. What do you think?"

"I think I need to sleep on it. Give it time to stew." Ellen kicked off her shoes and sat on the edge of the bed. "We only thought Gary Green was involved because of Lucy's suspicions. Now that those have been put to bed, I'm not sure if he's involved at all. And Tom? It would take a lot to convince me of that."

"Okay, maybe. But I don't want to give up on either of them too fast. But after my last meeting, I'm sure Angela is behind it all." Julie's pronouncement stunned Ellen.

"Last meeting?" Ellen scratched the nap from her agenda.

"What does that have to do with anything?"

"I met with a new doctor and his wife. They're working with Angela. She didn't refer them to us, which is odd in itself. But not surprisingly, Tom and Lucy did. They told me how Angela's managing everything for them." Julie's voice picked up speed. "And get this. She's doing it from her office in the

same building. Pretty convenient, don't you think?" Ellen's shoulders started to climb.

"Too convenient." Ellen stood up and walked over to the window. Her mind started to fill in the blanks. "Lucy talked with Tom this morning. Angela wants him to move into the same place. Hmm, her own little fiefdom. Did you tell them?"

"No. It was too early. But if Gary Green is really a good guy and she's getting ready to set up Tom again, just give the go-ahead, and I'll start tightening the noose. Maybe even get them to help?"

Ellen needed to tamp down Julie's excitement. She didn't want her passion to get them into trouble before they were ready.

"Not yet. Might be tricky. But it'd be great to catch Angela in the act. Easier to keep the police interested too. Let's sit tight until Monday when I'm back in the office. We'll work out the next steps then. We don't want to blow the whistle too soon." She wished Lucy was awake. They needed to stop Tom from doing anything stupid.

"Okay. I'll sit tight over the weekend." Julie didn't sound convincing. "Have a good flight back. And don't worry about me freezing in Maine. I'll be fine."

"Do you want some cheese with that whine?" Ellen heard Julie laugh as she hung up.

She turned away from the window's serene and sandy ocean view and looked at the connecting door. Her mind was swirling with questions about Angela. A nap for her was out of the question.

Was it too soon to wake Lucy?

# CHAPTER 68

## TOM

TOM STARED OUT AT THE OCEAN. SITTING IN Lucy's chair was the next best thing to having her here with him. The fragrance of her citrusy shampoo seeped from the cushions. It filled him with the same calm that enveloped him whenever he hugged her or bent down to kiss the top of her head. Mornings with her hands around a hot cup of coffee after her morning shower left its permanent imprint in this chair. He missed her. It was late afternoon, and he faced another night of eating alone. He didn't even want to think of sleeping without her in their cavernous king-sized bed another night.

He went back through this morning's phone call. Calling Lucy immediately after his meeting with Angela was a mistake. He was off-kilter, rattled by everything being asked of him. He didn't want a new office. He didn't want to start over. He didn't want a dead son. He never wanted any of this.

And then there was Angela. His sudden attraction. What was that about? He loved Lucy and everything about her. It wasn't just because she took care of him like she insinuated. Of course, he appreciated that. Who wouldn't? Maybe, if he were honest with himself, he did depend on her too much. But the truth was, she could do nothing but sit in her chair looking out the window all day, and he would still love her. He always had and always would.

Emotion pried loose from his gut, traveled through his tight throat, and spilled out. He slumped over in Lucy's chair and hugged his stomach. He didn't stop it this time. He let it erupt and engulf him until he was empty. "Oh God. I am so alone. Help me find my way," he prayed. Every emotion that he was too afraid to feel poured out. Sitting here in Lucy's chair, Tom felt safe enough to bear it. He forgot about time and place. He forgot about should-have-beens and responsibilities. Lucy's love surrounded and supported him. He heard her words whisper tenderly, "I'm here, I'm always here."

And then, "Stop blaming me."

He understood. Finally. He understood it all. His angst over Angela and his confusion were only a distraction to help him avoid all those other feelings. But now that he dumped the pain, the anguish, the frustration, and his resultant loneliness, he was free. Free to be fully here with all the good, the bad, and the ugly. Yes, the bad and the ugly were still here, but the good was piggybacking along. It bubbled up when he dropped the anchor tied to his soul. The beauty and good of his family: wife, daughter, and Ben surfaced. None of it was gone. It was here, along with his deep love for Lucy, the woman he loved, the one he always loved.

Tom picked up his cell phone that rested on Lucy's table next to her empty coffee cup from the morning she left. He was waiting for Lucy's call, the one he wrongly thought she owed him. He called her number and waited for her to pick up.

A sleepy-sounding "Tom" was all he heard. He needed to speak first and didn't hesitate.

"I'm so sorry Lucy. For the whining, the blaming, for everything. Even that silly ringtone I put on your phone. I love you so much. Can you forgive me?"

# CHAPTER 69

---

# BAHAMIAN BOB

BOB CHECKED HIS REFLECTION IN THE MIRROR. Eyebrows and eyelashes were still intact. Only the burnt fringe of his hair needed doctoring. The marina's bathroom was better than most. Clean, accessible, and, from the look of it, rarely used. He pulled his Swiss Army knife from his left pocket, a gift from his mother. She said she wouldn't worry if he promised to always carry it with him. It was his father's savior, and now it was his. Its McGyverish qualities bailed him out for decades. Whenever he used it, he thought of them both.

He used its tiny scissors to snip away his singed bangs. A few more clips around his ears, and it was just the haircut he needed. Free. All in the comfort of the marina's air-conditioned private bath. After crawling around the *Ocean Potion*'s steaming deck and sweaty cabin, the room's cool, dry air was a well-deserved breather. He stretched out on the teak bench to think about the task ahead. With any luck, he'd find his look-alike sailor at Monty's Tiki Bar after the tourists moved on to South Beach's nightlife. He doubted that Jared was right about meeting his doppelganger.

A sharp rap on the bathroom door jerked him from a deep sleep. "Anybody in there?" His body went on high alert. His brain was foggy, and his body was slow to follow.

"Yeah, yeah, I'm here. Give me a break. Can't a man relax?" Bob needed to collect his thoughts.

He opened the door a crack. An employee with the marina's logo on his shirt waited impatiently. "Give me another ten minutes, and it's yours. I'm with the *Ocean Potion,* slip 23. It's been a long day. I'm moving slower than usual." Good thing he trimmed his hair. He looked less like a homeless person. He shoved his keycard to Pier J through the crack as proof.

The guy glanced at the card and then walked away. "Okay. I need to get in to clean. We're locking up for the night."

What time was it? Bob looked at the marine watch strapped to his wrist: half past ten. The day's tension must have taken its toll. He had been asleep for almost three hours, and his back ached for every minute of it. A long hot shower would ease his tight muscles, and a final blast of cold water would clear his mind. He'd be ready for the night. And if it took longer than ten minutes, too bad. The cleaning could wait.

# CHAPTER 70

# GARY GREEN

GARY POURED THE REMAINING WINE INTO THEIR glasses and gave his wife a little extra. He needed to keep her on his good side. Cakebread Pinot Noir was one of their favorites, bought on their most recent trip to Napa Valley. Friday nights meant enjoying one of his wife's gourmet cooking adventures. He tried not to resent that he spent the week toiling over broken bodies while she fine-tuned her favorite French recipes. Tonight, it was Soupe a l'oignon and Boeuf Bourguignon, accompanied by her own crusty baguettes. His mother served French onion soup, beef stew, and homemade rolls as a child. They were still his favorites, even if his wife called them something fancier. The Crème Brulée she was bringing to the table was a new favorite. After much trial and error, hers almost equaled those of any Parisian restaurant they had dined at.

"To another fabulous dinner." Gary raised his glass. She blushed and clinked his glass with hers. He loved the admiration shining across to him and needed to keep it coming.

"Thanks. I'm getting better, don't you think?" She brushed back a blonde curl sticking to her sweaty forehead and wiped her hands on her apron. He loved seeing her dressed for the kitchen.

"Absolutely. No need to go to fancy restaurants ever again. I have all I could ask for right here." He tasted the first spoonful of the rich, creamy custard and caramelized sugar.

"Let's not get carried away, or I'll go back to my old favorites. Remember hot dogs and Kraft Macaroni and Cheese?"

He remembered it all too well.

Gary was able to relax and enjoy the main course, but now that dinner was ending, he found it tough to savor the final sweetness. He downed his last swallow of wine. "There's something I need to talk with you about." He looked across the table at his beautiful wife and watched her proud smile disappear. "Let me get this all out before you speak. This isn't easy, and I need to keep going if I'm going to say it at all." He saw her complexion fade. Was it possible for a tan to pale with fear and anxiety?

"I'm in trouble. Big trouble. I did something stupid." He pushed away from the table and started to pace. She stayed sitting, almost stoic, waiting. He winced at what he was about to disclose.

"I ran our expenses for the China adoption through the office. I knew it was wrong, but you wanted a baby, and we were running out of money. It was all so expensive, and I didn't know how to tell you. It was all a waste of time anyway. I'm not sure why we even went through any of it."

He watched her eyes soften at the mention of the baby. But with his stupid comment about it being a waste of time, her hard blink slammed a door shut between them.

"Don't make this my fault," she snapped. "You could've talked with me. But you never said a word. Just like you never do. I never would have asked you to do that. You know that."

She clapped her hand over her mouth. "Sorry, go on. I'll keep my mouth shut. That's what you prefer anyway, isn't it?" Gary never heard these biting words from her before and hoped never to hear them again.

"It isn't, you know that. And I'm sorry I shut you out. It's how I cope when things go wrong. But it's not working this time, it doesn't work at all. I need you to help me figure this out. I don't want to do it alone. I can't do it alone anymore. I promise." He stopped pacing and looked for her response.

"We'll see," she looked away.

He circled the dining room table again. "There's more. Angela knew what was going on and didn't stop me. She waited until I confronted her about some other discrepancies in the books. I found out she was embezzling, and she threatened to expose me if I said anything. I let her leave the practice without prosecuting and took Tom's place as Managing Physician." He stopped in front of her chair.

"No comment." She looked down to avoid his eyes.

"But Angela's still doing it. And Tom's about to hire her. I know she'll do it to him again. I have to come clean. I have to stop her." He knelt beside her chair, expecting her to take his outstretched hands. She folded her arms and looked down at him.

"Wait, is that why you let Tom go? To cover your ass?"

Gary was surprised by her choice of words but not offended. Maybe he underestimated her. Maybe she was more than a pretty face and could actually help him.

"I know it looks that way, but it happened a year before Tom left the practice." His excuses sounded weak, even to him. "I thought Tom would retire and take time to heal. He needed to recover from Ben's death. I wasn't the only one; all the other doctors agreed. It wasn't just my decision."

"But we both know the others do what you say. If you wanted Tom to stay, he would still be there. Your opinion carries a lot of weight, or at least it used to. What now?"

She would not lock eyes with him. Would he ever be in her good graces again?

"I already came clean with Daniel and asked for his help. He refused. I asked for time to speak with you before we told the other doctors. You deserve that much. I have until Monday."

He hung his head and waited for her soft touch. When it didn't come, he stood up again and resumed pacing. "I don't know what to do. I need your help. I know I never include you. I make decisions alone because I think I know better. I only involve you after the fact and expect you to help pick up the pieces. That isn't fair. I know that now. This time is different. I'm giving you the chance to be at my side now, to help me. I need your support. I can't do this without you."

She rose from her chair and walked towards him. He stopped, anticipating her embrace. There was none.

"Isn't that convenient; you need my support. Now. When your career is in danger. As a last resort. After you talked with Daniel? How am I supposed to feel? Flattered? Grateful that the big doctor is going to let his little wifey help? Get over yourself."

Gary stepped back from the vitriol she was spewing. It was not a time to defend or deflect. It was time to keep quiet. He waited like a properly chastised child.

"I need time," her cold voice stunned him. "Time to process all of this. Time to figure out who this man I married really is. You have until Monday to get back to Daniel? Then I'll get back to you Sunday night. I'll let you know if I want a role in this or not."

She grabbed the dessert plates from the table and marched into the kitchen. He heard the delicate French porcelain shatter when she threw them into the sink.

Gary faced a long, painful weekend. Alone.

# CHAPTER 71

## LUCY

LUCY FLOPPED BACK ONTO THE SOFT BED, LOOKED up at the ceiling, and smiled. Tom was back. Finally. His call lifted the thick fog enveloping them since Ben's death. Losing Ben changed them in ways that were still hard to articulate. Their world had shifted, and it would never be the same. As the distance between them grew, she lost faith that they'd find their way back to each other. She prayed that she wouldn't lose her husband too. Tonight, her prayers were answered with one simple phone call that rekindled her belief that together, they could find their way back to the love they so carefully tended for more than thirty years.

She closed her eyes and lay there, not yet ready to give up this feeling. She envisioned Ben looking over her, his signature grin spreading from ear to ear, saying, "See? I told you Mom. You worry too much." Ben was the optimist in the family, ready to push the envelope while placating those prone to overprotect. Wasn't that her role as a mother though, to be the keeper of safety, peace, and love? She wasn't able to keep Ben safe, and now her grief was contributing to the weakening of family peace.

Tom's call resurfaced the love and allowed it to breathe again. It was still there under the grief and sadness, under the anger and angst, under the frustration of unanswered questions. It waited for them to remember, to find their way back home. A different home for sure, but still a home she and Tom created together. For the first time in months, her grief-stricken body released its tight grip on her heart. Contracted muscles relaxed. Overfired nerves found relief. Sadness laced with joy filled her, and family memories flooded in. Ben was gone, and like it or not, there is no life without death. Ben would always be a part of them. Forever. She wept.

"Lucy?"

A soft tapping lifted the liminal veil between sleep and awake.

"Are you up?" Lucy stretched luxuriantly, feeling the new freedom coursing through her body.

"I am now. Give me a second. I must have drifted off."

Lucy detoured to the bathroom, splashed water on her face, and pinched her cheeks. She studied herself in the mirror. Puffy eyes and bedhead aside, she liked what she saw.

She opened the adjoining door and found Ellen's side unlocked and cracked open. Ellen was typing furiously on her laptop. Lucy rapped lightly to announce her arrival.

"Be right with you. I want to finish this email," Ellen called over her shoulder. "Did you have a good nap?"

"I did. Too short, but good enough. Tom called. I'll fill you in later. Finish what you're doing. I'll wait in my room so you won't be distracted."

Ellen's laptop snapped shut. "There, all done. I'm starving. What are we going to do for dinner?"

"How about room service or the hotel restaurant." Lucy leaned lightly against the door frame. "I'm not up for heading out in this heat and humidity. It saps all my energy. Give me Maine any day."

"I'll check in about that in January on one of those below-zero days with ungodly windchill," Ellen teased. "I could use a change of scenery from this room. Let's head down to the hotel's casual restaurant so we don't have to change clothes. They have a place called *Lolo's Cantina* or something like that."

"Works for me." Lucy looked down at her wrinkled t-shirt and used her hands to smooth away the worst creases. "I'm ready. Let's do it."

Lucy stuck to small talk as they headed down to the restaurant. She'd talk about Tom's call when they were seated and had Ellen's full attention. "Table for two, please. in a quiet corner, if possible." Lucy scanned the restaurant filled with parents trying to corral overtired children to finish their meals. It looked like most were losing the battle. Lucy smiled and remembered those days as if they were yesterday.

The host directed them to a secluded booth in the back of the restaurant.

"I'm sticking with water tonight," Lucy looked up at Ellen. "You go ahead and have a drink though. I want to keep my head clear and read more of Ben's journal. I've learned the hard way that alcohol's calming effect can spin on a dime when things get emotional."

"I hear you and will join you." Ellen's sigh said it all. "I need a good night's sleep. Alcohol is great for falling asleep, not so much for keeping you there. Tomorrow will be another tiring day. We have a long flight home after we meet with Bob."

"Two waters with lemon please. And keep them coming." Lucy skipped right to the waitperson's opening question.

"So, did you get to read more of Ben's journal?" As always, Ellen didn't waste time getting to the point.

"I did. More of what we already read. Most of it echoes our nightly phone calls with him—weather, water, and wonder. The real treasures are Ben's wonder at his natural surroundings and life in general. They were tough to read at first, but eventually, it was like he was speaking to me in ways I may never have heard. They aren't everyday mother-son conversations. I'm lucky to have them." A lone tear gathered at the corner of her right eye until it overflowed and rolled down her cheek. She let it dry in place without trying to wipe it away.

"You're lucky to have the journal. It's a gift, almost too personal for me to be privy to." Ellen reached across the table to hold Lucy's hand. "Let me know if you want or need to share any of it with me."

"Of course, you know I will." She held Ellen's hand and squeezed it to show how much she appreciated her. "Tom called. I do want to tell you about that. It went much better than that last phone call. For starters, he told me he was changing my ringtone to a normal one."

"The world works in mysterious ways!" Ellen almost choked on her water. "*1984* is here. All you have to do is think, and Big Brother delivers."

"Spooky. The big question is, who's Big Brother?"

"Another mystery to be solved at another time. Tell me more, what'd Tom want? Is he missing you?"

"Yes, and this time he wasn't whining about it." Lucy leaned back against the booth's red leather upholstery. "I think we're over the hump. It was good. We came together on a few contentious things." She looked across at Ellen, who was fidgeting with the napkin rolled around the silverware. "I want your opinion on some business things."

"You know me, it's hard to stop expressing my opinion whether I'm asked or not." Having released the silverware, Ellen fashioned the paper surrounding the bundle into a ring. Lucy was distracted by how she slid it on and off her finger. Did she have Ellen's attention or not?

"It's about Tom's new office space." Lucy waited until Ellen looked up. "Angela was pushing him to sign on the dotted line, and I told him he should wait until I got back. Something didn't feel right. I mean, there isn't any urgency. There's plenty of time. She didn't need to be so pushy about it."

"Angela?" Ellen scrunched up the distracting paper ring and leaned in. "Interesting. What didn't feel right?"

"I'm not sure." Lucy gave it some thought now that she had Ellen's full attention. "It's embarrassing to admit, and I might only be feeling guilty about not helping Tom. To be honest, I think I was jealous. I felt like I was being pushed out. Am I crazy? You've worked with Angela; am I totally off base?" Lucy cupped her neck in her hands and rested her elbows on the table. Not proper table etiquette, but Ellen wouldn't care.

"I haven't seen Angela since she left Tom's practice over a year ago," Ellen said. "I do know she's working with a variety of medical practices. Where does she want Tom to set up his office?"

Lucy was baffled that Ellen didn't comment on her jealousy confession. It wasn't like her to stick entirely to business. That's what she liked most about Ellen. She could be real, and talk business at the same time.

"That new building just off Congress Street. Angela's office is there too. Tom liked the idea of her being close so she could have full control, but it's feeling a little too close for me. What do you think? Am I just being a jealous fool?" Lucy relaxed into the red banquette and waited for Ellen's words of wisdom. She knew she could count on her honesty.

"I think you should trust your feelings. There's a reason for women's intuition. We're rarely wrong."

Ellen flipped open the menu. "What are you going to have?"

# CHAPTER 72

---

# ELLEN

ELLEN DIDN'T WANT TO RUSH LUCY, BUT SHE WAS dying to call Julie. She feigned having work to do before going to bed and suggested they skip coffee and dessert. She hugged Lucy before they entered their respective rooms. "I'll see you in the morning. What time are we meeting Bob? I'm anxious to hear about his night at Monty's and what he found on the boat."

"You and me both; with luck, he'll have some answers before we head to the airport. I told him we'd meet for coffee in the lobby around 9 a.m. It'll give us more time to pack up and check out. Sound good?" A huge yawn escaped from Lucy. She deserved to be tired after a day like today.

"Fine by me." Ellen was glad Lucy mentioned leaving. She was ready to get home. She wasn't sure if Lucy was, but it sounded like she had faith that Bob would deliver enough answers for her to head home tomorrow. "See you in the morning." Ellen unlocked her door. "Sleep well."

At dinner, Ellen was tempted to talk about Julie's suspicions. Her initial reaction was to go straight to Lucy and spill, but she resisted the urge. This was not time for speculation, suspicion, or assumption. It was time for facts, certainty, and proof. Things needed to be handled delicately until everything was in place. She would wait. It wouldn't take too long.

She glanced at her phone. It was only 8:30. Wherever she was, calling Julie shouldn't be a problem. Her phone never left her side, and for sure, she wouldn't be in the office on a Friday night, not even during tax season. Julie picked up on the fifth ring just before going to voicemail.

"Ellen, hold on a minute; I'm just paying the pizza guy."

Not much different from Ellen's Friday nights, minus three kids. Was it pizza for two?

"I'm back; pizza can wait. It's cold already, anyway. I stuck it in the oven on low. I'm all yours now."

"Sounds like you're having an exciting Friday night. No J's?" Ellen teased.

"Too crowded, not my scene. College crowd takes over Thursdays until Sunday afternoon. Then the fishermen and I get it back for the week. And, yes, I'm alone, so stop guessing."

"Got me," Ellen confessed. "I called because I need someone to mull things over with, and I'm not ready to discuss this with Lucy yet. I still don't think it's time to bring anyone else into this."

"I'm still trying to figure out all the angles too." Ellen heard Julie pop a beer before she continued. "The more I think about it, the more I think this is all Angela. It's too risky for someone else to be involved. I mean, how would it start? 'Hey, do you want to embezzle with me?' I don't think so. And why did she leave the practice so quickly? Was she fired? It was never called that, but now I wonder. And what about her new management crap? Pretty convenient setup if you ask me." Julie finally stopped to take a breath.

"Whoa, slow down, take a sip of your beer. I agree with all you're saying. I was just waiting for a little more proof of what Angela's up to. I think I just got it from Lucy." She heard Julie set down the can. "She just talked with Tom. Angela was pushing him to sign a lease now, and get this, she wants twenty-five grand deposited in a new account she can sign on."

"Are you fucking kidding me? She's getting awfully ballsy." Julie gulped her beer.

"Lucy convinced him to slow things down. She confided that something felt off, but I kept my mouth shut. It wasn't easy. I kept thinking about those new clients and Angela's control over their office. Sounds like Angela's expanding her empire." Ellen looked forward to Monday when she and Julie could talk in person. A phone call was slightly better than nothing, but being physically together to weave their thoughts into solutions was infinitely better.

"Well, then Tom's definitely not her co-conspirator. I never thought he was, and not just because I like the guy. I don't sense a dishonest bone in his body." Julie paused. Ellen waited. "Now Gary Green, that's another story. I still think he's involved; I just haven't figured out how."

"He's not my favorite person either, and I remember his early days in practice, when he adored Tom, hung on to his every word, and looked up to him as if Tom were God. I just can't believe he'd do that to him. Then again, Gary was part of firing Tom, and he could have stopped it if he tried. Was he trying to hide what was going on? But that was a year after Angela left. Seems too disjointed. Then again, he did dupe the practice with bogus expenses." Ellen stopped. Her logic was spiraling out of control and approaching a point of no return.

"What an asshole." Julie summed it up accurately.

Gary Green was an asshole, but was he a thief? Ellen doubted it. Embezzlement fell into a whole other category. "Agreed. Right now, patience is our best weapon. The dominoes are falling, one by one, and I have faith that all will be revealed soon. We're flying home tomorrow afternoon, and I'll see you on Monday."

She heard Julie's oven door creak open. "Enjoy your pizza."

# CHAPTER 73

## BAHAMIAN BOB

BOB CLIMBED ONTO THE BAR STOOL CLOSEST TO the server stand. It gave him an unobstructed view of all the seats surrounding the open-air tiki bar. From this stool, he might pick up an errant word or two between co-workers that might be exactly what he was looking for. The bar had emptied after the day's humidity erupted into a fierce downpour that sent the tourists ducking for cover. Most chose not to return.

He scoped out the locals who seemed to emerge from the woodwork when the tourists left. They arrived one by one, occasionally a couple, mostly loners who knew each other but kept their distance. Jared and Emily said the guy to talk to looked like him. In what way? Height, weight, age? Then he saw him. Leathery skin from too many days in the sun, bleached blonde hair desperately in need of a haircut. Is that what he looked like? Although, he had to admit the guy had a certain *je ne sais quoi*. Handsome, too. He'd take it.

Bob refused to make eye contact with others and kept a scowl on his face, hoping to keep the bar stool on his left open for the mystery guy. When the guy turned away from the come-hither looks of a bar fly who'd seen better days and the gnarly guy almost asleep at the bar, Bob turned off his scowl, and the guy sat down next to him. Bob remained silent. He didn't want to engage too soon. They both nursed their beers.

After twenty minutes or so, Bob started small talking with the bartender and steered towards the topic of Ben. He mentioned he was helping Ben's mother find out what happened here at Money's on his last night alive. It grabbed the bartender's interest as he intended. No one close to the sea, even if only to serve drinks to its seafarers, could resist a good story. Most couldn't resist helping a mother either. The bartender asked more and more questions until other patrons began tapping their bottles and glasses to get his attention. Bob returned to silence, stared out to sea over the patrons' heads across the bar, and waited.

"I think I can help you." A raspy, too-many-cigarettes voice broke the silence. Bob kept looking straight ahead, not wanting to spook the guy.

"Hmmm." Bob waited for more.

"I talked with a kid about three months ago. Heading to Eleuthera. Meeting his father."

"Sounds like Ben." No need to say more.

"He was excited about his first overnight on the open sea and his first glimpse of a truly dark sky. It was a perfect night for it. He talked about watching the stars with his mother. Nice kid." The guy looked up at the star-filled sky.

"Never got to meet him, unfortunately. I was with his parents when they found him. Bad news." Bob shook his head and grimaced.

"I'm Bob, by the way." He extended his hand.

"Curt." The guy nodded but ignored Bob's hand. "Like I said, I think I can help."

Bob took a slug of beer. "Go on, I'm listening."

"We talked. A lot. He liked picking the brain of someone who had sailed across before. I was happy to indulge him with my own stories. He liked the hairy ones, but I switched gears to my trips on calm seas when I noticed how the others shook him up. Told him what a treat it was to have the perfect weather for his sail. I wasn't exaggerating either. It was perfect. The skies above were amazing. Clear weather all around. He left around midnight. Said he was going to get a good night's sleep."

"That's it, huh? I was hoping for more." Bob raked his fingers through his newly shorn hair and set his beer down. He pushed back from the bar as if getting ready to leave.

"Hold on. There's more. I don't think it amounts to much, though. Some thugs, no other way to describe them, came in a few minutes after Ben left. Hooting and hollering, bragging about how they scared the bejesus out of some kid. I didn't know what they were up to. I knew better than to ask; just tried to keep them talking. They thought it was hilarious that they went to the *Ocean Potion* instead of the *Ocean Passion*."

"Ugh," Bob grunted. He could've said more but waited. He was still wary of the guy, not sure if he could trust him.

"They thought it was all fun and games. I didn't. I tried

to set them straight. We don't need to talk about that part." Curt motioned to the bartender for another beer.

"Make that two. On my tab," Bob said. "Go on, tell me more."

# CHAPTER 74

## CURT

CURT HAD A BAD FEELING ABOUT THE KID ON that boat from the beginning. Premonitions came often to him and, at times, played out. It was a family trait. But even without it, he knew he would have reacted in the same way: dry mouth, clenched jaw, and pounding heart. He hated bullies in any form, and taking advantage of a naïve, earnest kid like that only fueled his hatred.

"Angry was an understatement. If I could've, I would've ripped the guys' heads off." Curt hadn't told the story to anyone, and he could feel emotions from that night travel from his intestines up to his throat. He drained his beer and motioned for another. "After that first altercation, I let it drop. I didn't like the way their hands automatically reached behind their backs. I've watched enough TV to know what they were going for. I don't know who they were or who they worked for. I left well enough alone."

"Smart move." Bob shook his head no when the bartender looked over. Curt liked this guy. Clearly, he was here for one reason: to help that kid's mother.

"I decided rather than lock horns with them, I should check on the kid. I knew where his boat was docked from talking earlier, so I went over to find him. Don't ask how I opened the gate." Curt slugged more beer. The cold brew quieted the feelings erupting in his gut. Much more effective and cheaper than the therapy his ex-wife preferred. "That poor kid was pacing up and down the dock. When he saw me, he came running. I told him I knew what happened, had heard about it at the bar. Told him the thugs weren't coming back, that it was just a case of mistaken identity. I told him he was safe."

"You're saying he was alright? Are you sure?" Bob must care for the kid like he did.

"He said he was. He told me the thugs surprised him at the gate. That he was terrified when they threw him on his boat and that they started laughing because he obviously wasn't the big fat dude they were after. He didn't fight back or argue with them. They were drunk, and like me, Ben didn't trust them." Curt found some relief in finally telling someone the story of that night. He stopped short at sharing the sense of foreboding he carried when he left Ben that night.

"How long did you stay with him?" Bob asked.

"Long enough to know he was over it. We had another beer or two and told more stories. I told myself I wouldn't leave until he was laughing again. It took about an hour or two. He was fine when I said goodbye." Curt flashed a hairy eyeball at the dude across the way who was trying to listen in.

"Helluva way for Ben to spend his last night on land," Bob mumbled. "It must've been good to leave the next morning. Tough enough being alone in the middle of the ocean without something like that happening before you leave. Your mind can play foolish tricks when you're alone at sea with no landfall to ground you."

"Don't I know it. That's why I went back the next morning to check on him. He was already gone. Guess he got the hell out of here. That's what I would've done." Curt looked at Bob, who nodded in agreement.

"How did he die?" Curt wasn't sure if he wanted to know or not. He preferred to remember Ben chugging beers with him and laughing.

"Gas leak, as far as I can tell. Slow leak in the galley stove. It looked like it was just a worn and rusty fitting that finally gave out and did him in. We found him up on deck, near the hatch, trying to get to fresh air."

"Poor kid." Bob said nothing.

Curt took another big gulp of his beer. "That's the long and the short of it. You have your answers now." Curt didn't mention the dark intuition that shrouded him as he walked away that night. Better left unsaid; it was too late anyway.

# CHAPTER 75

# BAHAMIAN BOB

BOB LISTENED. THIS GUY CURT SEEMED TO BE telling the truth. There was no reason to believe otherwise. Still, he wasn't ready to part ways yet. He wasn't one hundred percent sure that Curt's story was exactly how things went down.

"Hey Curt," Bob looked straight ahead again. Curt was the type of guy who could get skittish if pushed. "The *Ocean Potion* is here waiting to go back to Maine. Any chance I can get you to check it out with me? I'd love another set of eyes to see if I'm right about the cookstove. I don't want to mislead Ben's mother. She needs the truth."

"Yeah, I can do that. I'll show you exactly where I left him. Let's do it." Curt hopped off his bar stool. Monty's was getting rowdy. Music was blaring, and outrageous flirtation was the name of the game. "Let's get out of here." Bob saw the same overused bar fly moving toward Curt and left his unfinished beer on the bar.

"We're out of here," Curt said. They headed down the eight steps from the tiki bar to the walking path to Pier J. Neither spoke until they approached the *Ocean Potion.* "Here it is." He let Curt board first. He was looking for some evidence that would prove that Curt was really there before.

Curt headed straight to the cooler housed beneath the captain's bench. "Oops, guess things have changed. This was filled to the brim when I was here with Ben. Do you have anything to drink?"

Bob had his proof.

"Not sure, we can check out the galley. I want you to take a look at that gas leak. See if you agree with me." He crossed over to the hatch and climbed down the ladder. Curt followed.

"Sad to think the kid spent his last night alone." Curt's voice was soft and reverent. "I hope he got to enjoy some of that dark sky he talked about. We really connected, you know. Something like this never should've happened." He coughed.

"I'm glad you were here to settle him down. He wasn't alone, you know. He had you." Bob made his first eye contact of the night.

"Don't get all maudlin on me. Where's that stove you want me to look at?" Curt's eye contact was short-lived, and he coughed again.

"Right behind you, in that nook." Bob pointed. He left Curt to do his investigation without any influence.

"One of those fancy stoves." Curt groaned as he bent over to get a closer look. "There she is. Easy to find, the stove is slowly rusting around the gasket for the gas line. It's happening on the other burner too. See? That's all it took. Probably did no harm until it did, you know. The proverbial last straw. Damn. It would've been so easy to fix with just a little bit of putty."

"I know. I'm not looking forward to telling Ben's mother. I really wanted to come up with something bigger, more exotic. I'm worried they'll blame themselves for not seeing the problem before he set sail." Bob raked his fingers through his clean hair.

"Yeah, but I'm thinking Ben got her good sense; he picked it up somewhere. They'll be fine. When he calmed down that night, he told me he understood that sometimes bad things happen to good people. That tonight was one of them. He believed it too. I assume he got that from his parents. They'll be alright."

Bob was skeptical of Curt's confidence, but his words were so assured that you had to believe him—or at least wanted to.

"How 'bout that beer?" Curt opened the small galley refrigerator. "Hooey! Something evil died in there. Guess we'll have to call it a night!"

Bob followed Curt up the ladder to fresh air. Ben's last climb. His discovery didn't make him feel any better.

# CHAPTER 76

## ELLEN

ELLEN HAD A ROUGH TIME TRYING TO GET TO sleep. Even her counting tricks didn't work. Ben, Lucy, and Tom swirled through her brain and intertwined with Gary and Angela. How did they fit together? Or did they? Was she trying to stuff a series of unfortunate events into a box too small and too shallow to contain them? By three in the morning, her mind was numb, and she finally drifted off. She woke at 8:30, a full five and a half hours later, unheard of in her sleepless world. She missed her early morning walk and had only a half hour to shower before she met with Lucy and Bob. She texted Lucy that she'd be late and shouldn't wait. She'd meet her downstairs.

The rainfall showerhead sprinkled her groggy mind awake, and the night's musings flowed away. What made perfect sense at two in the morning was now a ridiculous cacophony of misguided and mismatched assumptions. Still, she tucked the interesting ones away, knowing they might be a base for further rumination. Eventually, it would all make sense.

She missed the boys and cut her cleansing, creative-inducing shower short so she'd have time to call home. She threw on the hotel's fluffy robe to let it do a speedy job of drying her off. She picked up her phone from the side of the sink.

"Hi, this is the Hartmann's," Jack answered with the approved household greeting. They had debated long and hard over what to say with suggestions ranging from yo bro, through how can I help you, to a nonidentifying single hello. They finally settled on this. The boys were still practicing its delivery. Ellen heard Ethan whining in the background that it was his turn to answer the phone. The rivalry between siblings never seemed to end, but down here in Florida, living twenty-four-seven with the grief and reality of Ben's loss, their scrabbling was music to her ears.

"Jack, sweetie, I miss you guys." Ellen's mood lifted, and she shifted into mom mode. "Get your brothers and put me on speaker. I'm running late and don't have much time. I'll talk to everyone together." The bedside clock said she had ten minutes to dress and go downstairs.

"Kevin, Ethan, get over here! Now! It's Mom!" Jack screamed into the phone. Ellen deflated at the sound of another son slipping into the misguided role of man of the house. She'd have to remind them again that they were children, not parents. It was one of many disappointments from the aftermath of her divorce.

"Hi guys. Have you been having a good time with your dad?" She didn't wait for an answer. She knew it and wished she could occasionally have the role of fun parent instead of homework police, argument arbiter, and punishing judge. Luckily, her kids didn't require too much of that. "I miss you so much boys. I'll be home later today. Our flight leaves right after lunch, and I'll be there for dinner. Can you guys pick a place for us to go to eat without killing each other?"

"We can do it, right guys? It'll be worth it." Kevin, always the peacemaker, chimed in. "No more of dad's home cooking." Their father's penchant for plate-sized pancakes and massive undercooked burgers eventually took its toll. They'd be ready for some normal eating even if their normal came from a restaurant.

"Love you guys so much. I can't wait to see you. Soon." Ellen looked at the clock. Five minutes to get downstairs.

"Love you too, Mom," the three echoed as she hung up. The sounds of their voices for just those few minutes were enough to buoy her. Soon, she'd be home with her very alive sons to make their favorite waffles and to kiss them goodnight. Then they'd be off to school, and she'd be at the office. Life would be normal again. She grabbed yesterday's shorts and T-shirt, her last go-round, before donning Maine's long sleeves and pants.

# CHAPTER 77

# LUCY

LUCY LEANED AGAINST THE BACK OF THE WALNUT-paneled elevator and closed her eyes. She was ready for this, or at least that was the story she was telling herself. She didn't know if she wanted Bob to say he had no answers or that Ben was the victim of foul play (she couldn't bring herself to say murder). Black-and-white thinking eliminated any possibilities between the two alternatives, and she couldn't imagine anything that would ease her mind or help her find peace.

She counted eight rhythmic dings as the elevator descended to the lobby. It bumped gently, and Lucy inhaled deeply before pushing herself away from the wall to step through the spreading elevator doors. She scanned the lobby. No Ellen yet.

Bob stood at the top of the stairs leading from the hotel's street-level façade to its second-floor lobby. Their eyes met, and he smiled, but she didn't reciprocate because she was focusing on his steely green eyes, trying to decipher the story he'd be telling her this morning. He was unreadable yet somehow welcoming, an odd combination that revealed nothing.

The bank of elevators dinged behind her as she moved toward Bob.

"Good, I'm not late." Lucy never knew Ellen to be late, and she doubted she would be this morning. "Where's the coffee?"

"Morning to you too." Lucy pointed. "Bob's over there, by the steps. The hotel has its own Starbucks on street level with a few outside tables. How does that sound?"

"Fine by me," Ellen said.

Bob waited for them to approach. "Morning Bob," Lucy tried to sound light-hearted even though she wasn't feeling it.

"Lucy. Ellen. Sleep well?" Bob asked.

"Good enough," Ellen looked at Lucy.

"Oddly, I actually did. Home soon." She smiled to show her sympathy towards Ellen. "Let's get some Starbucks in her."

They followed Bob down the steps to the coffee shop.

"Get me a plain old coffee. Big one with cream and sugar. I don't know how to order at Starbucks, and frankly, I don't want to learn." Bob's response was abrupt, almost grumpy. "I'll find us a table."

He wasn't his usual diplomatic self, and Lucy's stomach spasmed in response. She turned to Ellen as they waited in line. "Let's get some muffins too. I'm feeling queasy this morning." They were silent as they waited to order. Lucy didn't feel like talking, and Ellen didn't seem to have anything to say either. Their barista was unusually quick and efficient, and their silence didn't have time to grow awkward.

"Here you go, one vente Pike Place. Remember that." She placed Bob's coffee down in front of him. "And a blueberry muffin without Maine's exceptional wild blueberries. It'll have to do. Enjoy."

Lucy sat across from Bob and broke off a piece of her muffin. She let it crumble and dissolve in her mouth before sipping her coffee. Despite the influx of caffeine, she settled down. She was ready to listen. "So, what's up?"

"Not much. And you?" Bob's green eyes twinkled, and his customary grin reappeared.

Bob's inane response broke the tension. Lucy felt untethered from the task at hand, and Bob was slowly bringing her back, first with humor. What was coming next? Her stomach clutched again. She broke off another piece of muffin and stuffed it in her mouth.

"Are you ready for this?" Ellen's gentle voice reminded Lucy that she was not alone.

Alone would not be good for Lucy, now or on the trip back to Maine. She was glad Ellen would be with her to help process things. She set her coffee down and looked across at Bob. "Yes, I'm ready. I thought I'd have an idea of what you're going to tell me from reading the rest of Ben's journal. But there was nothing, not a thing about Miami Beach. Every other night, he wrote something. His last entry was from Jensen Beach the night before. I even checked to see if there was a page missing, torn out, you know. There wasn't. It doesn't make sense." Her eyes dropped to her plate, and she picked a giant, cultivated blueberry from her muffin.

"I can explain that." Bob's words stopped Lucy from popping the berry in her mouth. "I met a guy, Curt, at Monty's last night. He remembered Ben. He was with him at the bar after Emily and Jared left, just like they said. Had great things to say about Ben. He thought a lot of your son."

Lucy dropped the berry on her plate. "Everyone loves Ben." She picked at another blueberry and moved it around her plate before looking up at Bob. "I mean loved." Ellen's hand moved to rest atop hers and delivered a subtle squeeze.

"Anyway," Bob cleared his throat. "Curt went back to the *Ocean Potion*. Sounds like they were up pretty late talking and drinking. I'm guessing Ben went straight to bed after Curt left, and that's why he didn't write."

"Okay. That makes sense, I guess." Lucy pushed her plate away. The muffin or single blueberries were not helping her stomach any. Neither was the coffee. She was ready to hear more. "What else did he say? I want to hear everything. Don't leave out anything, Bob. Promise?"

# CHAPTER 78

# LUCY

THE SOUND OF ELLEN'S WHIFFLING SOOTHED Lucy. On their flight to Miami three days before, Ellen buried her nose in a mindless romance novel and gradually dozed off as the plane taxied for takeoff. She confessed to Lucy that it was a skill she developed to cope with her latent fear of flying. She was doing it again, and Lucy agreed that Ellen's stress-reducing tactic was far more preferable than that of the babbling fool behind her who hadn't stopped talking since he boarded the plane.

Lucy and Ellen were quieter than usual after meeting with Bob this morning. After long goodbyes laced with on-the-verge tears and overflowing gratitude, they returned to their rooms to pack their bags and head to the airport. The reverse trip through Miami was the antithesis of their arrival. Gone was the hopeful excitement of finding a resolution to unanswered questions. In its place was a heaviness weighing down the sorrow Lucy carried each day. Her grief was like a pebble perpetually placed in her pocket, something she was always aware of, even on days when it didn't scream for her attention. Today, it was a boulder much too large to hold. She longed to have Tom at her side to help carry it.

The plane leveled out from its steep ascent, the seatbelt light dimmed, and the flight attendant pushed his way down the aisle with refreshments. The cart stopped a few rows before them, and the steward leaned across Ellen's aisle seat to softly ask for Lucy's drink selection. Despite Lucy's whispered reply, Ellen's eyes popped open. "Water please, no ice."

"Sorry about that. I didn't mean to wake you." Lucy fumbled to open the paltry packets of pretzels delivered with their drinks.

"I'm good now that we're up, up, and away." Ellen popped a tiny pretzel into her mouth. "Off the ground and clear sailing from here. I'm not even sure I need that crutch anymore, but why give it up? If it ain't broke, why fix it, right?"

Despite Ellen's joking, the boulder in Lucy's pocket grew heavier. How had they missed the broken stove? The rusting gasket would've been easy to replace, and it could've saved Ben's life. Tom will think it was all his fault. She tried to come up with words that wouldn't sound like an accusation. But that was in the future; there was something else to deal with now, something contributing to the heavy weight she was carrying.

She placed her hand on Ellen's, resting on their shared armrest. "Ellen, I need to apologize."

"For what?" Ellen shifted in her seat to face her.

"I'm sorry for making you come to Miami. It was all a waste. I was wrong to ask you to waste your time on my stupid intuition. You have better things to do than follow a harebrained client on a wild goose chase."

"I think your animal metaphors are off, and so is your thinking," Ellen teased. "The trip was well worth it on so many levels. First, we found the real story of Ben's death. No more speculation and assumptions. You were able to get closer to Ben when you found that amazing journal; it's a gift that will keep on giving. And don't forget reconnecting with Bob, your Bahamian savior. It was obvious that he made everything much easier for you to digest. I was glad he was there for you, and me. He's definitely one in a million."

Lucy relaxed her grip on Ellen's hand. She didn't realize she was squeezing it so hard. "But what was in it for you?"

"In it for me? Let me see." Ellen put two fingers to her lips. "Two and a half days in Miami Beach soaking up the rays instead of slogging through Maine's mud season. Rubbing elbows with Eleuthera's finest, the delightful, green-eyed Marley Roberts. Not to mention, my favorite client becoming a close friend while dining on stellar sushi and saké. All as a deductible business trip. It doesn't get much better than that."

Ellen dropped her head onto Lucy's shoulder, a gesture only a good friend or a drunk stranger would do.

"When you describe it like that, it sounds much better." Lucy leaned her head on Ellen's and felt the breeze blowing out of the plane's air vent. "I wanted the big reveal, a major plot twist or something. But that only happens in books and movies."

"I know what you're saying," Ellen said. "I was searching for more too. But the world works in mysterious ways. Things will eventually make more sense. I know it will."

Ellen's words were puzzling, but Lucy chalked it up to her penchant for looking beyond the details to find the bigger picture. She supposed Ellen was right. Eventually, everything made sense if you waited long enough.

# CHAPTER 79

# ELLEN

ELLEN LEANED FORWARD TO LOOK BEYOND LUCY for a glimpse of Maine's coastline before it disappeared when their plane headed inland to circle its approach to the Portland Jetport. She loved playing *Where's Waldo*, looking for known landmarks and the roof of her home. She never could quite find the red brick house camouflaged by the branches of the hundred-year-old trees shading her property. She could spot the boys' school and a neighboring church but never the house itself. She smiled when she remembered how her toddlers listened each morning for early departures. They had strict orders not to get out of bed until that first plane flew overhead at 6:06 a.m., a small perk of dwelling under the airport's flight path.

Lucy had been quiet since Ellen glossed over her longing for a plot twist. More news was coming, but there was more to do before sharing the closing chapter. Ellen would have the weekend with her boys, and on Monday, with fresh minds, she and Julie would somehow stabilize the wobbly third leg of the crime-solving stool: means, opportunity, and motive. With knowledge and access to the financial records, Angela definitely had the means for embezzlement and the opportunity to commit fraud both at Tom's former practice and the ones she worked with now. But what was her motive for such deceit? It had to be more than simple greed. And why was there a one-year gap between Angela's embezzlement and Tom's firing?

The pilot deployed the landing gears and stopped Ellen's speculation. The runway loomed into view, and she placed her hand over Lucy's when the plane's bump signaled their return to Earth.

"We're home. Back to our normal lives."

Lucy slid her hand out from under Ellen's and folded her hands in her lap. Ellen regretted her words as soon as they were out of her mouth. She was returning home to her normal life filled with three very lively sons, but Lucy and Tom were building a new normal, one they never imagined.

The words of a favorite Annie Lennox song sung through Ellen's mind: *dying is easy; it's living that scares me to death.* Too true. She squeezed her eyes shut and sighed.

# CHAPTER 80

# GARY GREEN

GARY TOSSED HIS TENNIS RACKET INTO THE TRUNK of his Mercedes. His wife was clear that she would not be his weekend entertainment, and he hoped to pick up a tennis match at the club. He was wrong. Like it or not, the world revolved around couples. Singles were not readily accommodated at tennis clubs or elsewhere, and even if they were, he was starting to think he liked, even preferred, being part of a couple. He missed his wife and the things they did that he too often referred to as wastes of time. Was being the poor, put-upon husband just a persona he absorbed from a father who could never find anything right about marriage or Gary's mother? One more instance of his father getting into his head and ruining his life.

He parked at the nearby Starbucks, skipped his usual harried and hurried drive-thru order, and headed inside to absorb some of the empty hours looming ahead. A feeling of spaciousness crept into him as his usual driving energy dissipated. He scanned the coffee shop and those in line in front of him. Once again, he was alone except for the singles at the surrounding tables in close relationship with their computers. He wished he had brought his laptop for company. Instead, he eavesdropped on others' conversations and noticed the variety of interactions around him, some intense and personal, some light and generic, and all fed by the addition of another.

Gary started to dig away at his role in the impasse between him and his wife. He never was party to the kinds of conversation he heard around him. He avoided deep interaction like the plague and feigned annoyance at mundane, shallow interactions with his wife or with others. To him, deep or shallow were the only options. Memories of his parents at the dinner table invaded him. They were not the couple to emulate, and his father, most definitely, wasn't either. Tom and Lucy floated into his mind and opened a floodgate of feelings.

Past transgressions marched through his mind like a film deserving fifty or less on his internal Tomatometer. His wife's words haunted him. Everything she said about him was true. Too many times, he dismissed women as stupid, unworthy, or frivolous. He criticized their physical appearance, putting beauty before everything else. He ignored their competence and experience and downplayed their struggle for equality and equity, all while expecting them to orchestrate every aspect of his life, from what he ate to how he felt. He did it both at work and at home and made it their fault when things went wrong but never when things went right. He was his father's son.

He finished the last of his Vente Espresso Macchiato and tossed the paper cup into the trashcan. He knew what to do. His wife was right; it wasn't her fault, and he shouldn't expect her to fix it. She was his wife, but it wasn't her job to make things better; her job was to be at his side and support him. She'd be so pleased when he told her that he took care of everything and had set their world right again. She'd remember how much she loved him. Everything would be alright. He sensed it in his gut. He wouldn't be his father; he'd be like Tom, the man he truly admired.

Gary began to imagine the phone call that would right all his wrongs. He would face the woman on a level playing field and do what he should have done a year ago. Soon, this would all be over, and he'd have his wife and Tom back again. He was doing the right thing. He'd make them both proud of him; he knew he would.

# CHAPTER 81

# ANGELA

ANGELA STARED AT THE COMPUTER SCREEN. everything was coming together nicely. Adding Will and Megan to her list of clients and Tom and Lucy (technically tentative but 99% assured) made her happy. She'd be even happier once Tom signed on the dotted line. She couldn't imagine what was holding him up. He was always putty in her hands. Not to worry, she saw how he looked at her when they met in the new office space.

She hated weekends when the world stopped to play. Play was not in her wheelhouse. She much-preferred work where she could contemplate, manipulate, and orchestrate her plans for the future. She loved quantifying the results of her efforts with complex spreadsheets forecasting the spoils of her labor. The one in front of her now verified what she had created: a system with multiple income streams that would make her a very wealthy woman. For once, she'd be the highest earner among the ego-inflated, highly paid, and overly praised doctors on her client list. It didn't matter that they didn't know; it only mattered that she knew. In fact, she loved how their lack of knowledge kept her in command of both her destiny and theirs.

She leaned back into the supportive hug of her Aeron chair, closed her eyes, and allowed herself a moment to remember why she was here. All she had asked for was good medical care for her mother, kindness during the nightmare of her preventable death, and to be made whole for the time and money wasted chasing pie-in-the-sky promises from incompetent doctors. Instead, she and her father were left with a mountain of debt. Pleas for financial assistance fell on deaf ears, even when she threatened malpractice. Then she took control. They would pay; she would not. Not now and not ever. Her father and the debt were long gone, but they would keep paying everything she was owed. She didn't care that the original *they* had morphed into something much bigger.

She checked the time on the Oyster Perpetual Rolex fastened to her wrist by its diamond-encrusted bracelet twinkling under the fluorescent lights. It was a gift to herself and represented what time and hard work could bring: beauty and worth. It didn't matter that she couldn't wear it around clients who would question her ability to own such a treasure. It was hers every weekend, and that was enough. Her index finger caressed the gems that perfectly surrounded the watch's clock face. Weekends with her watch, alone in her office, was all she desired. She was content. The muscles in her cheeks relaxed, taking with them the forced smile and sparkly disposition she donned each weekday. It was good to be herself again.

The phone jangled, taking her out of her reverie and pulling her back to the present. A brilliant smile rose from her depths and reignited the tension in her jaw and the duplicity of her soul. She answered on the perfectly timed third ring, "Angela Dunphy, how can I help you on this wonderful day?"

# CHAPTER 82

# JULIE

JULIE YANKED UP HER FAVORITE PAIR OF JEANS and noticed she tugged harder than usual to fasten the brass button. Time to trade Friday night pizza and beer for wine and salad. That, and more time at the gym, would get rid of her annoying tax season spread. She grabbed an oversized shaker knit sweater to hide the muffin top threatening to erupt, slipped it over her head, and looked over her shoulder to examine the rear view in her full-length mirror. The baggy sweater did its work and focused the view on her legs. Good enough.

She was surprised by his call. A weekend call or Saturday night meeting was out of character. He didn't give any details or leave room for questions; he only asked if she could meet him at the Old Port Tavern at 9 p.m. She hadn't been there in years but remembered, or partially remembered, too many Happy Hours with fellow staff and occasionally Ellen. It was the best place for half-price drinks and free Happy Hour fare of cheddar cheese, Ritz crackers, veggies, and wings back then. It was their favorite hangout until they aged out of the allure of cheap drinks and cheaper food in overcrowded bars. She assumed the place was different now, less packed, or he wouldn't have picked it for their meeting. He said they needed to talk. Of course, she said yes.

She parked at the office, walked down the empty pier, crossed Commercial Street, and turned right on Dana Street. The darkened sidewalks were filled with college students already half in the bag. They seemed younger every year, or maybe they were high schoolers trying to sneak into the area's many bars. For sure, it wasn't her that was getting older. She sucked in her gut which only accentuated her bulging waist. Gym tomorrow, she pledged, unless something more important grabbed her attention.

She skipped down the granite steps, pushed open the heavy oak doors, and paused on the landing before descending the final few stairs into the basement bar. The place was the same, dark with a damp, musty smell seeping through the old stones of its foundation. Before, the odor was carried lightly atop the scent of too many bodies packed into a poorly ventilated space. Tonight, it reminded her of her memere's cellar with its heavy, unavoidable stench filling every corner. The back room, once overflowing with unfortunate latecomers, was closed off. The Old Port Tavern seemed destined to become another Brian Boru, an old standby that disappeared when new, trendier places opened.

Julie waited to give her eyes time to adjust to the dark atmosphere. She scanned the bar, hoping she'd recognize him from behind. He wasn't there. Two women and a lone man, clearly not hers, were glued to their phones, ignoring each other and the bored bartender. She searched the room, looking for another lone wolf. She found him at a table in the back right corner, hiding from nonexistent patrons. He paid no attention to the slamming of the bar's heavy door and didn't look up. He, too, was buried in his phone, but unlike the blank faces of those at the bar, he wore a troubling expression.

She sucked in her breath, not to flatten her stomach this time, but to screw up her courage for a difficult conversation. She lifted her chin, planted a smile, and strode across the dank, dark bar to Gary Green.

# CHAPTER 83

## ELLEN

ELLEN SHOUTED ONE LAST *LOVE YOU* AS THE BOYS slammed the car door and ran to the playground. It was a wonderful weekend: warm weather, contented kids, and one pleased mother. Amazing what a little time away from each other could produce. As difficult as it was to be without her kids, weekends like this told Ellen they were well-adjusted and not the worse for wear, or divorce. She lingered in her car, watching them disperse. Jack tossed his jacket and backpack onto a pile by the basketball court. Kevin, loved by the girls, joined a circle of them under the big oak tree, and Ethan, sweet, shy Ethan, lingered by the chain link fence. His best friend Kwan joined him. All was well in her world.

The driver behind her laid on her horn, reminding her she was not alone. She glanced in her rearview mirror and mouthed an apology to the too-often-behind-her, on-her-last-nerve other mother. The scowl on the driver's face didn't change, and Ellen pledged to track the woman down at the next school gathering to deliver an in-person apology. She flicked on her left blinker, looked over her shoulder, and pulled into the downhill flow of morning traffic crossing over the bridge to Portland. The harbor's salt water shone as the morning sun reflected off the ebbing tide. It was going to be another spectacular day.

"Did you have a nice weekend?" Ellen called to Katie, who was always waiting with a pleasant smile to greet whoever stepped off the elevator. Constant interruptions that deposited who knows who in front of her desk must make a receptionist's job tough. She'd remember that for her next performance review. Katie was the visible heart and soul of the office.

"Not bad, and you?" Katie looked up from her computer. "Happy to be back with the boys?"

"Absolutely. And no calls from needy staff or clients. I'm back bright-eyed, bushy-tailed, and ready to go. Is Julie in her office?"

"Nope, in yours. She knew you'd want to see her. Sounds like she spent too much time in her office yesterday. Said she was giving herself a change of scenery. I just delivered her second cup of coffee; it looked like she needed it."

"Let her know that I'm here. I still need my first cup," Ellen headed to the kitchen confused. Julie working on a nontax season weekend meant something was up. She filled her favorite chipped pottery mug with the last dregs of the coffeepot and skipped starting another pot. Julie was waiting. "Do you mind making more coffee?" She breezed by Katie and didn't wait for an answer. Katie would cover her.

Julie stood at the sliding glass doors watching Ellen's friendly seagull peck at the glass. "I think he missed you. We're both happy to have you back. Fill me in. I have tons to tell you, but I want to hear from you first." She sat down in one of two client chairs.

Ellen sat in the other chair to keep things casual. Holding back news was unlike Julie, and she could see how hard it was. Julie's hands, usually flying in excitement, gripped the arms of the chair tightly to keep it oozing from her. Ellen decided to give the abridged version.

"With the help of Lucy's friend Bob and another salty sailor, we concluded that Ben's death was accidental. A rusty connection on the galley stove caused the propane leak. Accidental and tragic. Lucy gave the news to Tom this weekend. I haven't spoken with her since we landed."

"Damn, that's tough. How do you get over a death that could have easily been prevented?" Julie looked at Ellen.

"With love and faith. It'll see them through. I wish I carried one speck of what Tom and Lucy have. I'm giving them some time to adjust before I check in again. Hopefully, by then, we'll have the whole embezzlement thing figured out. It'll be another blow when they learn that people, friends really, took advantage of them. They're always so good, almost too good to others, but I know they'll see things in the right light. For them, it's just another case of flawed human beings to love and turn over to the Grace of God."

"If you say so, but if it were me?"

"You'd do the same." Ellen reached over and put her hand on Julie's knee. "You tell a good story, but when push comes to shove, you're no different. That's why I love you."

"Okay, enough of this shit, too much philosophy for one day. What else?" Julie crossed her leg, forcing Ellen to remove her hand. Typical Julie. But before she opened the floodgates for whatever Julie was dying to spill, there was more to share.

"We found the journal Ben wrote in every night, a gift from Gary Green."

"Really? Didn't know Gary had it in him. That's cool."

Ellen was puzzled by Julie's odd comment but decided to hold off asking questions for now.

"There was a lot of mundane stuff in it, but also deeper and more introspective thoughts that brought Lucy closer to Ben."

"Hmmm. Better than nothing, I guess." Julie didn't seem to care, and Ellen wondered why.

"It is. And the people who met Ben on his last night in Miami Beach had only good things to say. He was a son to be proud of. Such a big loss."

Ellen struggled to say more, but how does one adequately encapsulate the life of a young man. Less was better. Julie was right. She closed her eyes. Their moment of silence was brief but long enough to honor Ben. Ellen rested her right elbow on the desk and turned over an open palm to signal that it was Julie's time to speak.

"Sounds like an interesting three days," Julie squirmed in her chair, "but it's nothing compared to the meeting I've set up for this afternoon. Four o'clock today, the shit is going to hit the fan. Bobby's going to have one hell of a mess to clean up."

Ellen was stunned by Julie's wicked laugh. "What the hell have you cooked up now?"

# CHAPTER 84

# KATIE

THE STAGE WAS SET, AND KATIE'S NERVES WERE on high alert as she waited for the familiar ding announcing the elevator's arrival. She'd need all her skills to keep things normal: calm voice, sunny smile, mindless banter as she escorted them to the conference room. She couldn't forget to take their coat or offer water or coffee; nothing could appear out of the ordinary. She wiped her sweaty hands on her navy blue slacks and stared at the screensaver on her computer's monitor.

The elevator groaned as it lifted off the floor below her. Show time. Ellen and Julie's confidence in Katie ignited a desire in her to try even harder, and it tweaked her already overstretched nerves. Five years ago, straight out of a two-year business school, she wouldn't have been so sure she could pull it off. But now, with training and support from everyone at Hartmann Associates, she was well-prepared. Here, she was treated as an essential cog in the machine that made this firm successful. She could do this; she knew she could.

Her knee jumped as the elevator chimed and opened its doors. She buzzed the conference room intercom, breathed deeply to help smooth out the shakiness in her smile and voice, and stepped out from behind her desk. "Hi Angela, it's been a while. Can I take your coat? Oops, I guess you don't need one today."

Katie's smile and voice steadied as she slid into her routine banter. "Can't wait to get off work to enjoy this beautiful day. How about coffee or water before we go back? The others are already here."

"It has been some time, Katie, at least a year, I think. It is great to see you again. Thanks, but no coffee or water. I'm all set; I have what I need." Angela held up a turquoise water bottle.

Katie led the way to the conference room, happy it was close to the front desk. The long walk back to Ellen's office would have been too much of a challenge for her trembling legs to handle.

# CHAPTER 85

## ELLEN

ELLEN ACKNOWLEDGED THE SOUND OF THE intercom by putting her finger to her lips as a signal for everyone to remain still. Julie had arranged everything perfectly. When others arrived earlier, they were placed in separate offices to brief them before they all gathered in the conference room a few minutes ago. It was best to keep them apart in fear that speculation and assumption would run rampant and elevate noisy emotions. Just like any surprise party, silence was essential.

Ellen looked across the cherry conference table to where Julie sat at its head. This was Julie's show, she could handle it. Still, they decided to tag team the meeting. Ellen would introduce things and turn it over to Julie to tighten the noose. She shook her head to dispel the image of a lynching. That was not what this meeting was. She had no intention of slipping into the role of judge, jury, and executioner. She and Julie were simply accountants, number detectives of sorts, who stumbled upon deceit. Their only job was to inform pertinent parties and turn it over to the justice system.

She briefly locked eyes with all five seated at the table. There was no coercion getting them to the table. All were willing participants in Julie's plan, somber, silent, and prepared to disclose their piece of the puzzle. Once the pieces were revealed, the incontrovertible truth would paint a landscape of deceit.

# CHAPTER 86

## ANGELA

ANGELA DIDN'T LIKE GOING TO HARTMANN Associates, but now that they shared two, or almost two, mutual clients, she couldn't avoid it forever. Not to worry, she bamboozled Ellen before; she could do it again. And Julie? She was just Ellen's gopher.

She followed Katie down the hall, impressed by her cheery smile and sweet demeanor. Just like herself, she was trained to wear a pleasant, plastered grin that hid what was really going on. She could use someone like that and tucked Katie's name into the confines of her mind. She could be her first employee. She'd love to steal one of Ellen's well-trained staff.

As Katie opened the conference room door, Angela's bright red lips curled into a satisfying grin. She didn't know why her new clients asked her to meet with Ellen, but whatever a client wants, a client gets. She lifted her arm, extended her right hand to greet them, and quickly yanked it back. Ellen sat beside Will and Megan, but Julie flanked Tom and Lucy, and there was Gary Green, alone. What was he doing here? Her lips descended into a sinister scowl, and bile rose in her spasming throat. The silence in the room enveloped her.

"Thanks for coming, Angela." Ellen didn't stand up. "We saved a seat for you."

"I'll stand. I won't be staying." She stared pointedly at Ellen to avoid eye contact with her other betrayers.

"Have it your way." Julie's voice was almost jubilant. "Gary, would you like to start?"

"Thanks, Julie, I would." He cleared his throat. "I'm here, Angela, to do what I should've done a year ago. I cowered under your accusations, but that's over now. I'm not covering for you or myself any longer. I'm ready to face the consequences. It's over."

Dr. Green's glare could've melted most icebergs, but not Angela.

"What are you talking about?" Angela's voice had an edge to it that she didn't intend. "I saved you. Without me, you'd have been gone in a minute. No partners, no practice, no profession. You owe me." She didn't blink; she would not allow herself.

"And what do we owe you for an inflated lease and stolen dollars transferred from our account into yours?" Megan piped in from the other side of the table. "You misjudged us and forgot I was a banker. Getting a subpoena to review your bank records didn't take much effort. And our mutual landlord was more than ready to throw you under the bus. The gig is up."

Angela scoffed at the *Law and Order* language Megan used. Who did she think she was?

"Tom. Lucy. You know me better than that. I built your practice and made you the well-respected surgeon you are today. You'd have nothing without my help." Angela teetered atop her red heels and looked toward Tom. She rested her hand on the back of her unoccupied chair for balance. "It's all lies. Surely, you can see they're making it all up."

Tom looked down at Lucy's hand and stayed silent.

"I think we're done here, Angela." Julie turned to Tom and Lucy, then back to Angela. "Unless you want to apologize for your deception. I suspect you're not ready for that, though."

"You're goddamn right. That won't be happening. Who do you think you are? You think you're better than me? You're not. You're all just a bunch of pumped-up professionals who think you own the world. You don't. It's people like me who make your world go around. Without me, you'd have nothing. I earned every penny. I'm done here." Angela's instinct was to run out the door, but she would not give them the pleasure of seeing her panic. She turned around slowly to make an in-control departure. Ellen was already at the door.

"Wonderful, your next meeting is waiting. Let me get the door for you." Ellen pulled open the door. Two Portland police officers, black caps shielding their serious brows, waited.

"Angela Dunphy, you're under arrest for embezzlement. You have the right to remain silent."

It was all she heard. Angela's emotional brick wall ascended to muffle the rest.

# CHAPTER 87

# GARY GREEN

GARY WAITED FOR WILL AND MEGAN TO LEAVE the conference room. He owed them a lot for helping solidify the definitive evidence against Angela. The details Megan obtained from bank records cleared both him and Tom of any complicity in the crime. Gary's cursory thanks were enough for today, but he'd ask his wife to come up with something special to demonstrate his gratitude. She always knew what to do during times like this, and even though she chose not to be here today, he knew she still cared.

His Saturday night meeting with Julie set in motion the final denouement of this horrible chapter of his life. Soon, it would all be behind him. His face flushed, and sweat began to trickle down his neck. He trusted his black dress shirt would hide any pit stains. "I'd like to speak to Tom and Lucy if that would be alright." His eyes flitted from Ellen to Julie and back to Ellen before looking down at the inanimate conference table. He wasn't sure who was in charge.

"Tom. Lucy. How do you feel about that?" Ellen stood at the table after closing the door.

"Fine, but we want you and Julie to stay." Gary lifted his head and saw Tom nod in agreement with Lucy's request.

Gary gulped to control his trembling voice. He hated being this vulnerable. "A year ago, I found out that Angela was embezzling. When I confronted her, she didn't deny it. She didn't even apologize. She bragged that she only took what she deserved and that doctors like us were overpaid and ineffective. She said incompetent doctors killed her mother and left her father destitute."

He paused and waited for them to react. Certainly, someone would speak. Crickets. He looked down and tried to clear his voice, now froggy with emotion.

"She blackmailed me, found out my medical conferences in China were bogus, that I disguised them to hide personal trips. She threatened to tell everyone, to have me kicked out of the practice."

He scanned the room, hoping for some sympathy or at least understanding. He settled on Tom, his mentor.

"I didn't know what to do, Tom. I admire you so much. You're a god among surgeons and the father I deserved. How could I tell everyone that you messed up? Angela was embezzling for years, and you missed it. I thought it would be better just to let her leave and take over as Managing Physician. I couldn't expose you like that, so I let her go without prosecution." Silence. He looked at Julie and hoped their Saturday night meeting would encourage her to help explain.

"Tom and Lucy are already aware of all that. I filled them in," was all Julie said. "But there's still something missing that only you can answer. What does any of this have to do with firing Tom a year later? Your timing was less than impeccable."

Julie was not on his side. It was time to get real. He addressed Tom.

"When Ben died, I watched you struggle with your grief. I struggled too. I'm Ben's godfather. For god's sake, how could I not feel it? But what I was feeling was a snowflake compared to the avalanche burying you and Lucy. You needed to retire and take time to be together. I needed to take care of you. I thought I was doing you a favor. Was I wrong, Lucy?" Gary wiped the sweat threatening to drip from his hairline.

He couldn't decipher the look Lucy shot his way before she turned to look at Tom. She didn't speak. "When I saw you in the hospital that day, and you said Angela was helping you start over, I had to say something, to come clean. I couldn't let her do it again. Can you forgive me?"

Gary waited for someone, anyone, to fill the expanding void. Nothing. He looked at Ellen. She turned to the grieving couple. Both were silent and continued to avoid eye contact with him.

"Thanks for that, Gary." Ellen stepped in to speak for them. "I'm sure Tom and Lucy need time. This isn't the right forum for a mutual conversation. They'll be in touch, or not, when they're ready."

Gary knew he'd be back in their good graces one day; he was sure of it. It would just take a bit longer.

"Personally, Gary," Julie stood up from the head of the table, "I want to express my gratitude to you for starting this ball rolling. I want to say that we couldn't have done it without you, but that would be a lie. You just saved us a few steps. I think we're done. Ellen, do you agree?"

Gary lifted his head high and straightened his back as Ellen opened the door for him to follow Angela's trail of shame. He tried to remedy the situation. He didn't know if it was enough. Tonight, he'd try again when he met with his business partners. Facing himself and accepting that he had made poor decisions was tough. But in some remote corner of his mind, he was relieved to be doing the right thing. He prayed it was enough to get him back in his wife's good graces.

# CHAPTER 88

# TOM

TOM KNEW THAT AT TIMES LIKE THIS, SILENCE WAS his best response. But it was hard when the fury burning in his gut wanted to be unleashed, to engulf Gary with the same pain Tom was drowning in. Gary should feel the same guilt Tom carried from letting down someone you loved, to feel ashamed and less than. Tom wanted it to be all Gary's fault. But it wasn't. It wasn't anyone's fault that Ben was dead, not even his. Tom would struggle to remember that for the rest of his life. He released Lucy's hand, draped his arm around her shoulder, and pulled her close.

"I'm glad that's over. He's not the man I thought he was."

Lucy looked up at him. "I know, I'm disappointed too. It'll be a while, but I know we'll find forgiveness someday. We need time to process all of this. It's the only thing we can do." She rested her head on his shoulder, and he kissed the top of her head. Ellen cleared her throat, and Tom remembered that they were not alone.

"I think that's enough for today," Ellen waited by the closed door. "The final pieces are in someone else's hands. Angela will be prosecuted. The bank records prove she's accumulated quite a pile of cash, and with time, some of what she stole will be returned. Dr. Green is meeting tonight with his partners. Daniel tells me that some of your former partners want to give him a chance to rectify things, but it's not a done deal. It'll be a close vote. They're going to discuss bringing you back too. Whatever you decide to do Tom, you know that Julie and I are here to help."

Tom acknowledged her offer with a nod. Their help was the only thing he was sure of.

"There was a bit of truth in what Gary said." He tightened his arm around Lucy. She looked up at him but left her head on his shoulder. "The pressure of group practice made it easy for me to avoid the pain of Ben's death. When I was kicked out, it forced me to deal with things, to face my grief. It was tough, but it helped me move forward." A wave of sadness washed through him, and he was quiet for a moment.

They stood to leave, and he wrapped his arm around Lucy's waist. "But don't get me wrong, I'm not going to retire. Among everything else we discussed this weekend, Lucy and I agreed that a more laid-back, solo practice would be best for us. And we'll be doing it without Angela. Right?" Tom pulled Lucy close.

"Right, I'll help you find her replacement." She looked up at Tom and smiled. "We both agree that it won't be me."

Tom pulled her even closer. She turned her head, and they kissed deeply. Tom didn't care who was watching. He loved his wife.

# CHAPTER 89

## ELLEN

ELLEN DROPPED INTO ONE OF JULIE'S CLIENT chairs, rested her head on its back, and closed her eyes. It was over. If last week were a line graph, traveling its peaks and valleys would leave even the fittest mountain climber out of breath. With their trip to Miami Beach, Julie's stealth attack on Angela, and a weekend filled with her sons' antics, Ellen was exhausted. Lucy and Tom were gone, Katie was thanked and sent home, and Julie was taking a bathroom break. Ellen needed a moment to soothe her mind, heart, and soul.

"Wow, what a ride," Julie said when she returned. She sat behind her desk, kicked her shoes off, and put her feet on her desk.

"That it was." Ellen slipped her aching toes out of her black heels in solidarity. "I'm not sure how we turned from milquetoast number-crunchers to Sam Spade sleuths, but I'd say we did a helluva job. Never would I ever have guessed that this is where we'd end up." She pushed a satisfying whoosh from her lungs. She rubbed her eyes, massaged her temples, and cradled her neck in her clasped hands. She rested her feet on the desk next to Julie's.

"You never know what lurks beneath a bunch of numbers." Julie's laugh was deep and sinister. "Numbers don't lie—until they do. But they don't teach that in school. If they did, more kids would go for accounting instead of criminal justice. We're much more than financial historians. Our number crunching can change the course of history!"

Ellen loved Julie's temporarily inflated ego and had to admit that she liked helping people solve their problems. Even if she was only an accountant. Money controls too much of this world and drives people to make poor decisions. Gary Green was a prime example.

"Let's not get carried away there. Change the world? I doubt it. But this was a pleasant and satisfying detour from tax season and our 'regular' job." Ellen unclasped her hands and added the requisite quotation marks.

Their version of accounting used both sides of their brains: right for facts, left for nuance. It expanded her life view, diversified her take on people, and stoked her curiosity. She hated to admit it, but sometimes accounting bored her. Excitement like this kept her from looking for adventure elsewhere.

"Hey, don't rain on my parade! Let me enjoy it for a while." Ellen heard the squeaky, creaky wheels of Julie's favorite, fact-finding sidekick's trash barrel.

Julie's eyes widened, a smile crept across her face, and she placed her feet back on the ground and leaned in. "In fact, we need a celebratory drink. Don't you think? How about J's?" Ellen removed her feet from the desktop and stood.

"I have a date with three young men that I can't miss. But I'm sure there's someone else you can invite who can help keep that parade going." Ellen turned to their handsome, trash-picking renaissance man.

Julie flipped her dark, curly hair over her shoulder and smiled.

# EPILOGUE

---

*Four months later*

# THE OCEAN POTION

SHE BOBBED ON HER NEW MOORING. SHE MISSED the more familiar one, the one she had known for so long, the one encircled by her companions, *Sea Sharp, She Said Yes, Maine Squeeze.* She saw them in the distance next to someone else, someone who had taken her place. Now, she was surrounded by not-yet-known-to-her vessels, the aftermath of a missed sailing season.

She was happy, nonetheless, to be resting in the chilly waters of Maine where green slime didn't accumulate from the always warm water that slapped her sides for over six months. Here, back home, she was refreshed and well-tended. Before she'd tremble in wintry winds when her deck could become a receptacle for windswept snow, they would tenderly lift her from the icy waters and lovingly wrap her until warm spring breezes brought dawn's light lifted on sweet bird songs to illuminate the greening shores.

She was glad to be back after that long, joyless journey from Eleuthera to Miami Beach, where she waited months to be brought back up the East Coast. She shivered, recalling the youthful adventure that carried her down. The brilliant mornings when she and Ben would sail out of cozy harbors to unknown waters filled with surprises and wonder. And then, there was the trip back to Maine. It was hard, a family of three instead of four, trying to relive the joys of their loved one's final journey down the coast.

If only her creaking deck could speak, and her lines could sing. She'd tell them of sunrises that called Ben to open seas where they rode like dolphins, rising and falling to the rhythm of the waves. She'd tell of evenings, snug in harbors, of new friends calling with kind invitations for comradery, drinks, and music. Oh the music. How her decks vibrated, and her sails danced to the tunes they played. She never tired of it. She dreamed it would play forever. Until it didn't.

She wished she could tell them the end of the story. Of their last night together under a dome of stars made brighter by a moonless night. She'd tell them his heart was filled with magical rememberings of Mom and Dad and sister together under the same miraculous sky. She'd tell them he was happy. And, she'd say, I'm sorry. I loved him too.

www.ingramcontent.com/pod-product-compliance
Lightning Source LLC
Chambersburg PA
CBHW030521120726
47904CB00005B/1560